I0611954

THE CRIPPLE GOAT

A Novel

By
Michael Warren

Righter Books

Copyright 2016 by Michael Warren
All rights reserved

This is a work of fiction. All characters, events and circumstances portrayed in this story are products of the author's imagination. Any resemblance to actual people and events is purely coincidental. No part of this book may be reproduced without written permission by the author and publisher.

Righter Publishing Company, Inc.
1112 Rogers Road
Graham, North Carolina, 27253

www.righterbooks.com

First Edition
May 2016

Printed and bound in the United States of America

ISBN: 978-1-938527-34-0
The Cripple Goat
By Michael Warren

Also in on Amazon Kindle

IN MEMORIUM

Robert McConnell Rice

DEDICATED TO

Kevin George Carle

CHAPTER 1--MEDICINE SPIRIT

Olivia was seized at sunup. In the instant of her possession, she knew that the medicine spirit had flown from the canyons of the other world on the bright rays of sunlight that broke above the dark trees along the Glory River. The golden phantasm, she immediately understood, had erupted from the depths of the ancestral soul, spilled into her room, splashed into her nostrils and rushed into her mind as she had slept. The old woman sat up in her brass bed with a shivering start.

"Matthew!" she cried plaintively for her husband of fifty three years. The dying echo of her voice in the cold, empty house brought a tear to her eyes. In the manner of those forced to live alone in the same space a departed loved one had shared, Olivia often spoke her thoughts aloud as if she could invoke her missing husband.

"Foolish old woman," she muttered, "get up. Matthew's not coming. He's been dead six years. That's why he sent this spirit message. Cale will be home from the war soon. You've got to do it now, in time to help Cale. Besides, Matthew is always here. He loved himself into every inch of this place, and into you."

Olivia had inherited an eighth of her blood from the Choctaw and it had given her olive-brown skin, black eyes, a square chin and coarse, lustrous black hair, which was now silvered by age. The blood of those wild ancestors had also given her countenance a warm, pensive air that seemed jovial when her broad smile revealed a gold tooth.

Because of her Indian blood, Olivia had an abiding connection to the land and she cherished the days that she and Matthew had spent tilling and tending to their fields and pastures. Her love for being in the earth was deep and flew into farm and wood and creatures she encountered-- man or beast. Being descended from a people who once lived free, Olivia was occasionally possessed by spirits which drove her out of her home to a hidden spot where she could confront a pressing trouble and vanquish the unsettling possessor.

She had not been to her secret place in years, not since her own sons, coming home from World War II, had abandoned the farm. Now her grandson was returning from his war, and the medicine spirit was driving her to that hidden sanctuary. She would climb Toenail Hill until she reached a massive hemlock tree whose down swept branches enveloped a smooth granite boulder. There she would sit until the waters of her heart and the waters of her mind ran clear and strong with conviction and rightful purpose.

Olivia put on a housecoat and went into the dim kitchen. Even though it was July, a freak cold front had suddenly dropped down from Canada and chilled the countryside; the refreshing air was not cool enough to damage the large pink and white flowers of the poppies that grew by her gate but the spoiled magnolia blossoms that hung from the trees in Swede's Pasture were a harbinger, she thought, of an early winter. She opened the firebox and threw a handful of kindling on the glowing coals inside the great cast iron cook stove that stood in the far corner. The wood crackled as she set a pot of coffee to boil.

Olivia looked at the pearled horizon and trembled as a wisp of sorrow sailed through her heart. The promise of morning was cruel. Since Matthew had died, Olivia knew at the first light of every day that the sun could never shine upon her vanished joy. The earth held her husband in a simple grave on Toenail Hill. Though Matthew's spirit still dwelled in the house and in the cornfields around her, nothing in creation could ever put light on that loving face again.

Olivia poured a cup of coffee and sat in the waxing light at her lonely kitchen table. She thought of the strong will that had driven Matthew to build the sturdy two-story farmhouse with his own hands. She remembered the great love for the land that had seized Matthew in the south of France during his war and his fierce determination, once home, to stay out of the Adluh Cotton Mill. So many of his returning comrades, beaten down by debt and worn out land, had trudged into the dim, hot, noisy chambers of the textile factory and, baptized with their rank sweat, had accepted machines as their master, had moved farther away from nature, had accelerated the journey their race had begun to return to the spirit of the beast.

Olivia had been proud that Matthew had bowed to no lord, including the heavenly one decried with frenzy within the numerous churches with white steeples that flickered in the pines of the low hills of the Red Bank country. Matthew had stayed on the land, working from sun to sun across the seasons that spanned years to transform the poor red clay of his fields into dark, loamy soil that grew tall green stalks bearing bright yellow ears of corn whose kernels were swollen with rich milk.

She recalled, with a smile that wrinkled the dark olive skin around her mouth and eyes, how Matthew had been a powerful and purposeful man yet also a loving man. He had always cared for her tenderly, surprising her with bunches of wildflowers from the meadow in Bride's Woods or, when he had returned from town with feed and supplies, by suddenly pulling some womanly notion from beneath the wagon seat. But mostly, he had always swept her up in his great love for life and had cherished her with the same passion he had for his children, for his land, for the wildness of the game he hunted, for the beauty of a rose, for the honor of friendship, and for the dignity of knowledge.

"In this moment," Olivia said aloud, "I wish you were sitting here, Matthew. The medicine spirit is on me. I have to finish what you started with Cale. He's coming home from his war, after being missing for a long while. His daddy says he's probably been hurt bad.

"Cale will want comforting. Only natural. He'll turn to his momma and he'll turn to me. Mostly, he'll turn to you, Matthew. Only he can't have you, so he will pour his sorrow into your land. Cale loves this farm because we showed him how to love it and he wants it to be his home. Matthew, that boy thinks your legacy can be his life.

"I can't let him make that mistake. He doesn't know the other part, Matthew, the seeking part. Give me the strength, husband, I can't let him come back alive from the war just to die in your shadow."

CHAPTER 2--PLOUGHSHARES

The old passenger bus lumbering through the countryside was not crowded. The tide of students flooding in and out of the central piedmont from the colleges to the east and west had not yet begun to run. Apart from the farmers and working class people who had settled in the front of the bus, a solitary young man sat in the rear section opposite the exit. Hopeful of glimpsing their destination, the forward passengers sat up straight to gaze eagerly at the piedmont landscape but the tall, slender figure toward the back of the bus slouched in his seat. Cale Haines could no longer engage the world, so he tried to content himself with just letting it pass by. Drinking helped him let go of the passions he could no longer feel but it did not help him let go of the war.

The grey eyes of Cale's handsome face stared languidly out the window, seeming not to notice the low hills and forests, not glancing at the numerous roadside produce stands brimming with red tomatoes, golden peaches, purple plums, glistening blackberries and deep green collards. Ringlets of tightly curled long black hair fell across his face as he dipped his head to take a sip of bourbon from the small flask he kept hidden in the dark blue pea coat folded on his lap. Only when he wiped his thin moustache with his sleeve did Cale attract the attention of someone looking his way.

When the bus arrived at New Cana, it swerved into the gravel parking lot of the general store that served as the terminal and the post office. While the driver unloaded a few packages, Cale peered into the dispatcher's tiny office

9

and noticed a calendar on the wall. He read the large black type, "July 1971".

Cale knew the date, but seeing it posted authoritatively this close to home made him shudder. He had been at war four years. Cale sneaked a large gulp of whisky. He could see that the tiny hamlet where the bus was idling had changed very little since 1967. Cale was confident that Adluh, the small village for which he was bound, would look much the same as it had since he was a boy. Cale beat back the tears that tried to flood his eyes as he felt a profound longing to live innocently in the world again, to exist solely in dimensions of love that joined his whole being to the full glory of being human. His innocence and his glory had been gored to death by the warrior he had been in the jungle.

As the wages of war, service to his country had exacted from him much more than if it had taken his life. "If I had been lucky," Cale thought grimly, "my captors would have killed me. Dead men should not be allowed to live."

Before leaving home to serve in the war, Cale remembered that he had been a young man in love with life, in love with a pretty girl, in love with a dream of one day inheriting his grandfather's farm, in love with the idea that he would live his life as a happy, robust spirit. Now, watching the dispatcher sort papers, Cale recalled that as a lad he had asked his grandfather, "Grandpa, are your cornfields paradise?"

Matthew stroked his chin. "In fact or in feeling?" he responded.

"I don't know," Cale complained. "My teacher said that in the Garden of Eden, life was full of happiness. No trouble or sadness was allowed. She said it's called paradise when everything is happiness and everything is beautiful and you have everything you want."

"I 'spect she's right about that," Matthew confirmed.

"When I'm at home," Cale confessed, "I feel sad because my daddy is always gone, and my momma is always working at the grill, and my brother is in the Army and my sister is a girl. Nobody wants to fish in the river, or catch grasshoppers or look for rainbows after a storm. Nobody sings. Nobody is happy.

"But when I'm on the farm with you and Grandma, we are always exploring, or telling stories, or fishing, or picking blueberries, or working with the mules or making something in the shop. Everybody's happy here. Grandma is always singing. She says it's because of your cornfields. I can't remember the next part."

"Well, son," Matthew advised, "in fact, my cornfields are a lot of backbreaking work. But in feeling, the part that really matters, raising corn is my insides flowing out into the world. It's the love I have for the land, for my animals, for the critters of the woods, for my life, for your grandma, for my sons, for my friends, and especially for my grandchildren. So I guess my cornfields are paradise. But paradise only comes when you make it. And you can only make it out of the things you love."

The loud clanking of the bus door as it closed disturbed Cale's remembrance. In 1967, when he had reluctantly forsaken the Red Bank country to engage in battle, Cale knew he had loved everything. Going home from war now, Cale thought of how love had been beaten out of his soul in the jungle. "I have nothing left inside," he mumbled as the bus gained speed, "and hell is the only thing you can make out of that."

When the bus reached Graniteville, a strange young man wearing a field jacket came aboard. He wore his long black hair in two pigtails, each wrapped in thin strands of brown suede leather. Around his forehead was a headband made of snakeskin. Piercing black eyes and thick black eyebrows gave his oval face a slightly menacing look. The odd young man was tall, had an athletic build, and moved

11

quickly and precisely as he climbed into the cabin. Seeing the pea coat of the slumping passenger, he quickly strode to the rear of the bus. The soft leather of the Apache boots on his feet made no sound, but the sheath of the long knife he wore on his belt slapped against his jeans as he approached the secretive man cradling the flask.

The man with pigtails slipped off his battered rucksack and settled in the seat across the aisle from the bourbon drinker, who cocked his head and scrutinized the commotion. The sailor's empty eyes suddenly focused and he raised up with a start. He scanned the field jacket, then the snakeskin headband that secured the intruder's long pigtails, locks of hair so black that, in the July sun, they had a bluish sheen. The imbiber's eyes narrowed when he saw the stag horn handle of his sudden companion's knife. "Ranger?" Cale asked the man in the field jacket.

"Marine," the man replied, stretching his legs as the bus lurched onto the highway. "You?"

"Naval intelligence. How long you been home?"

"Two years," the Marine responded gravely.

"Today is my homecoming," Cale said, attempting a swagger. "Want a snort?"

The Marine nodded and tossed his rucksack over to the Navy man, who dropped in the flask and heaved the canvas bag back to its owner. Shielding himself with the rucksack, the Marine quickly sipped the whisky. Palming the flask, he reached toward the Navy man as if to shake hands. "Name's Dakota," he said as Cale secretly took the flask.

"Cale Haines," the sailor said as he sat up and shifted to face Dakota.

"The Navy must be loosening up. Your hair is very long for someone who just got out," observed Dakota.

"I got out several months ago. I'm just now making my way back home. Didn't see any need to hurry. It won't be the same, anyway."

12

Dakota nodded gravely.

"So what was your Area of Operations during our little conflict?" asked Cale.

Dakota's eyes clouded and he looked away. "I Corps. They sent me into Khe Sahn and Hue," he replied.

"Bummer!" exclaimed Cale. "Which was your favorite, being surrounded and fired on from the high ground across the Laotian border at Khe Sahn or fighting house to house in Hue?"

Dakota drummed his fingers on his knife sheath. "Hue. I felt like a warrior there. In Khe Sahn, I just felt like bait for the North Vietnamese Army. Where did you see action?"

"Officially," Cale began slowly, "nowhere. Unofficially, I was hiking in Thailand and looking for evidence of Chinese influence on Thai culture."

"Hiking. Never heard it called that before," Dakota said with a grin. "Did you have to hike in or did they give you a ride?"

"I got a very good ride going in."

"How about coming out?" Dakota asked as he peered expectantly at the sailor.

Cale's eyes were looking at something very far away and Dakota saw that they were filled with anguish. The Navy man laughed hollowly. "Let's just say I let myself out."

Dakota's nostrils flared. "The Navy left you in that shit hole?"

"I was unavoidably detained," Cale answered grimly, "by some very skilled detainers." They rode in silence as Dakota stared at the floor to give Cale the privacy to repulse the horrific recollections that Dakota knew were now overwhelming the sailor. Finally Cale said falteringly, "I never felt like a warrior. Warriors stand for something. I had a mission, not a purpose. From the moment I was in country, I felt like a robot with a killing

13

license. Leaving the war revoked the mission, but it didn't turn off the robot."

Dakota gripped the handle of his knife. "I hear you, man. It was different for me when I first got home. Nobody here understands what it is to take a man's life. Nobody here knows that when the enemy is begging and screaming, he has just seen how precious life is as you are ripping it away from him. And when you see him bleed out, you <u>know</u> that his blood is actually regret that he lived without really knowing why."

"For some, maybe," Cale objected. "If he was like these happy bastards we came home to, then the world lost nothing with his death."

"Sometimes," Dakota agreed solemnly, "I wish I had my piece and lots of ammo. I'd take out these pleasantly numb sonsof--".

"The war's over for us, man," Cale retorted.

"<u>That</u> fucking war is over for us," Dakota declared, "but the real war never stops. That's why I joined a commune, on an old farm just outside Saluda. We call it the Potlatch. It's basically a refugee camp for freaks. To keep the place going, we plan to start a food co-op and Dargan, he's the dude with the money, bought the old train depot in Saluda.

"We want to convert it into a cafe and head shops. Then we can use the stuff we grow on the farm for the menu in the cafe and our artists will be able to sell their creations in the shops. We're trying to create a little society of folks who want to live their lives with passion. If you're in Saluda sometime, dude, look us up."

"I'll actually be living in Saluda soon," Cale explained. "I'm renting a house there. I'll move in after I go to Adluh and have the big homecoming. Then I'll pack up my truck and get my tools and head to Saluda."

"What kind of tools?"

"When I'm not farming my grandfather's land, I'm a fair carpenter. Frame and finish."

"Do you have a job yet in Saluda?" Dakota asked excitedly.

Cale shook his head.

"Look us up, man, seriously. We've got plenty of freaks who can dig in the dirt. The head honcho is a plumber and I'm an electrician, but we need a carpenter bad. When you get back to Saluda, come down to the old train depot. I'll introduce you to the dude who runs the show. He'll pay top dollar. He's using his daddy's money to pay for his social experiment. The Potlatch isn't real for him. It's not even real for a lot of the freaks. But for a few of us it is. As my Oglala grandfathers would say, 'It is a place of spirit where a man can see the limits of his body.'"

"I'm afraid I don't have much spirit left. The war took most of what I had," Cale said sadly.

Dakota smiled and laughed. "Yeah, me too. But it didn't get it all. And the Potlatch is the kind of place that helps you get it back. At least it did that for me."

The bus slowed and turned into the terminal at Saluda. "One for the road?" Cale offered.

As passengers began retrieving their luggage, Dakota took the flask and drank quickly. "Look us up when you get back, Cale."

"I lived with spirit once," Cale said icily, "before."

Turning towards the front of the bus to depart, Dakota counseled, "Every robot has an off switch. You just have to find it. Later, dude."

CHAPTER 3--SILKING

When the sputtering passenger bus clattered across the rust-colored Campbell River on an old wooden bridge, Cale looked up. He was in his home country now, the Red Bank country. Thick deposits of red clay covered the limestone bedrock in this part of the piedmont. River banks, ploughed fields, tidy gardens near kitchen doors, and the trusted paths lovers took into the pine thickets all shone a creamy reddish-brown in the glaring light of July. Only the emerald cornfields and home gardens burgeoning with the glaucous foliage of cabbages and melons broke the sanguine palette.

The sailor remembered his grandfather Matthew's words about this country. "If there had been a god, and he had wanted to make an image of himself out of clay and give it life," Matthew often said when they had walked his green corn fields, "he would have come to the Red Bank country to create man. Here, on the banks of the Glory River, grows the finest corn on Earth. Raising the best corn completes the circle of farming. All of the critters, all of the tools, all of the land, and all of the man have a part. Making a proud corn crop is as much spirit as it is sweat. That's why we carry the cripple goat."

Cale scrutinized the fields of tasseled corn he now passed for signs of silk. At highway speed, his examination was impossible, but Cale knew that soon he would be walking his grandfather's fields to check the corn crop his brother Marsh put in for their grandmother. First, his family would welcome him home from the war. Cale drained the flask and stowed it in his seabag.

"I'll be glad to see them," he thought, "and they will make me feel welcome. I don't know if I'll ever feel like I'm home."

***

The smell of freshly moved earth pleased him as Marshall Haines eased the bucket of his front-end loader through a weedy meadow to clear an infield for his baseball team, the Haines Construction Lions. Fresh, new blue-and-white shirts and pants lay in a cardboard box on the front seat of his pickup truck, and the stocky, sandy-haired owner of the construction company smiled as he anticipated giving the young boys their uniforms and shoes with real cleats. He looked forward to watching them swell with pride as they realized they were actually a team. He knew that sponsoring and coaching the team would cause conflict with his wife, Linda, who feverishly tried to commit all of his free time to performing chores for her church, but he also knew it would give him some peace.

Marshall Haines was renowned in the county for feats of strength and, every year in the cool air of October at the county fair, opponents in the volunteer fire department's charity tug-of-war contest braced themselves when they saw his tattooed left forearm on the rope. Those standing close enough to see his mutton chop whiskers gritted their teeth. The ones standing nearest, beholding his resolution, grimaced.

As he prepared the infield, Marsh's green eyes sparkled, which they had rarely done in the five years since the doctor had informed the hopeful couple that Marshall Haines was sterile. The general contractor's eyes glowed with delight now because, for a few months of the year, he would be a coach and almost a father to his team. Part of the shine in his eyes was also pride for his younger brother, Cale, who was coming home from the war.

A strident voice suddenly beckoned him. "Marsh! Please stop that foolishness for a minute!" his wife

17

demanded from her car at the edge of the field. "Preacher Darnell phoned. There's a broken water pipe in the church basement. You need to hurry over there!"

Marsh switched off the loader. He looked at Linda. Her harsh tone, which had begun in earnest shortly after learning of his condition, was now as raw as her ring finger, which she kept inflamed by frequently pushing against her wedding band with her thumb. Each time he heard that unhappiness in her voice, he flinched, expecting her to say she was leaving him. But she stayed, exacting an undeclared vengeance by giving her life to the church and her waxing indifference to him.

Marsh checked his watch. He would have enough time to make a simple repair before heading to his family's restaurant to join in the reception for Cale. He got into his truck and sped along the graceful flow of the river thinking, "Cale was missing in action for a long time. I know he is more broken than God's water pipe." When he reached the church, Marsh stood and watched the ejaculatory spray that was soaking the holiness out of the basement. He applied a simple clamp which, like his wife's nervous tick, stifled the outcry but did not mend the rupture.

***

As she left the ramshackle house on the outskirts of Adluh and walked past the chrome-laden motorcycle of the man she had just angrily left, Julia Haines felt it. As she hurriedly jumped into her car and sped away towards the secretarial school on the Saluda highway, it moved again. At the bridge that crossed the Glory River, Julia pulled her car onto the shoulder of the road, got out and slowly walked out into the middle of the span.

She still carried her slight frame like a dancer-- lightly, with a poised rhythm--even though stage lights had not shown upon her rich auburn hair and sharp black eyes since her senior year in high school. Before an audience,

18

Julia had delighted in gracefully expressing powerful emotions.

Now, she couldn't cry. She could not scream in rage. Julia wanted to feel pain--sharp, cutting torture or deep, abiding agony--she wanted to feel it. She wanted to feel it now. She wanted desperately to hurt so that she would know that her insides had not become the cold stillness that had filled her boyfriend's eyes as he had stood in the doorway, casually smoking a cigarette.

He didn't want it.

She wanted to sob so hot, burning tears would stream down her face and she would know that she could still feel touch.

He didn't want her, now.

Julia looked at the streaming waters beneath her and her mind reeled with despair. "That dark water could take away the need to feel," she projected. "It would be quick. If I have the courage to breathe in those muddy waters. If I have the strength to let myself sink and drift with the current. If I have the mettle to demand the wages of my sin."

Suddenly her eye caught a golden glint as the sun passed beyond the mill and its light streamed onto the water. A golden sparkle was Julia's earliest memory and, as she grew older, she knew that it must have come from her grandmother's gold tooth when Olivia smiled. That golden sparkle came to embody countless happy moments on her grandmother's lap and, as her childhood passed, it had included the sunlight that fell through her grandmother's kitchen window on frosty winter mornings, and the smell of hoecake sizzling in a pan on the great cast iron cook stove that warmed the bright room; still later, that gleam had embraced the tattered yellow cover of the storybook her grandmother read to her when Julia had feared that goblins raced in the night winds that sometimes blew fiercely outside the farmhouse; stitched in time to that marvelous golden glow was the yellow Easter dress her grandmother had sewn for her, and the color of the roses that had lain atop her grandfather Matthew's coffin as it was lowered into the ground, and the yellow box that sat on the top shelf of her grandmother's hall closet, the yellow box that Matthew had made and that her grandmother called Julia's hope chest.

Standing disfigured on that lonely bridge, Julia suddenly felt the warmth unleashed by the memory of that golden sparkle. As that wonderful glow spread through her, it moved again and Julia realized that the baby was now a part of her fabulous golden sparkle. Then she thought of Cale, and Julia stepped back from the edge of the bridge.

Her brother was coming home from the war today. Her mother's long enduring agony would finally cease. Julia was deeply shamed that she could have thought, even for an instant, of taking her life and adding to her mother's misery on the very day that Cale's arrival would end that great sorrow. She carefully sat down in a bed of blue chicory flowers on the soft grass beside the road and wept, rejoicing in the golden splendor that had been hers as a child and was hers still, sobbing until hot tears finally drove the coldness from her abandoned heart.

***

The driver shifted to a lower gear and the bus growled as it slowed and swerved into the broad parking lot in front of a dingy white brick building. Bright strands of red, white, and blue bunting draped the large sign above the door that read RuSam Grill. In the large window to the left of the door, a hand-lettered poster declared "Welcome Home Farm Boy!" As he stepped down from the bus with his seabag on his shoulder, Cale shuddered.

From this very spot, he had left to go to a distant war; now the war lay thousands of miles behind, yet its chill was in him and he knew the warmth of home could not drive it out. Failing to notice that the normally bright cafe window was dim, Cale opened the door and stepped in quickly. The afternoon light that followed him inside briefly illuminated several figures who were then quickly enveloped in darkness as the door closed.

Cale instinctively froze. He trembled in memory. "They are so close! I must be very still. Maybe they will pass by like the others. Maybe they will light cigarettes, talk, laugh, and forget they are looking for me. If I just don't move.

"I can't remember what happened. My wound could be infected again. When I crossed the river, chunks of fresh green elephant dung floated by me. Could be that. Or the meat I ate from that bloated water buffalo carcass could have been more rotten than it looked. Maybe it was bad water. Or no water. I can't focus.

"My head is spinning but I don't feel any pain. I could be delirious again. Maybe it's just a normal day and I am just lying in the pit with my dung and my piss and my vomit. But who are they? Only one comes to give me the moldy rice. Only one. The rice is the worst. Hunger makes me eat it, and it makes me sick.

"Why don't they just kill me? The one with the scar on his left cheek is tired of trying to break me. I'll break soon. All men break. And no man knows where that line is inside himself until the time comes. It is simple, really. What can you live with, and what can you not live with?

"Scared men find that line inside themselves first. They cannot live with pain, but they can live without honor. Despairing men find it next. Pain and honor are the same for them. Then come the brave men. For them, pain finally triumphs over honor. Last to reach the grim line are the idealists. Pain hurts them the most but their hearts are made of honor. When they go down, it is as if the spirit of all humanity has been struck down in the reeking muck.

"They still give me foul rice so I have not broken yet. Broken men get better chow. Soon I will be broken, and dead and rotting in this stinking jungle. There should have been more love while I had life."

Suddenly the lights came on and his awful remembrance was dispelled by a chorus of "Surprise! Welcome home, Cale!" Only then did he see the jubilant faces. First, he saw his mother. Ruth was taking baby steps towards him, fearing that, if she lunged, he would disappear again, rejoining the legions of vanished servicemen. Ruth held her arms out to her son. Her eyes were streaming with tears, but she did not make a sound. Cale could see that she was trying to say his name and he knew that no one else would make a move until his mother had reclaimed her son.

Cale dropped his seabag and hurried to her. He gently took her in his arms.

"It's ok, Momma, you don't have to say anything," Cale stammered, "I'm back. I'm really here."

Ruth trembled in Cale's arms. She whimpered and then burst into long, agonizing sobs. Cale touched his mother's hair softly. "I'm safe now, Momma, I'm back in the Red Bank country," he said reassuringly. "Your boy has come home."

Cale held his mother until his grandmother, Olivia, approached. Her fierce black eyes regarded him with wild pride. She kissed him on the cheek and whispered, "Tend to your momma real good, Cale. You come see me when you can."

Cale took his grandmother's hand and squeezed it. He nodded as Olivia stepped away. Cale's father, Sam, hugged him lightly and said, sniffling, "Welcome home, Cale. I'm proud of you, son." Sam helped Ruth disentangle herself from Cale, then led her away from their son.

Cale's sister, Julia, flew at him, sobbing loudly and exclaiming, "Cale! Cale!" Julia threw her arms around Cale's neck, clenched him tightly and cried softly. "We thought we had lost you," she confessed--for herself as much as her brother.

When Julia finally released Cale, he turned to his older brother and started to grin. "Hello, Construction Boy," Cale said to Marsh.

"Welcome home, Farm Boy." Marsh choked back tears as he hugged his younger brother. "I don't know what to say," Marsh blurted awkwardly.

"Say you'll beat my ass if I do it again," Cale teased.

Marsh took his brother's face in his hands. "If you do it again, little brother, I'll beat your ass," Marsh said lovingly. The brothers hugged vigorously then parted.

Cale walked slowly to the back of the cafe and sat in his usual place in the family booth. This familiar action released them all from homecoming. As she would have at any other time when Cale walked through the cafe door, Ruth asked, "Are you hungry, honey?"

"I'm starved," Cale answered gleefully.

Sam and Julia immediately took their stations behind the counter. Sam began frying a fat burger patty while Julia tossed fresh fries in hot oil and threw a bun on the grill. Olivia and Marsh joined Cale. Ruth was humming now, as she sliced a ripe tomato. Julia filled a large glass with sweet iced tea, took it to Cale, and tapped him playfully on the head. Marsh stretched his large frame and relaxed against the back of the booth.

Only Olivia remained poised with purpose. "Tell us what you can, now Cale, so we won't have to draw this out," she insisted.

"Good idea, Grandma," Cale said with a hollow laugh. "The details I can never tell you. I was never missing in action."

Olivia gasped.

"I was in operations that were not officially recorded. The Navy didn't really lie to you though. Only a few people even knew what my missions were. Nobody knew where I was."

"So you were not a lost fighter?" Olivia asked tenderly.

Cale's eyes became guarded. "I wasn't lost until I came out of the jungle, Grandma," Cale said solemnly.

***

Broadus Cottle emerged from a small brick building in Saluda and ran out into the empty street yelling, "Whoopee! I did it now!"

Strangers were startled by the leaping, shouting young man. He was tall and muscular and wore a white tee shirt whose sleeves had been torn away, leaving their jagged sockets to encircle his bulging arms. His closely cropped hair was everywhere askew. But it was his eyes, deep-set in his broad, angular face, that inspired alarm in the passersby. Those agitated eyes were animatedly open-- as if his insides were filled with some volatile energy--but they remained unfocused, eerily suggesting that he beheld, not a premonition, but a looming nothingness. He had the frightening look of seething wildness.

Broadus ceased his antics, lit a cigarette, jumped into his car, thrust one arm through the open window and pounded on the door as he switched on the radio and jammed the accelerator, tearing out of town with squealing tires, blaring music and a tortuous cry of sheer release.

Broadus sped through the countryside towards Adluh, and swerved into the parking lot of the massive Adluh Mill. He quickly found the car he sought, a sleek sedan parked in front of the mill supervisor's office. As he leapt from his car and hurriedly opened the trunk, Broadus thought briefly of the car's owner, Grady Johnstone.

Inside the gloomy, foul air of the mill, Broadus had felt the stinging lash of Grady Johnstone's rule over the lives of toiling workers like a patroller disciplining slaves on a plantation. Broadus had worked inside just one brief summer but his uncles, aunts, and cousins had suffered Grady's cold cruelties for years. Most of Broadus' friends,

24

like himself, newly graduated from high school, now labored to attend Grady's machines. His eager, happy classmates would still be on Grady's payroll when they fell dead from exhaustion and deprivation of the land that had nurtured their families for generations.

Broadus cackled as he unloaded his supplies and began methodically vandalizing the sparkling sedan. When he finished his attack on the vehicle, Broadus jumped into his car and raced away from the mill. He drove to a modest house on the banks of the Glory River, plunged into the driveway, stomped on the brake pedal, and slid to a halt just in front of the man emerging from the garage, his best friend, Cale Haines.

"What the hell are you doing, man?" demanded Cale as Broadus proudly stepped from his car.

"I'm coming to welcome you home from the war!" Broadus exclaimed as he heartily embraced Cale.

"It's good to see you, man," Cale declared.

"I want to hear your tales of glory. First, your daddy told me you stopped writing, then he said you were missing in action, and the last time he came to the gas station—he thinks I can keep that damned old Studebaker running forever—he said you were coming home. But that was months ago. You sure took your time getting back here. You must have been getting pussy in twenty different states to take so long getting back. So tell me: what happened to you over there?"

Cale regarded his friend thoughtfully. They had shared their first cigarette, their first drink of whisky, and their first picture of a naked woman. They had backed each other in fights, double dated, and exchanged their knowledge of tools and mechanics. They had hunted deep in the woods and fished far downstream. They had speculated together about the mysteries of females.

Cale wanted to tell Broadus about the bamboo cage in which he had been held captive, and the torment and the

25

hopelessness of mere animal existence—but it would not come. Cale clenched his jaw and shook his head. "Not now, man. The time's not right. We can talk about it when we go backpacking for trout in the mountains this fall."

Broadus threw his head back and roared with laughter. "No can do. No can do after what I done!" he screamed, arching his back and beating his chest. Then he flashed a knowing grin at Cale.

"What is it, shithead?" Cale asked seriously as he walked up to his red-faced friend.

Broadus lit a cigarette. "Want one?" he inquired casually.

Cale nodded and Broadus flipped him a cigarette and some matches.

"Well," Broadus began as he took a deep drag on his cigarette, "just two little things. I went by the mill and egged Grady Johnstone's new car."

Broadus paused as Cale's face contorted into simultaneous mirth and astonishment.

"Then, I just kind of smeared it with mule shit. And to top it off, I wrote 'BROADUS WAS HERE' with a can of white spray paint."

Cale hurled the screwdriver he had been holding into a toolbox. "Are you crazy? Grady will never let you into the mill now! You'll be stuck at that gas station forever. Marsh told me Grady's car was brand spanking new."

"Not now, it ain't," Broadus replied devilishly. "Got any beer?"

"Beer," Cale retorted sharply, "aren't you drunk already? Mule shit on Grady's new car!"

"No, I'm not drunk," Broadus insisted. "Besides, it was very fresh mule shit. I got it myself from my old man's barn this morning before I went to Saluda."

"What were you doing in Saluda?" Cale asked as he washed the grease from his hands with gasoline, after carefully putting his lit cigarette aside.

"Well, that's why I don't give a damn about Grady."

Cale paused and scrutinized his friend. Broadus' eyes brimmed with agitation. "What else have you done? When I talked to you from California, you were supposed to start in the weave room next week," Cale said sternly.

"Fuck the weave room! I joined the Marines!" Broadus declared jubilantly. "I'm not going into Grady's goddamned mill, I'm going into the President's goddamned war, just like you did!"

Cale hugged his friend. "The Marines!" he exclaimed. "Are you fucking crazy?"

"No," Broadus said with a grin. "It's just like momma's always telling me. I'm out of control! Only she says it's because my daddy went away when I was a baby and she hasn't been able to make a proper home for me. That I haven't been socialized right. But I say I was just born a wild man."

"Listen, jackass," Cale lectured, "this isn't like your other stunts. There is a war on. There's some serious shit going on where you're headed."

"You made it back alive," countered Broadus.

"You big ape! I made it back, but I don't know how alive I am. Anyway, in that shit over there, you can get killed without even trying," Cale explained.

"Staying here with these dull-ass crackers will kill me quicker, knucklehead. That's why I'm shipping out to Parris Island next week," Broadus said frankly.

"Have you told Bernice?" Cale asked.

Broadus stooped, picked up a piece of gravel from the driveway and tossed it into the shrubbery behind the garage. "She doesn't know that I did it yet. I'll tell her when I see her tonight. But it won't be much of a surprise,"

Broadus answered. He drew a large pocket knife from his jeans and began peeling the bark from a dead branch.

"Why?" asked Cale.

"Because I've been telling her for months that I'm a wild man and a wild man craves glory. There ain't no glory in this goddamned mill town. And there ain't no wilderness left where a man can find glory. So that leaves war and learning. I ain't got no head for learning."

"You would have if you ever put some learning in your head, jackass," Cale retorted.

"There's glory where you've been," Broadus asserted roughly, "and I aim to get some of it. All I have to do is shoot to kill and throw some grenades around."

Cale grabbed Broadus' knife hand and quickly turned the blade towards his friend's throat. "Listen, Marine," he said menacingly, "and listen good."

Broadus had always been the stronger of the two. He was surprised that Cale had instantly and easily seized control of the knife. He was not troubled by Cale's threatening voice. They had fought before. Cale's eyes made him uneasy. They were not filled with friendship. They flashed agony, as if Cale were drowning in a vast sea, beyond all hope of rescue, his love extinguished without ever passing into purpose.

"There's no glory in war. Repeat after me, Marine! There is no glory in war!" Cale howled.

Broadus knew that Cale had been overwhelmed by memory and could not even see him now. Cale shook with ferocity.

"There is no glory in war," Broadus said softly.

The spirit in Cale's eyes dissolved. He released his grip on Broadus' wrist and turned to face the brown waters of the Glory River. A moment later he spoke, sadly.

"Before I went over there, my life was constant glory. When the sun came up, the world was filled with beauty and excitement. I spent every hour exploring the farm, the river, the countryside, and the inside of my head. I worked in the natural rhythm of the livestock and the fields. I sang the joy of achievement and relished the peace of rest.

"I thought that living on my grandpa's land, keeping his cornfields tall and green, and holding on to a good woman's love, was all the glory I would ever need. It would have been too, if the war hadn't taken it away. I got nothing left inside. No glory. No heart. No mind. War takes away glory, Marine. Remember that when you've got blood on your hands."

Broadus recoiled from Cale's intensity. "There ain't no glory in dirt farming, country boy," Broadus declared vehemently, "you've always got shit on your hands. It's only one rung above the mill. You ought to know that, hayseed. How about that beer?"

Cale drew two beers from a noisy old refrigerator in the garage. He opened them, handed one to Broadus and lifted his bottle in a toast.

"You better not die on me, Marine," said Cale somberly.

To the clinking of the glass bottles, raised so that for an instant they were filled with shimmering sunlight, Broadus confirmed, "I would if I went in that mill, from lack of glory. Me and Grady Johnstone both."

***

July's heat returned with a vengeance in the afternoon as Cale Haines walked the rich brown cornfields of his late grandfather Matthew's farm and examined the thin green ears for corn silk. While he had been at war, Marsh had diligently worked the land and raised the crops that kept Olivia out of the poverty that drove most of the county residents into the Adluh cotton mill.

As he inspected the slender ears of corn, Cale remembered that he once dreamt of the day these cornfields would be his, when the lush, broad pastures, the sweet waters, the tangled forests of Bride's Woods and the slopes of Toenail Hill would be put in his hands. Since childhood, his dream of living on the farm had been so blissful that Cale had never imagined any other life. Until the war. Now he didn't deserve to be on this land, this ground that he had dearly loved for so long.

The farm covered eight hundred and sixty acres of gently rolling, shallow hills, bordered on the east by the great bend of the Glory River. Near the center of the land sat the farmhouse and the barn that Matthew had built from chestnut lumber salvaged from an abandoned farm in the mountains. The house and barn were surrounded on the west by cornfields, and on the east by Swede's Pasture, a broad meadow where the heavy clay soil gave way to white sand and grasses grew thick and lush. The heavy forest of oak, hickory, yellow poplar and white pine known as Bride's Woods stood in the northwestern section of the farm, and the abrupt promontory of Toenail Hill, along with a large grove of scarlet oak trees, lay to the northeast.

Within that dominion, typical of many farms in the Red Bank country, Cale had found wonder and excitement in the enthusiasm of his grandfather, and they had happily explored the land as if they had ranged the world and probed its mysteries and revealed its majesties. During these exploits, Cale had questioned Matthew incessantly about the mechanics of nature and the intrigues of man.

He had eagerly received from his grandfather an earnest and passionate tutelage of the cruel harmony that governed the natural world and the chaos that was a man trying to put his heart into the human world. If Matthew failed to satisfy Cale or himself on some matter as they tramped about the farm, his grandfather had, after supper, gathered Cale and Olivia in the parlor and read to them from his red encyclopedia.

Those evenings with the red books were some of Cale's fondest memories. A day spent traversing the farm, marveling at the beauty and the secrets of the season, was completed by rummaging through the pages of fascination that those red books offered for history, for art, for geography. He had been in love with the world then, and everything in it.

Cale suddenly stopped. Gripped by terror, he was lost once again in a tangle of green. He dropped to the ground and frantically searched for his radio. It was gone. So was his rifle. He must have been forced to leave it behind. His memory was really bad now. Was he doing recon or was he running? His knife was missing and he had no grenades. He must be running. From what? For what?

"Think, Cale, think!" His body trembled as he slowly crawled towards the tree line. He couldn't let them catch him again.

When he heard his grandmother ringing the iron triangle that hung outside the back door, Cale returned to himself in the present. He was ashamed that the flashbacks were still coming. He thought he had washed them out in the gin mills of California.

Cale stood up and focused on the corn plants. Then he hurried through the tall corn to the white farmhouse. He washed his face and hands quickly and went into the kitchen, where Olivia was removing a tray of biscuits from the oven.

"It's plenty hot out there, I reckon," Olivia said with a wide grin as she brought the biscuits to the table. "I thought you would have supper at home on your first day back."

Cale took a long drink of sweet iced tea. "Momma said she was fine and that I better get down here and check on the silking. That's just her way of saying she's knows I'd rather be on the farm than anywhere else. You know how true that always was, Grandma. But I can't stay here now."

Olivia put her hands in her lap and stared at her grandson. She was surprised and puzzled, and waited for an explanation.

Cale eyed his grandmother sharply. "I am all cold inside now. I don't feel anything like I used to. I can't be on Grandpa's land when I'm dead inside. This is the place I was always most alive. I've rented a house in Saluda. I'll still come home and help Marsh work the corn. But I'm going to get a job and live in Saluda for a while, until my insides recover," he said sadly.

Olivia winced and bit her lip.

"You know I don't want to go," Cale said despairingly.

Olivia sighed and her black eyes moistened. "Those same words are the last words your grandpa ever said to me."

"They are?" Cale questioned.

Olivia brushed away a fly that had landed near a bowl of field peas. "When the big flood came and the river jumped out of its banks, Matthew hurried us up to the top of Toenail Hill--me, your daddy, and your uncle Buck. We stood beside the holly tree and watched that muddy water race across the fields and surround the house and barn. You could tell that the whole county was going to flood.

"Matthew had already run the stock out of the feed lot, and the cows and the horses had moved to higher ground. But those damn mules wanted more grain to eat. Your grandpa hadn't gotten around to fixing the latch on that gate, so when Silk and Sack pushed on it with their muzzles, the thing opened. Naturally, those mules went back into the feedlot. The wind had just started to come up strong, and it blew so hard it slammed that gate shut behind them and the lock caught. A mule ain't smart enough to unlock a gate, so those mules were trapped and the water was rising fast.

"You know your grandpa loved those mules. So when they laid their ears back flat and they started kicking and snorting and neighing with the most terrified sound you ever heard, he started down the hill.

Olivia paused. The corners of her mouth grew taut and she inhaled with a gasp. She would lose him again with the telling.

"I begged Matthew not to go--you could already see one house floating in the river--but he was determined. He said to me, 'I can't let 'em get swept away, Liv, they'll drown for sure. They've served me faithfully. I have a duty, woman. You know I don't want to go!'

"I was clinging to him mightily, but Matthew was a man of strength and he was honor bound to go. He tore away from me and ran down to the feed lot. He splashed through that quick rising red water to the gate. He was fumbling with the latch when Sack suddenly charged. The gate snapped open and knocked Matthew in front of those frantic mules. Silk and Sack trampled Matthew, lost their footing, and stumbled into the water. Matthew floated in the water and those mules panicked and swam into the current towards the river. Matthew and those mules were swept downriver and were drowned."

"I'm sorry, Grandma," Cale said softly. He waited until the reverie no longer flickered in Olivia's eyes. "But I have to go. Everything here reminds me of what I used to be. I need to be in a place where I have no past. I know this is my real home, but I just can't stay now."

Olivia's eyes grew stern. "Don't matter anyway, Cale. I had to lease out the farm. I need the money. But boy, home is not a place!" she exclaimed. "Home is the way you live your life, according to the truest things you know in your heart and mind. The body can rest in any place. The spirit can only rest in what the heart loves and what the mind loves. A restful spirit is the only home a man can truly have. Matthew must have taught you that."

Olivia gazed through the kitchen window to the bed of red geraniums and purple impatiens that ran alongside the clothesline. Clusters of blue hydrangea flanked the bushy fig tree laden with setting fruit. "Don't worry about your insides. They will heal. Just try to love the things you've always loved. And pay special attention to the beauty in this world. That is what first separated us from the beasts."

***

"Diane, honey, come here a minute," Mabel Barnes called to her daughter from the kitchen where she was preparing to stew a chicken.

"Just a sec', Momma," Diane replied from her bedroom. The lithe young woman sat before the mirror of her vanity and slowly brushed her curly brown hair. Her quick brown eyes scrutinized her face and reflected irritation at the barely discernible square set of the tip of her chin. With that minor exception, she was quite pleased with her face and her figure--although she thought her firm, well-formed breasts tilted upward slightly. Gravity and pregnancy, she had been assured by her mother, would provide the necessary correction soon enough.

But it was levity, not gravity, that Diane was planning to achieve with her attractive looks and carefully pleasing manner. "Out of this miserable little town," she thought as she touched her uplifting young breasts, "I want these babies to raise me up out of this hick town." She squeezed her nipples firmly, waved goodbye to herself and went into the kitchen.

"Yes, Momma," Diane said as she appeared in the kitchen doorway and inhaled the scent of caramelizing onions.

"It's nothing to be bothered about," Mabel said as she covered a large pot and put it in the oven. "I just wanted to talk to you about Cale before your father gets home," she added with a quick smile.

"Let's hear it, Momma," Diane rejoined sternly.

Mabel felt herself blush so she turned towards the kitchen counter. "Your father and I have raised you to be a good girl, and we know that you have been."

"Yes, Momma. The whole town knows that Diane Barnes is a good girl. So what is it, Momma?"

Mabel remembered dusk in a cornfield many years earlier. She turned to face her beautiful daughter, eyes downcast. "Well, it's just that Cale has come home from the war, and he's been gone a long time, and I know he's going to come by for you tonight. And a girl's emotions can get pretty confusing at a time like that, especially when the whole county knows she's probably going to marry her boyfriend, and, lord knows, it would be easy to--." Mabel stopped. Her eyes welled with tears. Suddenly, she pulled her apron up to her face and, gently sobbing into it, cried, "Yield."

Diane hurried to embrace her mother. "Don't be silly, Momma," Diane explained with a laugh, "Cale is very handsome and I care for him, but I've got something stronger than Preacher Darnell's sermons to help me keep my bloomers on."

Mabel's reddened eyes transformed distress into a questioning demand.

Diane kissed her mother's forehead. "Ambition, Momma. I intend for my womanly delights to buy me a ticket out of this mill town, not just a cab ride to Grady Johnstone's front door. God gave me plenty of desire, Momma, but, thank goodness, escaping Grady gives me sense to use it wisely. I'll be fine, Momma."

***

Cale arrived at the foot of Toenail Hill, parked in the shade of a Chinaberry tree, and sat in his truck, smoking a cigarette and nervously awaiting the arrival of his girlfriend. In all of the odd moments he had experienced since he had returned from the war, this moment was the

35

strangest. Diane had refused to let him pick her up and had insisted on meeting him at the bottom of the hill. Since his sophomore year in high school, Cale had always driven them. As he anxiously tapped on the steering wheel, Cale thought that he should be sitting in Diane's parlor, listening to Mrs. Barnes' unceasing prattle as Diane fussed with her hair and clothes.

As Diane's car approached, Cale stepped out of his truck. He walked over to the path that led to the top of the hill and waited for her. Diane got out of her car and paused for a moment to gaze at Cale. The slender young woman with curly brown hair and warm brown eyes smiled shyly at Cale and walked towards him slowly.

"Why did you want to drive your mother's car?" asked Cale hesitantly. "I could have picked you up."

Diane stopped. Since Cale had called her from his base in California three weeks earlier, she had been rehearsing this moment. If she had told him then, he would not be standing before her, a returning warrior, so handsome, so needing her affection, so unprepared to hear her words. In the second that she hesitated, Diane saw the love they had known—and she swept him out of her heart for the last time.

"Cale," she said falteringly, "I had to drive myself because you won't be taking me home."

Cale halted and looked at her. She seemed tired and withdrawn but her eyes had energy--dispassion coolly swirled in them. She had made no move to hug him.

Diane dropped her head and stared at the daisies that grew along the path up the hill. "You were gone for so long. And they told us you were missing in action and--"

"You've met someone else," Cale said coldly.

Diane backed away from him. The harshness of his voice reminded her that he had recently been in battle. "That's right," she began bravely, "I waited for you. I waited for a long time. But no word came."

36

She stopped. Cale saw that her eyes were sad but resolute, like a banker denying credit for new seed.

"I had to do what's right for me," Diane declared as she looked away from him.

"You did the right thing, Diane," Cale said hollowly.

Diane glanced at Cale. She was startled but her eyes suddenly flooded with relief then clouded with suspicion. "Do you really feel that way? Everybody in the county expected us to get married--if you got back. Did you find someone else too?"

"No. I can't even find me anymore--that's why I am going away, to Saluda. The war broke me up inside. I feel so cold. I can't feel my love for the farm, or my family, or my friends, or you. I'm glad you moved on. I just hope I can someday."

Released from guilt, Diane opened the door of her car and stood behind it. "I once loved you very much, Cale. I dreamed of us getting out of this place and going to a real town. I waited as long as I could. You have to believe that. I'll always remember you, always."

Diane began to cry. Now that she could never have him, she felt trapped in the shabby mill town. Her dream of a graceful home, distinguished appointments, and pleasant friends seemed to withdraw to an unbearable distance. She whimpered with desperation not sorrow. Cale was unmoved. "Believe what you want to believe, Cale," she sobbed. "I couldn't wait anymore. I wish the best for you, Cale, and someday you'll know that I was right. Goodbye. Take care of yourself." Though he did not approach, she waved him aside, got into her car and drove away.

Cale watched numbly as the woman who had owned his heart—the woman he had first loved, the woman he had longed for from his bamboo cage in the jungle— adjusted her rear view mirror to check her makeup as she drove out of his life. Mechanically, he turned, lit a

37

cigarette, then walked up the path to the summit of Toenail Hill. When he reached the top, Cale strode to the massive holly tree that erupted from a small thicket of young pines on the pinnacle of the ridge.

Between the cloaking foliage of those pines and the sweeping branches of that holly tree, Diane had first declared her love for Cale, and he had first experienced the compelling power of desire; there, above the land which had held him since birth in the certainty of its duties, labors and customs, he had first felt his mind take flight, wondering at the creature that he was and marveling at his discovery that life could not fit into the patterns society had made for it, that it bulged with textures that made his spirit spark, like the strike of flint against steel; there, he had first kissed Diane and felt himself burst out of himself with longing and irrepressible excitement; there, he had first seen Diane's firm creamy breasts, had suckled her tender stippled nipples and touched her supple, moist, undulating genitals; there, he had first understood that, as himself, he was alone in the world and that his solitude was both beautiful and terrifying.

Cale walked over to the small headstone of Matthew's grave. He knelt in the grass and gently rubbed the granite marker.

"I'm all messed up now, Grandpa," Cale said sorrowfully. "I got home from the war but I didn't get back alive! I don't feel anything!"

Cale looked down at the river. What had always been to him a liquid mystery, a sweep of beauty, a rustle of intrigue was now nothing but a dull, dirty current sluicing through low hills of red clay.

"I used to feel the sunrise—the warmth on my skin and the beauty in my heart. Everything on the farm used to stick me like I was a pin cushion. I could feel the glory of the river on a frosty morning, and the harmony of new corn plants pushing up through the ground, and the grandeur of a full moon in summer, and—"

Cale kissed Matthew's headstone.

"I'm just so cold inside now, I have to go away. I can't be here, in this powerful place, and feel nothing. Marsh will be here to take care of Grandma. Bye, Grandpa."

CHAPTER 4--GRACE HOUSE

The first week of September, after he had picked the last of the ripe figs from the tree by the clothesline and given them to Olivia, Cale sadly returned home and began his move upstream to Saluda. He loaded his headboard, footboard, mattress, box spring, slats, radio, bulging seabag and two suitcases onto the bed of his truck. He eased the frame of his dresser against one wheel well then shoved the drawers in place. He slid a black footlocker against the other wheel well. Then he took two large toolboxes from the garage, placed them snugly against the other cargo, and closed the tailgate.

On the front seat, interleaved with an old quilt, he carefully laid his 20-gauge shotgun, 58 caliber flintlock rifle, 30-30 lever action rifle, and Matthew's 22 caliber hog rifle. Atop the quilted bundle, he placed his bow and quiver of arrows. Against the passenger door, he leaned the aluminum tubes that contained his Tonkin Gulf bamboo fly rod and his fiberglass spinning rod. On the floorboard, he stowed his hunting vest and his fishing vest. The final item he packed, nestling the leather tool apron between the two vests, was the set of Solingen steel woodworking tools his grandmother had given him after his grandfather's death.

Cale lit a cigarette and stopped to gaze at the red 1949 Ford, flathead six, three-quarter ton pickup. In the six years he had owned it, the vehicle had not been driven out of the Red Bank country. "Now, we're both going upriver for a spell," Cale said uneasily as he climbed into the cab.

***

At ten thirty in the morning, Cale arrived in the College Hill neighborhood of Saluda and quickly found

Grace House, a two-story white clapboard Queen Anne-styled house surrounded by clusters of sassafras and pawpaw trees. He had arranged to rent the once grand structure along with two roommates, as yet unknown to him. He parked beside an unpainted garage behind the house whose sagging doors hung from their jambs like the jowls of an old bloodhound. As he stepped from the cab, Cale glanced up to the curious little room with a cone-shaped roof that rose unexpectedly from the second floor on the south end of the house and gave the appearance of being a tower. Since the odd little room only suggested a castle turret, Cale wondered if the original owner had been seeking dominion over this college town or had been besieged by it.

"I'm just going to endure it," Cale thought, "until my insides are fit to go back home." Cale bounded up the front steps, strode across the veranda, unlocked the front door, and entered Grace House. He found himself in a spacious parlor which opened onto a dining room and a long hallway. At the end of the hallway was a stairway and a large door. Cale strolled down the hallway, casually examining the adjoining kitchen, bathroom, and bedroom. He saw that the door led to a small back porch. Cale scrambled up the stairway in the hall and looked at the three bedrooms on the second floor of the house. The larger bedroom gave access to the tiny room in the tower.

Because he had always kept some kind of shop at the farm, Cale planned to set up a basic workbench in the old garage. The bench would give him a place to tinker and provide proper storage for his tools. Not wanting to walk up and down the stairs to get to the shop, Cale decided to occupy the bedroom on the first floor.

He quickly unloaded his truck, assembled his bed, and arranged his meager belongings; then he sat on the bed and examined his new room. The dingy green walls were dimly illuminated by a single bulb weakly shining in a

41

dusty glass fixture. The stained window sills, the missing doorknob on the closet door, and the uneven, scarred wooden floor seemed like shards of countless lives whose purpose had perished in this room. Sitting in that dreary, forlorn, menacing chamber, Cale felt unconnected.

Home was little more than an hour away. Because his spirit was no longer equal to the enthusiasm, joy, and hope his grandfather's farm had always inspired in him, Cale had abandoned Matthew's land. The girl he had cared for so deeply; who had shared his thoughts and his desires as they both stepped across the threshold of adulthood; who had understood his fear of going to war and the sense of duty that drove him to enlist; whose remembered countenance had been a pinpoint of delight in his dark, unending sea of agony—was lost to him forever and he could not mourn her.

He could not grieve himself. The excited, curious, adventuresome boy he had been, ardently examining the world for its beauties, puzzles, enchantments, and spectacles--from the first whiff of coffee to reach his nose in the morning until he at last hung his baseball glove on his bedpost and wearily accepted slumber—that bubbling, studious, playful boy, embracing fate and death in the chase and the hunt and the kill, touching wildness with a taut line furiously whipped by a hooked trout, that questing, reverent youthful intelligence perished in the darkness of deeds that were his and others in that terrible jungle.

What remained of him was a passionless young man whose empty heart enveloped him like a prison. He was not certain if he still believed in freedom. But he knew he could not live much longer in confinement. Cale recalled what Broadus had said about being forced into the mill. It was true. No man can live without glory.

Cale hurriedly left his bleak bedroom and went to inspect the garage. The paint had long ago blistered and peeled from the clapboards and the side walls were swayed beneath the sagging roof joists. But the roof was intact and he judged from the dry, unstained walls inside that the shingles didn't leak. The floor was littered with trash and there were no intriguing old boxes to explore, just years of discarded junk which he would have to throw out before he could set up a woodshop. In the rafters, Cale saw gray planks of rough cut lumber.

There was no electricity in the garage, so he took a heavy-duty extension cord from the cab of his truck, connected it to an outlet on the small back porch and ran it into the garage and looped it over one of the rafters on the back wall. He knew he would have to buy a couple of work lights and a kerosene heater. "I can make it work," Cale thought as he carried his tools from the truck and put them in the middle of the dirt floor, "it is roomy enough and dry enough.

Cale took measurements along the back wall, retrieved several boards from the rafters and began to build a basic workbench. Using a handsaw, he cut a cleat, rails, legs, and braces. The familiar heft of his framing hammer soothed him and began to minutely bind him to this alien place as he nailed the cleat to the back wall then joined the rails to make a frame for the bench top. He attached the legs to the frame and stabilized the legs with braces. Cale measured and recorded the outside dimensions of the frame and left the garage in the early afternoon to get some dinner.

He quickly strode two blocks down the hill on Rancileer Street to the market on the corner. The market faced Station Avenue, which was busy with traffic and crowded with students flocking to buy supplies to clean and decorate their rooms, and to celebrate the beginning of the academic year.

All along the street, new roommates walked together, gossiping and talking happily, and here and there, small groups of friends, re-united after summer vacation, were discussing their recent adventures. It was a friendly excitement, though it made Cale feel lonely because he knew not a soul and his roommates had not yet arrived.

Station Avenue was lined with an assortment of shops catering to the college trade--a clothing store, a pizza shop, a record store, a drug store, a bookstore, a barber shop, a bar, a Laundromat, and a beauty salon.

At the upper end of the street, Cale saw a hardware store and the old train depot. A crude sign had been posted on the abandoned station door--FUTURE HOME OF THE COLORADO CAFÉ—and around the placard flowed a lovely floral mural. This was the building Dakota had told him about and Cale decided he would visit the soldier soon. But now he needed a drink and a burger, so he stepped into The Red Onion bar and sat on the stool nearest the door. The bar was cool and dark and nearly empty. Several members of a motorcycle gang were involved in a raucous discussion at a booth in the back and a lone businessman sat midway down the bar.

The bartender, a skinny man with a pencil moustache and a nervous face, limped toward him. "What'll it be?"

"A bottle of cheap beer and a burger and fries," Cale replied.

"You got it," the barkeep acknowledged before calling the order to the kitchen. When he brought the beer, Cale asked, "You got any whores in this town?"

"You bet," the nervous man answered as he lit a cigarette, "but they're all married and respectable. You don't need to buy it anyway. Just come in here on a Friday or Saturday night, you can get it to go home with you."

"Thanks for the tip. Got a good poker game in this town?"

"You just get here?" the bartender asked irritably.

Cale took a long swallow of the cold, crisp beer. "Yep. Just got back from the war. Couldn't stand to go back home yet."

The skinny man laughed a nervous laugh. "Got some unwinding to do first?"

"I'm not sure what I have to do first. I just can't go home for a while."

"Go to the hardware store down the street," the barkeep advised. "It's run by a bootlegger. Ask him if he has any Cajun alligator wire. He'll know what you mean. He can get you a bottle of moonshine and tell you where you can find a game."

Cale ate quickly, gave the bartender a good tip, walked back to Grace House and drove his truck to the hardware store on Station Avenue. He bought a sheet of thick plywood and two work lights then asked the clerk, "You have any Cajun alligator wire?"

The pudgy middle-aged man smiled. "Sure do."

"I'll take a pint and a tip on where I can find a good game," Cale requested.

The clerk scribbled on a brown paper bag, filled the bag with a bottle he took from beneath the counter, and handed the package to Cale. "Big George runs the only game the cops allow. Number's on the bag. Just say you're looking for Cajun alligator wire."

Cale paid the clerk, got some groceries at the market and drove home. He put the groceries away and returned to the garage. Cale marked and cut the plywood and screwed it to the workbench frame to form a tabletop. From the plywood scrap, he made a shelf under the bench. At sharp angles to each other, he drove nails into the back wall above the bench. From the cab of his truck, he retrieved a leather bundle and carefully unrolled it on the workbench, revealing finely crafted woodworking tools. These had belonged to his grandfather and the sheer presence of Matthew's elegant chisels and gouges added a little warmth to the strange space he was attempting to adopt. Cale hung the tool apron on the nails above the workbench.

After stowing his toolbox on the shelf beneath the bench, he attached the work lights to the large extension cord, hoisted them up to the rafter, then drove a staple into the wall to secure the cord. He closed the garage doors and went into the house.

The sun was setting and the empty house was bleakly dim. Cale took the bottle of moonshine into the living room, which was flooded with the pale red light of the dying day. He looked out at the darkening neighborhood and deliberately thought of home. Alone in a new place, beyond the welcome embrace of family and friends, absent from Matthew's land, from the only place on earth he had ever felt sacred, Cale desperately wanted to feel that his spirit still lived, that it still loved something.

It did not.

Cale sat on the bare floor and quickly took a drink of the burning whisky as darkness gathered in the corners. He took another drink and wished a dog would bark. No dogs barked in the jungle. The jungle had no corners. It had only darkness, blackest in full sun. Blackest because then you could see yourself and you could not deny what you were. You were the unnatural force, slithering upright through the jungle, hissing, spitting, unclean and unrelenting. You were the unnatural fingers of death, restlessly combing the dense green foliage.

A single star now shown in the night sky. Cale toasted its arrival with a large gulp of whisky. "Star, you are my true brother. We know the real meaning of cold. Warmth vanquished. Those who have never been warmed can never know cold for what it is. Loss. Utter loss. Shit, I need a drink."

Cale drained the bottle and tossed it across the floor. Outside, a truck backfired and Cale dove away from the pale starlight and curled up in a dark corner. He lay trembling in an infinite, eternal jungle until the alcohol took his mind away and let his soul stop bleeding for the night.

***

Cale was awakened the next morning by a loud, rapid banging on the front door. Swinging the huge door open with a frown, he encountered a young man on the steps who held a suitcase in one hand and a key in the other. The stranger spoke first, "Cale?"

Cale nodded.

The young man extended a hand. "Henry Reid Kelly. Poet--and if I'm at the right place, your roommate. I go by Hank, unless I'm submitting a poem and need to sound more dignified. That's my dad in the station wagon."

Cale smiled. "Glad to know you, Hank. You can have any one of the three bedrooms on the second floor. Just pick one out, and you and your dad can move your stuff in. I'm still setting up my jackleg woodshop in the old garage out back, so I'll be out of your way."

Hank nodded with a shrug. His life was ruled by omens and symbols, and he had hoped that his appearance at his student apartment could, in the tiniest dimension, be ceremonious. His dad had barely acknowledged that he was starting college.

Cale retrieved a wood vise from the cab of his truck and positioned it on the top of the workbench. He marked the location of the bolts for the vise base, carefully drilled the holes with a brace and bit, and fastened the vise securely. Hank and his dad were struggling with a bed when Cale drove slowly down the drive and headed to the hardware store.

The clerk remembered him immediately. "You get that special wire we talked about?"

"Yep. Now I'm in the market for a small kerosene heater," Cale responded.

47

"Got just the thing," the clerk assured him. "They're left over from last winter, and there's not much call for them in September, so I can give you a real good price. Two or three months from now, those professors in the big, drafty old houses on College Hill will be in here begging for one."

When Cale returned to Grace House, the station wagon was gone. He hauled the kerosene heater into the garage and put it on the dirt floor in a corner near the door. Cale sat on the workbench and examined his shop. When he was a kid, Matthew had built a small shop for him in the rear of the tractor shed.

Working with his hands had connected him to his imagination, and he had loved the excitement of creation. The production from that first childhood shop had been simple--rough boxes, crude shelving, sharpened blades, and hand tools fit with snug new handles. Matthew had welcomed these contributions and had assured him that life on the farm was better because of them. Now Cale hoped his new shop would help connect him to his heart so he could go home, back to the place where he had felt truly magical, back to the family farm, back to Matthew's cornfields.

As he turned the corner of the house after leaving the garage, Cale saw a strange young man on the stoop who was searching feverishly through his pockets while swearing heartily. Parked at the curb was an old Volkswagen Karman Ghia loaded with clothes and boxes that jutted through the windows; the rear end sat low to the ground on partially deflated tires and the whole car had been hand painted in a camouflage pattern of olive, brown, and black, which was accentuated with patches of rust.

"Jack?" Cale hailed cautiously.

"Hell yes!" roared the tall, lanky, mustachioed young man, "John Patrick O'Donnell--known in the great Blue Mountains as Mad Jack! Have you got your key? I can't find my goddamn key. All keys ought to be orange, big as a pancake and worn around your neck so you could find 'em!" he thundered in mighty disgust.

Before Cale could answer, Hank suddenly opened the door and beheld the blustery stranger.

"I'm Cale Haines and this is the third roommate, Henry Reid Kelly, a real poet." Cale extended his hand to Jack, who stared suspiciously as they shook hands.

"I go by Hank," said the poet as he also shook hands with the newcomer.

"Have a look-see at what you're paying rent for," said Cale as Jack marveled at the spacious living room.

"Damn, what a fine room," Jack declared. "Cleaned up, it would be plumb elegant. A fine place for a drink of good whisky and a good-smoking pipe." Wiping dust from the bay window, he stared down Rancileer Street to Station Avenue and beyond to the college and its imposing chancellery. "A little elbow grease and this'll be a parlor for a gentleman. Either of you flatlanders got any decent furniture for our parlor?"

The roommates shook their heads.

"No matter," Jack retorted, "I'll bring something down the mountain. The family's got a little trade in antiques. Nothing fancy. Mostly junk to peddle to the snowbirds on their way to Miami. I could bring a stick or two of the good stuff."

"I like your battle wagon," Hank said tentatively, a smile at his lips.

Jack wheeled and glared at him for an instant; then he sensed Hank's humorous intent and exploded with laughter. "Ha! Ha!" he shouted and sucked in a huge breath as he slapped his knee; pointing to his car, he began to guffaw rhythmically until tears rolled from his eyes, and Hank and Cale joined him with genial chuckles. "That's the Bismarck," Jack said weakly, "ain't it a sight?"

"Want to see the rest of the house?" Hank timidly inquired of the explosive third roommate.

"What I really need to see is the bathroom," Jack responded. After Cale pointed the way, Jack slapped his thigh with his hand, as if it were a riding crop, and marched stiffly down the hall.

The ancient toilet roared, and directly Jack appeared in the doorway. "That crapper is a real howitzer," he said with a chuckle.

"Ready to move in?" Cale asked.

"If you mates heave to and lend a hand," Jack said sanguinely, "I'll fork over the pieces of eight for a fat supper tomorrow night."

Cale and Hank agreed, and the three of them emptied the Bismarck quickly. When the last thing was tossed on the floor of his room, Jack rummaged through the mess until he found his pipe and some tobacco. He lit the pipe and sat on the windowsill. Cale lit a cigarette, took a deep drag and exhaled slowly. Hank unwrapped a stick of gum and chewed it nervously.

"The phone will be connected soon. It's in my name and I don't mind paying for the local calls," Cale advised his new roommates officiously, "but if you make any long distance calls, you have to pay up when the bill comes. I can't give anybody credit. The first time anybody's late or comes up short, I'll jerk the cord out of the wall. There's a phone booth on the corner at Station Avenue. I'm going there as soon as I finish this cigarette. I guess you boys will be going to the cafeteria for supper."

Jack scowled. "I pay my freight," he grumbled. "Don't use a phone much anyway. I'm sure the food won't be much to speak of at the cafeteria, but I'll bet we'll be surrounded by some very fetching pussy."

"Then you should eat well tonight," Cale said with a wink as he walked towards the door.

When he entered the phone booth, Cale pulled a crumpled paper sack from his back pocket and called the number written next to the name Big George. Cale gave the code to the muffled voice on the other end of the line and received a time and a place. As he walked up the hill to Grace House, Cale gazed at the campus, now glowing in the evening light of September. "Tomorrow morning," he thought, "Jack and Hank will begin a new life. A life of purpose. Tomorrow morning, I will still be missing in action."

CHAPTER 5--THE THREE PUSSKETEERS

As they had their morning coffee at the wobbly turquoise dinette table in the sunlit kitchen of Grace House, the exuberance of Jack and Hank's conversation rang through the house, and Cale listened sadly until they had gone. He felt hollow. He knew they had not deserted him but their excited, expectant voices carried the promise of a happiness that did not include him, that eluded him, that left him still adrift in a cold sorrow that would not ebb.

The old pipes in the bathroom clanged and squealed as Cale showered, and he stood in the spitting hot water and tried to weep. He was not away. He was not home. He was not lost. He was unplaced--and he was losing ground. Maybe having a job would help stop the slide, would begin to ground him in Saluda.

After a filling breakfast at the coffee shop on Station Avenue, Cale walked up the busy street to the old train depot. Entering the spacious lobby, he encountered three strange looking young men. Each had long hair and wore bell-bottomed jeans.

Cale easily recognized the first young man as Dakota. He was tall and slender, kept his black hair in braided pigtails, wore a snakeskin headband, a buckskin shirt and Apache boots.

The second fellow was short and stocky, wore a chambray shirt and crowned his curly brown hair with a black wool Fedora hat. His open countenance bore an easy smile, as if he were constantly bidding welcome to the world.

While his companions appeared to be in their early twenties, the third guy was much older. He wore a florid, multi-colored, blousy shirt and a red leather vest. His thin face had a secretive look, and his wet eyes were focused, dispassionate, and calculating.

"Cale! Good to see you, dude," Dakota exclaimed as Cale came through the door. "This is Dargan, the founder of the Potlatch," Dakota said, gesturing to the man in the red vest.

Dargan approached Cale calmly as a mellow smile emerged on his bearded face but he did not offer to shake hands. His green eyes, framed by locks of ginger hair that fell over his shoulders in thick masses, reaching his breastbone, seemed to Cale to be distant, almost as if they belonged to a different body. He wore a loose tunic of a delicate fabric patterned in rich, iridescent colors, above jeans whose fanned cuffs rested on his sandaled feet. Around his neck he wore a leather thong from which a stone talisman hung.

"Peace, dude," Dargan said in a soft voice.

Pointing to the clean-shaven one with the Fedora, Dakota said, "This is Boss. We call him Boss because he always knows the sensible way to get things done, and he always has a plan. In a group of hippies, that's a trait that stands out."

Boss cheerfully extended his hand, "Glad to know you, Cale."

"Hello, Boss," said Cale. "How much of the depot are you going to renovate?"

A big smile emerged on Boss' squarish face. "We haven't finalized the plan. We are going to put in a cafe and some shops."

"The basic idea is simple," Dargan declared. "We want the commune at the farm, the Potlatch, to be the place where we grow stuff and make stuff. We bought the depot so we could have a restaurant that serves the food we have grown and to have shops to sell the stuff our artists create. We might want to have another space or two, for yoga or politics. But the restaurant, that we call the Colorado Cafe, and the retail shops are for certain. Dakota says you are a carpenter and a farmer."

Cale nodded. "I'm a fair carpenter," he admitted frankly. "My father is in the real estate business and my brother, Marsh, is a contractor. I can frame to code and I can finish to fit. On jobs I've done, Marsh signs off on the work and gets it passed by the inspectors. He could do the same for any work I do here. I've been working the family farm with my brother for years, so I know a little about farming."

"Do you have a tractor, dude?" Boss asked excitedly.

Cale nodded. "I've got an old red belly Ford."

"Cool. Are you looking for work?" Dargan inquired.

Cale eyed Dargan cautiously. "Sure. What work have you got?"

"Carpentry, here and at the Potlatch, and plowing fields at the Potlatch," Dargan replied. "I've got all the helpers, gardeners, and field hands I need. I need somebody who knows how to actually build things, and who can manage field crops."

Dargan noted Cale's skeptical gaze. "I can pay top dollar. I've got the trust fund thing going. We all want the Potlatch to be self-sufficient. I need somebody who can help me get it there. Dakota will organize whatever crews you need, and Boss will get the supplies you need. Boss will pay you too. Boss handles the money."

"I don't know," Cale said reluctantly.

"Hey, dude, I'm not asking you to be one of us. Not everybody's head is into the commune thing. I'm just asking you to do some work for us. You'll get paid in cash every Friday evening, and I'll pay for your gas to drive out to the farm," Dargan offered.

"I would need a flexible schedule. I help my brother with the family farm. And I like to hunt and fish," countered Cale.

"That's cool with me," Dargan said. "Just keep track of your time, and give it to Boss. Like I said, he handles the money. That's another reason we call him Boss. That, and his plans and his killer hat."

Boss chuckled and doffed his Fedora.

"When would you need me to start?" asked Cale.

"Let's see. Today is Thursday. I'm getting a delivery of building materials on Tuesday," Boss answered.

"You would be working mostly here at the depot until we finish the renovation projects," Dargan explained. "Could you could start Wednesday?"

"Ok," Cale agreed. He shook hands with Dargan to seal the bargain.

"Looking forward to working with you," Boss called as Cale turned to leave.

Dakota offered his hand to Cale. "I'm glad you looked us up, man. We can rap anytime you want to about readjusting to society."

"Thanks," Cale answered sincerely, "but it's not society I'm worried about."

***

Hank returned home from his first day of classes and found Jack in the parlor holding a large flashlight and staring at the hearth. "We gotta get on the roof," Jack said enigmatically. "We gotta get on the roof."

"Why?" Hank demanded.

Jack grimaced and handed the flashlight to Hank. "Stick your head in there and look up."

"This thing's filthy," Hank declared after a momentary inspection.

"It's a fireplace, Longfellow," Jack said disdainfully. "See any daylight when you look up at the sky?"

55

"No," Hank replied sheepishly.

"Right. It's clogged up. We gotta clean it out before we can use it. Can't see not using it. I got wood up the mountain. I could haul a pile down here and we could build some nice fires. In two weeks, it will be fall. Be cooling down right smart pretty soon. A crackling fire and a jug of whisky would be mighty comforting on a frosty night. Not to mention setting the mood for the ladies," Jack advised.

Hank accepted the scheme. "How can we get up there? We don't have a ladder."

"Don't need one."

"Why?"

"The tower. We can climb out on the roof from the windows there."

"Hey, that's right."

"We could unclog it real quick. I been studying on that during my smoke," said Jack posturing, as he always did when away from home, in the manner of a salty mountain man. "There's two ways to do most anything–the wrong way and the mountain way. The mountain way gets shed of the silliness of doing things with a bunch of fancy tools and modern procedures. Mountain people are used to gittin' by and making do. We'll have to make do."

Jack reclined elegantly against the mantle. "The way I see it, all we gotta do is drop something heavy down the chimney and all of the trash will get knocked down, and we can just pick it up and throw it away. We ain't got to clean the chimney–even a fool knows the fire's going to muss it up directly–all we got to do is open 'er up so the smoke can get out."

"But what if we got something stuck in there?" Hank asked nervously.

"Wouldn't be no worse off. We can't use it now 'cause it's blocked up–besides, if we git something heavy enough and small enough it'll just fall right down through."

"I don't know what we could use," Hank countered hesitantly, worried he could be held at fault.

"I do!" boomed Jack, and he rushed upstairs to his room. Hank listened as Jack searched through his belongings, cursing and kicking things aside until he heaved a small ball from a carton. The heavy black ball struck the floor with a loud whack, rolled around the uneven boards and came to rest against a pile of clothes.

"What's that?" squawked Hank when Jack returned with his prize and an old wooden pallet.

"A genuine cannonball," Jack announced proudly.

"Where'd you get it?" Hank asked in amazement as he picked up the ball.

"On the mountain," was the gruff reply.

Hank carefully examined the war relic. "Seems like it would hit bottom pretty hard," he warned.

"That's what I dragged out this crate for. Jam it in the fireplace and when the ball comes down, it'll land on all that trash and that crate'll get smashed but it ought to stop that ball without busting up the hearth none."

"We're liable for any damages, you know."

"Hell fire! If you don't want to help me, by jing I'll shinny up on the roof and do 'er myself," bellowed Jack. He shoved the crate into the hearth and started for the tower, cannonball in hand.

"All right," complained Hank. "But I'm going up first," he added authoritatively and raced past Jack to the tower door.

Climbing the stairs from Hank's bedroom into the tower, they came to the small landing which Hank, upon moving into the adjoining room, had claimed as his poetic meditation space. Two large windows faced the street, one looked northward to the college and the other opened southward towards the river. A small window on the east wall offered access to the steep roof.

"Hop out and I'll pass you the ball," said Jack.

Hank squeezed through the narrow window, stood up cautiously, got his balance, and took the ball from Jack, who had great difficulty bending his long frame enough to follow. When Jack emerged, they crept up the roof to the chimney.

The view was exhilarating: they could see the top of the chancellery and the sweep of the campus and the town down to the dark swath of the river; the leaves of the poplar trees had already turned yellow and tinges of yellow, red and orange appeared in the crowns of the oaks, the hickories and the maples; far beyond the steeples of the churches and smokestacks of the cotton mills, in the purple ribbon that lay along the horizon, stretched the uplifting of earth that was the Blue Mountains.

"Damn," exclaimed Jack, "that's a fine sight. And a comfort, too, to know I can at least see the great Blues from the roof."

"Umm," Hank murmured. Captivated by the romance of such a grand vista and the crisp late summer air, Hank pondered the collegiate adventure he had just begun. He knew there must be a poem somewhere in the powerful emotions that gripped him as he observed his place in the world, as he beheld the specific place from which his journey as a collegiate poet would begin. What delicate words, properly and deliberately sounded, could capture the majesty of this moment?

"Well, let 'er rip!" Jack declared after inspecting the black column.

Diminished, Hank handed the ball to Jack who ceremoniously raised it above the chimney. "Bombs away," the mountain man cried gleefully, and in the instant he released the ball, they heard, echoing up the chimney, the sound of the front door slamming shut.

As Cale closed the door and turned toward his room, a loud roar filled the parlor. Suddenly a violent crash shook the room and a cloud of soot and ash burst from the fireplace amidst the sharp splitting and cracking of wood and the clanging of metal.

Cale dove away from the grenade blast and rolled behind the stairway to get protection from the mortar rounds that would be coming. He had walked into another ambush! He was tired of running, weary of ants and beetles, fatigued by thirst and hunger, spent from wet clothes and damp feet, disgusted by incessant fear and longing, impatient with darkness and shadow. Desperately, Cale wanted to rest, to be dry, to be content, to be in full sun—or to be dead. He remained crouched, waiting to be assailed by fate.

A small black ball bounced from the fireplace and rolled across the floor. The soot and ash cloud belching from the hearth rose and dissipated through the sunlit room. Cale lay motionless and watched as the myriad particles drifted across the room and settled on the walls, windows and floor. Then he heard Jack's voice resonating in the chimney.

"Thar she blows, mate! Clean as a scraped hog."

"Cale, is that you down there?" echoed Hank's tremulous voice.

"What the hell are y'all doing?" Cale shouted as he jumped to his feet. He heard not an answer but feet scrambling across the roof and clattering down the steps in the tower. Hank was the first to break into the dust filled parlor.

"Holy smoke!" he exclaimed as he ran to the fireplace and discovered among the litter and smashed remains of the wooden crate a large crack in the hearth. He saw also the obstruction dashed from the flue by the plummeting cannonball. It was merely a bird's nest which had been covered by leaves, and it had offered little resistance to the ball which easily crashed through the crate and struck the hearth with a jolting wallop. "Damn," Hank muttered. He stared angrily at Jack who had retrieved the cannonball and stood gaping at the long crack.

"Hell fire! We cleaned the damn thing out so we can use it," Jack insisted to Cale.

"That was a fool thing to do," Cale replied angrily. "That crack will have to be fixed and you boys have a big mess here to clean up."

Jack stared at Cale in alarm. The parlor was filthy now, and as his compatriot was sulking and glowering at him from across the room, Jack contrived a deal. "Hear me out mates," Jack began in a silky voice, "I've got a proposition on this matter. Hank, if you will get the trash out of the fireplace and sweep up all this dust, and Cale, if you'll patch the crack in the hearth, then I will paint the parlor and provide some furnishings for it. That way, we'll have a proper parlor for entertaining the ladies."

"I'm in, you goddamn scalawag!" cried Hank, relieved that Cale had not exploded in fury. When they had first met, something in Cale's eyes had seemed cold to Hank, and he had feared that it was some hidden rage.

"I'll patch the hearth but I'm not cleaning up one speck of this crap," Cale said firmly. "Deal?"

"Deal!" Jack agreed. "Let's do 'er tomorrow then, so she'll be spic and span for the weekend. One of us might get lucky," he said heartily. "I promised to buy a good supper tonight, and I'm good for my word. What'll it be mates?"

"I don't know my way around yet. Do you know some place, Jack?" asked Cale.

"I prospected a place on my way down the mountain. It's out on 611. The 611 Diner. A diner's the only place fit to eat around here," said Jack adamantly.

Hank shrugged.

"Let's go," said Cale. They piled into Cale's truck and quickly arrived at the diner, a drab cinder block building a few miles north of town.

"Looks like my momma's cafe," said Cale as they walked past the jukebox and slid into a booth at far end of the diner. Cale ran his finger across the table a saw a trail in the thin film of grease which covered the surface. "Maybe hers is a little cleaner."

"Your momma runs a diner?" asked Jack who, because of his size, had claimed one side of the booth for himself.

"Yeah, my daddy got the family into it. It makes a nice gathering place where my daddy can work some of his real estate deals. He's got this plan for a family business. My brother Marsh is a contractor, so he can build whatever project my daddy cooks up. The RuSam Grill—momma's name is Ruth and daddy's is Sam--brings in cash and gives him a place to talk business with the customers."

Hank nodded but he was intently watching the waitress working the counter. Her lovely body evoked a lusty desire which had never been--and, he feared, would never be--fulfilled.

"Oh," Hank said absently, "I wish she'd come on, I'm hungry."

"For what?" teased Cale, who had also noticed the buxom young woman.

"I just hope they got good swill," Jack commented. "I ain't had much luck with vittles in the flatland."

Hank watched the waitress flirting with the customers at the counter. Finally, she turned from the counter and ambled towards the booth.

"Hell fire," Jack said quietly, "she's a handsome figure of a woman."

Though she was as young as the three roommates, the waitress had been seasoned by several years' work, and she decided as she approached the booth, that the awkwardly disguised leers of the three young men could produce a good tip. She wore uniforms which had been altered to accent her voluptuous figure, and when she

61

worked, the top button of her blouse was always unbuttoned, revealing the smooth deep cleavage of her full breasts. She never tolerated unseemly advances, but she knew that a man with a little hanker and a little money usually found enough change to leave her a generous gratuity.

"Evening, boys," she said as she leaned across the table, "I better give this table a wipe." Eagerly the roommates stared at her sensuous, outstretched body as she slowly washed the table. When she stood up, she drew her pad from her apron and concentrated on the blank paper so the young men could openly admire her figure. "What can I get for you boys?" she asked warmly.

"I'll have the country-style steak with rice and gravy and peas and tea," Cale responded.

"I'll have the same, lassie," Jack replied with a smile.

"Make it three," said Hank shyly as he gazed at her shapely body.

"Dessert?" the waitress asked and looked up suddenly into Hank's longing stare. His eyes were so filled with desire that he turned quickly away.

"None for me," said Cale.

"Got any cobbler?" inquired Jack.

"No, but we have pie--pecan, chocolate, and apple."

"Humph," muttered Jack.

"I'll take chocolate," said Hank. He watched her soft red lips as she tabulated the bill. Desperately he longed to kiss those lips and caress her supple body.

"Be ready shortly," the waitress said, and she walked back to the counter, confident that the three young men were watching her every step.

"Damn, she is nice!" cried Hank.

"She sure is," said Cale, "I think I'll have a better look." He rose and strolled over to the counter to examine the slices of pie which sat in a small glass case. The waitress posted their order as a customer sat down at the counter. "Coffee?" she called, and when the man nodded, she bent over to get a cup. Cale framed her between two pieces of apple pie and gazed wondrously as her blouse fell open, exposing her creamy breasts nestled in a white brassiere.

"Change your mind?" the waitress asked when she noticed Cale.

"Yes," said Cale, "once I saw it, I had to have a piece." He smiled suggestively. "I'll have apple."

"Ok," she answered with a knowing smile.

When Cale slid into his seat, his roommates were laughing quietly.

"She's got gorgeous tits," Cale declared.

"Did you see 'em?" Hank asked seriously.

"Hook, line and sinker," said Cale. "She gave me a smile too."

"Hell fire!" roared Jack in appreciation of Cale's boldness. "I can shore see myself spending some time in this little diner," Jack observed with a grin, "can't you, Cale?"

"Sure," said Cale cockily.

The waitress returned a few moments later and filled the table with their plates. "I've got a bet going with these boys," Cale said playfully.

"Yeah?" the waitress responded cautiously.

"If I lose, I can't pay so I hope you can help me out," pleaded Cale.

"Right," the waitress said quickly, expecting the punch line.

"I bet them that if I asked you your name," he said slowly, watching as she braced for the rest, "that a pretty girl like you would get mad and not tell me 'cause you'd think I was getting fresh, instead of just being friendly."

The waitress was charmed by the clever, handsome young man with grey eyes and long black hair that grew in ringlets. "Everybody that comes in here regular knows my name."

"But I ain't never been here before," argued Cale.

"When you come back again, I'll tell you," she said with a wink as she turned and walked away.

"Hell fire!" Jack cried and he giggled with delight.

Cale laughed and took a large drink of tea. Hank was very quiet, deflated by a hopeless lust and a gnawing envy of Cale's easy manner with women.

The roommates ate a leisurely supper, while competing with tales of valor and bravery, of romantic conquests and unfulfilled longings. Jack delivered a tirade against the hypocrisy of life in the flatlands, contrasting it to the virtue, hardiness and purity of mountain people. Several times, the meal was interrupted by interludes with the lovely waitress, and all were convinced by the time Jack searched his pockets for the money to pay the bill that Cale would not only be remembered by her when he returned but would be well received to boot.

Secretly, they each planned to return alone and try their luck at seducing the pretty young woman. Jack thought it a fine sport for a displaced, lusty mountain man, while Hank envisioned a sweet, soulful encounter with her upon his return. Cale was attracted to the waitress, but memories of Diane clouded his excitement.

"Of course, getting this waitress filly in the sack," Jack opined as he finished the last of his coffee, "is not the crux of the matter. The question really is how can we meet lots of fair lasses so we can have a chance to see their bare asses?"

"What do you mean, Jack?" Hank asked.

"Golldangit, Longfellow!" Jack roared, "The two of us gonna be here for four years and Cale for as long as he likes! In my book, that means a man is going to need a lot of mud for his turtle. I'm not going to be able to dip my wick on a regular basis unless I can meet a variety of females. I'll bet you boys won't be able to either."

Hank stared forlornly at the table. Cale pondered the scope of Jack's remark.

"Don't git so long in the face, Longfellow," Jack counseled. "I been studying on it up the mountain and I have an idee how to skin this cat."

Hank's face brightened. Cale regarded Jack with interest.

"They got this high falutin' literary magazine here at the college. Called the Epos. But the way I figger it, it should be called the Epuss. Girls just love arty things. Flatlander girls, anyway. I believe that three enterprising young blades such as ourselves could work this trait to our advantage.

"I propose that we band together as the Three Pussketeers and that we adopt this motto: One get some. All get some. And I propose that our first adventure in the land of pudendum should be to host a poetry reading at Grace House in our proper parlor. Hank is a poet, I'm an artist with the camera lens, and Cale is a budding cabinetmaker, verily, an artist with wood. I'm telling you boys, the girls would flock to us in a flutter and the Three Pussketeers could be waist deep in pussy. All in a lather to pursue my palaver, say aye!"

Hank leapt to his feet. "Aye," he declared boldly, "and I'm a calligrapher, too," he added as he sat with a flourish.

Cale started to laugh. "Aye, Jack, aye. Damn that's brilliant. But no shirking here. There's real work to be done by all. If you really can get us some decent furniture for the parlor, and you slap a cheap coat of paint on the walls, we might just have a respectable place for such an event. And with fall fast approaching, and a fire crackling in the newly patched fireplace, we might just be able to set the mood for some of these girls. But I'm no artist with wood--all I do is make basic boxes and shelves in my sad excuse for a woodshop."

"You mean," Jack added with a grin, "that's what you did before you became a Pussketeer. From this day forward, you shall have the soul of an artist and you shall express it in exquisite cabinetry. And we shall henceforth enjoy the finest pussy in the land."

Jack extended his hand to the middle of the table. First Hank, then Cale, placed one hand atop the other.

"One get some. All get some," said Jack somberly.

"One get some. All get some," Hank and Cale repeated.

Returning to Grace House, they stopped at the market on Station Avenue and Jack bought a half gallon of red wine and a packet of cheap cigars. When they got home, since the parlor was dirty, Jack proposed that they camp out in the kitchen and drink a spell, so they sat on the linoleum floor and Jack opened the wine and passed it on to Cale. Jack then drew three cigars from the box, and they began to smoke. After a few quick drinks to numb their inexperienced gullets to the sharp taste of poor wine, they leaned back against the wall and puffed on their cigars in solemn ceremony.

After another deep draught, Hank finally broke the silence, "Jack and I are here to go to college. What brought you to Grace House, Cale?"

"I'll tell you," Cale answered reluctantly. "But I can't say with such a dry throat. Jack, pass the jug and give a man a drink!"

"Ho ho!" Jack cried as he swung the bottle through the air in salute to the speaker.

Cale hoisted the jug and took a long drink. His bragging manner instantly infected the others and they joyfully demanded the jug.

"My home is a little wide spot in the road called Adluh," Cale began, "on the Glory River, a bit south of here in the Red Bank country. I just got back from the war, and believe me, I wanted to go home, I really did. I've never wanted to be anywhere else.

"All my life, I couldn't wait to grow up so I could leave my daddy's house and live on the family farm. On my Grandpa Matthew's land. Matthew's dead but my grandmother, Olivia, still lives there. It's a beautiful farm that Matthew put his whole heart into every day. I spent as much time there as I could when I was growing up.

"When I was on the farm, I felt really alive. I was connected to the land, to the animals; I was caught up in adventure everywhere, in the barn, in the fields, in the river; I wondered about everything--clouds, spiders, mules, river critters--and my grandpa had answers to my questions and more questions of his own. My grandparents seemed to be in some great romance with the land, the river, the sun and moon, the seasons, and most of all, each other."

Cale stopped. He seemed to be considering something as he slowly examined his cigar then relit it. He puffed several times before continuing.

"It wasn't that way in my father's house. Life was routine. No sense of excitement. No clue that there could be great things stirring in this world. No hint that great things should be stirring inside you. Just live, work, die. Just talk about living, working and dying. No talk about being.

"I enlisted in the Navy to do my duty and then go back home. I miscalculated. Doing my duty screwed me up so much I can't go back home. So I rented this house in Saluda to give me a chance to work things out so I can go back home. I figured I could get a job, lease out rooms to students, and survive until I was ready to move on. That's all there is to my sad tale."

"How about you, Jack, what dragged you down off the mountain?" Hank asked.

Jack gulped some wine, and a studied look appeared on his face as he stared at the floor. He drew on his cigar slowly as he gauged his thoughts. He was uneasy with the question. He was a young man accustomed to looking at others--the flatlanders, the hated tourists--or looking back to examine the past. Rarely did he look within; he lived like a cat, moving and acting in the drift of impulse and sensation, never allowing his mind to settle for an examination of itself. Now he was picturing, not himself, but a friend, a fellow photographer who had recently departed from the mountains.

"Ain't much call for photographers on the mountain. Most folks fend for themselves and they ain't got the money to trifle away on pictures, 'less it's family concerns--weddings and buryings--and a dime store camera takes care of that. A man can't sell art on the mountain because the mountain is art. 'Sides, if a man wants to make out with a camera, there's lots of techniques he needs to master."

"Don't they have tech schools on the mountain?" asked Hank.

"Yes," Jack said impatiently, "but there's that other thing. Ain't so awful many women on the mountain these days. Mountain people usually get pledged in high school. Come graduation day, all the girls are spoken for. That's the mountain way. If a fella is unlucky in high school, he has to pack up and hunt up a woman somewheres else."

"Shouldn't have no trouble here, from the look of things," said Cale.

"So you'll go back to the mountains after school?" Hank casually suggested.

"Hell fire yes!" Jack bellowed. "Maybe 'fore then if I find a good woman." He lifted the bottle to his lips and drank the last of the wine. "This damn thing's empty!" Jack declared and he rolled the jug down the hall; he tried to stand but he could not raise himself, and he fell back against the wall. "I'm so drunk I can't get up. I'm gonna pee all over myself."

Cale helped him to his feet, and Jack staggered down the hall to the bathroom. Moments later Cale and Hank heard the toilet rumble and Jack's feet stumbling up the stairs; suddenly the house rang with wild, exotic music and Jack returned with a dark bottle in his hand.

"What's that?" asked Hank.

"This," Jack said as he raised the bottle, "is fine Irish whisky and that"--he flung his other hand towards his room--"is ancient Irish music and I, Mad Jack O'Donnell, am a fine Irish fellow--have a snort."

Hank took the whisky, sipped it quickly and passed it to Cale. Cale drank and then, stupefied, he and Hank and Jack succumbed to the blissful weariness of drink, and they fell asleep.

***

The next morning, the bleary-eyed roommates revived themselves in the sunny kitchen with several cups of strong coffee. Jack then took off without explanation, leaving Hank and Cale to munch on stale doughnuts.

"I'm sorry we made such a mess with Jack's hair-brained idea about the chimney. Ol' Jack's pretty convincing when he wants to be," Hank confessed.

"Jack is that," Cale replied with a grin.

"I'll do the cleanup in a few minutes. Why don't you meet me at the cafeteria for supper. I can cover you with my meal ticket. You'll see plenty of pretty girls--and we might even run into Jack."

"Ok. But I wouldn't be surprised if Jack was taking his evening meal at the diner."

After Cale left the house, Hank grudgingly cleared trash from the fireplace, carefully swept the parlor, and washed the hearth. Then he dressed quickly and hurried to his classes. Jack did not appear at the cafeteria while Cale and Hank were eating supper but when they returned to Grace House, he was sitting on the front steps, lazily smoking his pipe.

"Evening, boys," Jack called as his roommates drew near.

"You done with all your chores, Jack?" chided Hank.

Jack stood and eyed Hank sharply. "I 'spect I mostly do what needs to be done," he replied coolly.

"Damn!" exclaimed Cale as he opened the front door and stepped into the parlor. Hank scurried after him and they were astonished at what they saw: the parlor had been painted a light gray color and had been furnished with a large Oriental carpet, an antique settee, three side chairs and a small coffee table.

"Jack, what happened?" cried Hank.

Jack puffed up his chest and chomped on his bushy moustache. "Well," he began with a high-pitched voice, "I moseyed on down to the coffee shop for some breakfast and then made a call up the mountain. After breakfast, I bought some paint. I was just finishing up with the parlor when my cousin Donny showed up with a few items from my family's antique store. They give the room a classy look, kind of a finger sandwiches and high tea appeal, don't you think?"

"Damn, if you don't beat all, Jack," Cale said with a chuckle. "Except for chasing pussy, I never figured you to be the enterprising type."

Jack snorted and shook his head. "I don't do it regular, not regular at all. But this is a special occasion. We have to make the parlor respectable enough to hold a poetry reading."

They settled regally in the chairs, savoring their grand drawing room and imagining the females they would woo.

"I spoke to Dr. Randolph, my English professor," said Hank. "I told him about our idea and he thinks it's great. He offered to read some poems and to make an announcement to his classes--once we set a date. He also said we should make some signs and put them up around campus."

Later that night, Cale repaired the hearth while Hank hung several of Jack's framed photographs in the parlor and Jack created posters in the kitchen that artfully announced the coming poetry reading at Grace House.

"By jing, we're under way, mates! Three cheers for the Three Pussketeers! We'll cruise the bountiful main, and in the main, we'll snatch snatch from the jaws of modesty. One get some! All get some!" exclaimed Jack.

CHAPTER 6--HARVEST HOME

As promised, Cale arrived at the old train depot on Wednesday morning to begin working with Boss and Dakota. After inspecting the interior of the building, Cale reviewed the notes Dargan had given Boss, took measurements and drew a blueprint to frame space for a cafe with internal bathrooms, a central hallway, public bathrooms and three large rooms. After burgers and beer at the Red Onion, Boss added the plumbing details to Cale's blueprint and Dakota inserted the electrical wiring drawing.

Cale and Boss smoked cigarettes while Dakota aimlessly whittled a piece of scrap wood with the large hunting knife he wore on his belt.

"If we all work on stubbing in the main lines," Boss suggested to Cale, "then Dakota and I can help with the framing. While I am running lines and setting fixtures and Dakota is pulling wire and installing outlets, you can build cabinets and shelves."

"Sounds like a plan," Cale agreed.

"Boss always has a plan," Dakota remarked with a grin.

When Cale returned to Grace House, Hank and Jack were sitting in the parlor. "We put up the posters on campus," Hank began excitedly, "then I went by the campus newspaper office and they are doing a story on our poetry reading. Oh yeah, I talked to Dr. Randolph again. He said he would get a couple of his female students to serve whatever refreshments we have."

"Great," Cale replied.

"I sashayed by the college radio station and gave them a note about our gathering," reported Jack. "They said they will add it to their events news. The word's going to get around--we saw lots of girls reading the poster we put up in the student union. We'll have a bevy of winsome lasses gently shaking their asses and drinking cheap wine from plastic glasses."

Hank pointed to the hearth. "And if cold air the coming fall nights keep producing, we'll have a crackling fire to assist with seducing--"

"And separate bedrooms for pleasure introducing," Cale added.

"Speaking of bedrooms, Jack. I measured the closet in the bedroom where you are setting up your darkroom. I can make a simple table out of scrap to hold your enlarger and your developing trays. I'm going to start on it after I get some supper," Cale said.

"Much obliged, Cale. I can pay for the materials," offered Jack. He was not accustomed to receiving favors. It smacked of charity, which was not the mountain way.

"No need. There is some old lumber in the garage and lots of scrap at the job site."

"Then thank you kindly. How do you like working with those hippies?"

"The boys I'm working with are journeymen in their trades. A plumber and an electrician. Clothes and weed don't change that. They're in pursuit of the honey pot just like the rest of us."

"One get some. All get some--real soon," Jack predicted.

***

The nervous bartender was on duty when Cale ordered a burger and a beer. "Is that game on tonight?" Cale whispered. The barkeep nodded and held up seven fingers. Cale ate slowly and thought about Diane and the happy life that had been torn away from him by war. For an instant, he glimpsed the dark place where they had held him and the darker reality they had inflicted upon him--

then he pushed that hellish image back into its hiding place and tried to seal the door.

***

Cale did not return to Grace House until after midnight. He was ashamed that he had not worked on Jack's table as promised. He could not banish the memories that plagued him or expel the coldness that gripped his heart. But he could control his honor, and he had given his word. He had to make an honest start on the table so he could look Jack in the eye in the morning.

He pulled from his back pocket the measured drawing he had made for the table, and lit a cigarette. It would be a very long night and an even longer day on the job. He had it coming. As he worked, he suddenly became aware that the split, cracked clapboard on the rear wall of the garage reminded him of the bamboo pen where he had been held. That siding stabbed at a tender cell of memory that Cale did not want to burst. He found a discarded quilt in an old box and tacked it over the disquieting boards. After assembling the frame for Jack's table, Cale left the garage to get a few hours of sleep before going to work.

***

In the middle of September, the sky deepened in color as the sun's track signaled that the end of summer was near. The cerulean heavens struck a somber chord in Hank because the end of summer was more than a change of season for him. Losing light from the day frightened him as if somehow the diminished illumination inexorably drained promise from his life. As was his habit, Hank climbed the staircase from his bedroom into the false turret that, upon moving in to Grace House, he had claimed as his poetic refuge.

Though he had furnished it with a lamp, some large pillows, and a small table, the cramped cylindrical room that jutted above the roofline and offered him a splendid view of the student quarter and the college campus in

74

Saluda had not yet beckoned his muse. Discarded greasy pizza boxes proved that Hank's special room had provoked his appetite for food and the nude magazines hidden by pillows were a testament to the isolated place's ability to unfurl his lust. But, perched above the college town where he could reflect on his new life and the torrent of knowledge his classes had unleashed upon him, Hank had not yet written a line.

Munching on potato chips he had left behind the night before, Hank absolved himself. "How can I write great poetry?" he thought. "I am just a middle-class kid from Raleigh. I grew up in suburbia in modern times. A hallmark of modern times is that men no longer have quests. They have careers."

Hank rummaged beneath the pillows on the floor and found a slice of stale pizza. "I know I have a great soul. My passions are strong and driven by beauty and truth and the tragedy of the unrealized spirit. My own death haunts me. Why don't the words come?" The morsels he had eaten ignited his hunger and Hank grew irritable.

"Shit," he muttered. He thought of the poetry reading. He had already made calligraphic copies of two poems he had written in high school. "I need to have something I've written since I got here. These chicks aren't going to be impressed if I don't have any college stuff. Jack just has to push a shutter button and Cale just has to cut a piece of wood. I have to see humanity—poignantly."

Hank reached for his favorite magazine and opened it to the photographic spread he had dog-eared. The female was fantastic. Everything he desperately hungered for was before him: a beautiful woman's face with accepting, beckoning eyes; large, pendulous breasts with a globular fullness that seemed to need relief through the impassioned suckling of her stiff nipples; curvaceous hips with taunt, rounded buttocks that called out for caresses and correction; a delicately tufted crotch beseeching stimulation and penetration.

Such a woman inspired romance and lust, devoted service and wringing wet sheets, sublimity and deeply satisfying pleasure. The Trojan War, the struggling poet reasoned, had not been started by a misunderstanding or a territorial dispute. That heroic conflict was undertaken by something a man will always fight for—an alluring woman. "Never had one of those," Hank grumbled.

The hapless poet was not a virgin but the experience he had with a freckled girl in high school was sex only if measured by the most scientific criteria. Hank wanted a woman he desired to also desire him and to express that desire in word and deed, and for one of those deeds to be torrid physical passion. The other deed he craved was for his imagined siren to love him—unquestioningly, eternally.

"I can't write about that," the poet ruefully concluded. "Everybody needs love and everybody needs sex. There's no greatness in that. I need something new for the poetry reading. Above the vulgar world I sit, a sensitive man reflecting on my fate yet sidetracked by a wondrous set of tits. Were it not for this fatal flaw, I could instruct mankind in the resurrection of his soul. And the women would reward me, and their number would be legion."

Hank grasped his pen and wrote two lines.

"If the death knell of humanity rings in my heart,
Do I hang in a cathedral or a gallows?"

***

Fall arrived with deep blue skies, scattered ribbons of white clouds, and a refreshing breeze that hinted of a coolness to come. The tall proud sunflowers and the burgeoning hydrangeas were gone; the blossoms of pinks and blue daze were spent; and the zinnias, asters, and begonias had dropped their petals. The sober colors of coleus and marigolds gained ascendency as a forewarning that the diminished sun has consequences. Only the scarlet and gold cockscomb maintained a tribute to the power of light.

Cale finished the table for Jack. He lit a cigarette and studied the piece. It was plumb, square, level and functional but it made him unhappy. The table was not ugly, but it had no beauty. He had no reason to expect the hastily crafted utilitarian furniture to be pleasing to the eye but Cale was sad that it was so plain. It looked like one of the projects he had made in his high school shop class. "Hell, nothing makes me happy," he muttered as he put the table in Jack's darkroom.

***

A few days before the poetry reading, Jack began to fret about his attire. From thrift stores and scattered relatives, he had acquired a broad array of Edwardian clothes. When the parlor at Grace House would be packed with available females, Jack intended to present his dashing best. He filled a pipe and lit it and anxiously opened his closet door.

The first garment he spied was a navy blue wool frock coat. In it, he looked like a railroad baron of yesteryear but he couldn't wear it inside. Because he was hosting and not leading a tour through the countryside, Jack had to pass on his Norfolk jacket as well.

"More's the pity," Jack grumbled as he beheld the splendid houndstooth tweed belted coat. Box pleats adorned the front and back of the single-breasted jacket which also boasted patch pockets which Jack thought were quite sporting. As he replaced the coat, a hat tumbled from the jumble of clothes stuffed onto the shelf above the closet rod.

"Can't wear a hat in the house," Jack complained loudly as he picked up the black felt Homburg. The slightly rounded crown and the curled-up brim gave him a rakish look and Jack loved to wear that hat around susceptible women of class. He threw the hat onto his bed. Someday he would arrange a proper place for the Homburg, his pork pie, his derby, and his Fedora.

"Get down to business, mate," he said to himself.

The first two shirts he retrieved had band collars so Jack put them back in the closet. The third shirt was the right one. The white dress shirt had a full button front with a finely pleated bib and a winged collar. The neck of the shirt closed with a stud. Jack laid the shirt on his bed.

Jack then selected a pair of brown wool trousers with silver pinstripes. The pants had narrow, boot-cut legs and side-entry pockets in the front with button-fastened pockets in the rear. The dressy trousers closed with buttons and the waistband had big buttons for the black canvas Y-back braces Jack would attach to hold them up.

The only jacket that matched those trousers was a sack coat made of the same fabric. This jacket was cut close to the body, with no back vent, and featured narrow arm holes and high, thin lapels. The two flap pockets were situated slightly above his hips and the rounded front hem, when closed with four buttons, trimmed his silhouette. Jack knew his manly frame would indeed be accentuated by this coat.

Jack had several waistcoats to choose from but most of them were too casual for the upcoming cultural occasion. He skipped over the brown corduroy, and the blue one, and the black canvas one and snatched the shiny one from the closet. This double-breasted vest was made of a silver and maroon paisley fabric, had covered buttons, a curved watch pocket and a black satin back. Jack added it to the pile on his bed. From his top dresser drawer, Jack retrieved a gold-colored watch with a gold watch chain.

The handsome timepiece was engraved on the case and the stem, driven by a 17-jewel mechanical movement and displayed its intricate wheels and gears through the open glass face of a skeleton dial. Jack placed the watch on top of his bureau.

Jack turned his attention to ties. He immediately dismissed his array of four-in-hand ties and his two cravats. He dismissed his ascots and settled on a dark crimson silk puff tie. "Not one in a thousand men alive today knows how to tie one of these," Jack observed, "but I do. The trick is, after you have attached it with the hook and adjusted the slider, you must keep the ends facing forward as you cross them and tuck them under your vest. You can't fold them, just gently kink them so that, when you stick your thumbs under them and pull up, they puff and hold their shape."

Jack stared in the mirror and imagined himself dressed in the carefully chosen wardrobe. He was very pleased with the imagery then troubled by a nagging thought.

"Why have I never done a portrait of myself? All great artists create self-portraits and I am certainly a great artist."

Jack swept aside the clothes on the closet rod to create ample space to hang his selected attire together. "Must be a reason. I need to study on it."

Jack closed the closet and went into the parlor. Hank was in class and Cale was at work. "I don't know if poets can render themselves or not," he thought as he lit his pipe again, "but I know cabinetmakers can't be bothered by this self-portrait nonsense. They can't put their image into their work. Why do I care?"

Jack was about to brew some coffee when he heard a sharp rapping on the front door. He grudgingly answered the knock.

"Good afternoon, sir," a fresh-faced neatly dressed young man said as Jack scowled at him. "Have you accepted the Lord into—"

"Goddamn you!" Jack bellowed as he slammed the door. He rapidly paced the room, stomping emphatically. "That's why I can't do a self-portrait!" he boomed. "The instant I develop it, it becomes an affirmation of the present. Goddamn the present! The age of the zombies and the jackals! I won't have it! Goddamn it, I won't have it!

"My work affirms the past, the Golden Age when noble humans walked the Earth. I won't honor the lizards who have taken their place. I am a gentleman. I have a human soul. Goddamn the lizards who surround me in their leisure suits! Goddamn them all!"

***

The Saturday of the poetry reading at Grace House arrived in the middle of October and the three roommates began preparing immediately after their morning coffee. Jack hung his three best artistic photographs in the long hallway that led from the parlor. Hank framed two of the poems he had rendered in calligraphy and placed them on either side of the fireplace. From his shop, Cale took a small bookcase which he had made and painted Williamsburg blue, carted it inside and positioned it between the settee and one of the chairs, and watched as Jack and Hank filled it with books of poetry and art.

After lunch, the roommates grudgingly cleaned the kitchen, the first floor bathroom and the parlor. They were strangely quiet when they gathered on the front porch for a breather, as if they had just noticed that the world around them had changed greatly. The leaves of the sassafras trees and the pawpaw trees that enclosed Grace House were brilliant yellow. The maples bore bright orange foliage while the oaks and hickories were covered with red and auburn. This florid milieu would soon collapse and they could sense the brown, bare death that would strip its bones until spring.

As night fell on that chilly evening, Cale struck a match against the hearth and lit the fire while Jack, elegantly dressed in his most commanding duds and moving slowly and formally, lit the candles Hank had placed in the parlor.

"The trap is set," Jack observed with a satisfied smile. "Now we shall see what manner of females we can catch."

Just before seven o'clock, Dr. Randolph and his wife, Claire, arrived. Randolph was a man in his early forties with ordinary looks, a slight build and a haughty manner that made him seem occupied with a great secret and generally impatient with the world. He wore the standard costume of a Bohemian academic: a corduroy sports coat, blue jeans, a turtleneck shirt and a pair of hiking boots.

Dr. Randolph's wife presented a contrary character, as she was intensely engaging, both in appearance and demeanor. Claire was a radiantly beautiful woman of perhaps thirty years, whose voluptuous body swept into the room with a confident, mirthful air that proclaimed she required--and was accustomed to--much flattering attention. Her eyes were quick, and they flashed between swirls of her long dark hair when she turned her head about in several rapid scans of the parlor.

Claire seemed to be looking for something--until her eyes fell upon Cale. Then the gorgeous woman seemed to relax and let herself idly accompany her husband as he chatted with the two female students from his classes who had volunteered to serve the modest refreshments.

Within minutes, the parlor hosted several more faculty members and two dozen students, mostly female. The students sat on the Oriental rug while the faculty seated themselves on the settee and the chairs. Hank stood shyly in a far corner of the room while Jack positioned himself near the hearth and Cale leaned casually against the doorway to the hall.

With a grand manner, Jack tugged on his watch chain and checked the time. At precisely seven-thirty, Jack stepped in front of the fireplace and raised his hands. His guests, beholding their host as a specter of the past, displayed the proper awe. When the suddenly stilled conversations settled into murmurs, Jack addressed the gathering.

"Welcome this crisp night to the first Epos poetry reading at Grace House. My name is Jack O'Donnell and I hail from the Great Blue mountains. I fancy myself an artist with the camera. My roommate, Hank Kelly--raise your hand, Hank—unfortunately has origins above the Mason Dixon but is a fine poet. And my other roommate, Cale Haines--give us a wave, Cale—comes to us from the Red Bank country and is an artisan with wood. We are happy that you could join us in our humble abode for an evening of fine poetry and intelligent discussion. The poems will be read by Dr. Randolph and Hank. Hank, if you're ready."

Hank walked to the fireplace and faced the group. Quickly scanning the crowd, he saw among the eager faces several attractive girls. He cleared his throat and stood erect. "My first poem is called The Bell Curve."

The students briefly giggled then quieted. A stunning red-head from his English class gave Hank the eye. With the gravest voice he could muster, Hank began, "If the death knell of humanity rings in my heart, do I hang in a cathedral or a gallows?"

With those words, the reading began. As the guests listened closely to the forceful, musical, evocative words Hank and Dr. Randolph delivered, Cale uneasily inched towards the kitchen. When the commentary began, Cale knew that the assembled faculty and students were sharing a special knowledge known only to college folks.

Cale quickly saw that this stiff, mannered exchange was not like the exciting lessons his grandfather had read from his great red encyclopedia. The ideas batted artfully about like a shuttlecock would have interested him if they had sought truth, but these aerial verbalizations were merely for show. Cale inched towards the kitchen then slipped out the back door and trotted through the frosty air to his woodshop.

After lighting the kerosene heater and the lantern that hung above his workbench, Cale grabbed a slip stone and began sharpening one of his wood gouges. He made harsh strokes against the curved blade. But the work did not release him from the miserable feeling that had caused him to flee the parlor.

"Except for the bullets and bombs," he thought, "the war was just like those college types putting on a circus for each other. It was about prevailing, not truth. I should be working Grandpa's farm instead of sitting here like a dope."

Suddenly the garage door opened, and Cale turned to see Mrs. Randolph hobbling into his shop.

"I broke a heel," Claire said quickly as she stumbled towards him.

Cale leapt up and caught her as she fell forward. He tried to grab her outstretched arms but she raised them as she reeled against his chest. Claire's ample breasts settled firmly on his bracing body as she let herself be arrested by, then hang limply against, his rigid frame.

Cale was electrified by the feel of her, the crush of her breasts, the smell of her hair as it brushed his face and the soft, whimpering sound she made as he steadied her. For a long moment, Claire embraced him and lightly nuzzled his throat.

"Are you all right?" Cale asked excitedly.

Claire threw her head back, exposing the creamy flesh of her neck and her bulging cleavage. "Yes, yes. This broken heel made me trip. Thanks for catching me. It's Cale, right, your name is Cale?"

Cale looked at the floor and nodded. "Yes, ma'am, Cale Haines."

Claire smiled graciously. "I'm Claire Randolph, Dr. Randolph's wife. When this heel broke a few minutes ago in the kitchen, I remembered that Jack had said that you worked with wood. I was hoping you might have some glue that would fix this heel for now, just enough so I can walk home after the poetry reading."

"I don't know, ma'am. I'll take a look at it and see what I can do."

"Thank you," Claire said as she handed him the shoe. "And please call me Claire. All of Harley's students call me Claire."

Cale took the shoe. "Sorry, ma'am. I'm not in Dr. Randolph's class. I'm not even in the college. I just got back home from the war," Cale said, "and that was education enough for a while."

Cale gestured towards a stool. "This will take a few minutes. Would you like to sit down?"

"Thank you," Claire said coquettishly as she slid onto the stool. As she sat, her dress rode up her legs and revealed her inner thighs. She did not adjust her hem.

Cale looked away from her exposed legs as he examined the shoe. "Looks like a clean break. I could mix up some epoxy and glue the heel back on for you."

"Thank you," Claire replied cheerily. "Where are you from?" she asked as he began to work.

"A little hick town named Adluh. It's in the great bend of the Glory River," he replied without looking at her.

"You didn't go back home after the war, you just came to Saluda?"

"Yes, ma'am."

"I guess Saluda must seem like a different world to you," Claire suggested.

"There's no war here, at least not the military kind," Cale muttered as he placed a clamp on the shoe. "This epoxy will set up in about five minutes. Then we'll see if it worked."

Claire began smoking a cigarette. "You got a girl back in Adluh?"

Cale shook his head as he lit up.

"A handsome country boy like you. That's hard to believe," Claire said suggestively.

Cale looked at her. She smiled invitingly and slowly scratched her upper thigh with her long red nails. He saw the white of her panties as she spread her legs to rake herself. Cale relished the moment then looked away. "I was MIA for a long time. She moved on," he confessed bluntly.

Claire looked at him intently. "Don't worry. I know a good looking soldier like you can have any woman you want. You just have to pick one and show her that you want her," she said with an entreating flutter of her eyelids and a seductive pout of her glistening red lips.

Cale turned back to the workbench and scrutinized the repair. A few minutes later, Claire was able to walk gingerly in the repaired shoe. She kissed Cale on the cheek.

"Thanks for the favor, country boy," she said in a soft, breathy voice. "I'll do something sweet for you, real soon. Goodnight."

Cale's pulse was racing as Claire walked out of the garage and went inside Grace House. He thought of how beautiful she was, of the instant when he had actually held her in his arms and felt the wondrous press of her firm breasts against his chest, of the soft brush of her luscious lips on his neck as he had steadied her, of the wild beckoning of her open thighs, of the intoxicating scent of her hair, of the enchanting lilt of her voice, of the enticing look in her eyes, of the softness of her kiss.

Cale sat at his workbench for a few minutes but he could not calm himself. He walked to the house and went into the kitchen. Jack was brewing a pot of coffee.

"Are you that scared of college folk that you've been hiding out?" Jack asked with a grin.

"No," Cale replied irritably, "I had to tend to something in the shop."

***

A few days after the poetry reading at Grace House, as Cale went into his shop, he noticed a bright red fabric stuffed into his nail apron. A scrap of paper tumbled onto the workbench as he withdrew the silky cloth and discovered that he was holding a pair of panties. On the paper was a note that read, "My husband will be away at a conference for a few days, disseminating knowledge and, if he gets lucky with some pretty young girl, himself. You did me a good turn in your shop, now I will do you one in my bed. If you want it, country boy, be at my back door Friday at 8pm."

Claire had not signed the note. Cale raised the crotch of the panties to his nose and inhaled the musky, sweet, exhilarating scent of Claire's loins. Images of Claire's naked body tantalized him: exposed neck, hair swept onto her bulging breasts, nipples erect, legs spread, hips arching urgently, lips full, wet, open, and eager.

What Cale knew of honor demanded that he refuse her. In the Red Bank country, he would deny her. Yet, as he touched his lips to the patch of cloth that Claire had perfumed with her crotch, Cale knew that in this place, in this college town, in this Grace House, the stars that had shone so clearly above Toenail Hill were lost in the muddled glow of the electric town, and he had no bearing. Just as he had in the jungle, he lived now solely by instinct.

For the next few days, as he worked at the depot, Cale thought of the cruel proposition that Claire had made to him: she knew how beautiful she was and how eager any man would be to sleep with her, and yet she knew that she was married and that to offer herself to another man was wrong. An irresistible offer and an indisputable wrong, that was the pact Claire presented. To accept, Cale reasoned, was to accept the shame of deliberately committing a wrong; to deny her, and himself, was unthinkable. "If I had only stayed in Adluh," Cale feverishly concluded to himself, "if I hadn't left home, I would have never gotten into this mess."

Cale decided to confide his dilemma one evening when the roommates, as had now become their custom, gathered in the parlor after supper. Hank regarded Cale with interest, and Jack eyed him with skepticism, as Cale told them about the encounter with Claire. When he read the note and produced the red panties, his roommates were thunderstruck.

Finally, Hank said, "Claire's a heavenly woman. She's so beautiful, and she has such a great body. Damn! You lucky bastard."

"Ain't no luck in it at all," Jack growled. "She's the kind of woman who can get a man in a heap of trouble. By jing, she is gorgeous but she's married, to a college professor nonetheless. Even if he doesn't shoot you, which is what husbands in that situation do up the mountain, he could make a lot of trouble for you, Cale."

"I know, I know," Cale protested. "The reason I even told you guys about it was so I could see it out in the open, so I could see how wrong it is."

"Do tell," Jack declared contemptuously.

"If pussy like that had my name on it, I'd be in a whale of trouble. What are you going to do, Cale?" Hank demanded excitedly.

"I don't know," Cale said. "I don't know about a lot of things since I came back from the war. This wouldn't have happened if I had stayed at home."

"Happened in the good book and it happens up the mountain. What's so special about Adluh that it couldn't have happened there?" Jack insisted gruffly.

"You've got a thorny problem, Cale. I mean even a simpleton can see that it's wrong to screw another man's wife, even if she is asking for it. But that simpleton can also see that men don't usually turn away a gorgeous piece of ass like Claire," Hank declared freely.

"It's just plain wrong," Cale said confidently.

"Ain't nothing of the kind," Jack retorted brusquely. "If it were, you wouldn't give it a second thought, and you sure as hell wouldn't be talking about it. What you're really saying is that if Claire were an honest woman and truly faithful and in love with her husband, that it would be wrong if you attempted to violate that bond. But that ain't what's going on here. In marriage, Claire wears the mantle of loving trust, but she is willing to hike up that mantle and give you a crack at her. So the truth is, banging her could not be morally wrong but it sure as hell could be messy."

"I hate to say it," Hank said reluctantly, "but the mountain goat is right--it ain't really wrong but you sure as hell don't want to get caught."

"It's just crazy," Cale said with exasperation, "I don't know what I'll do."

Jack's eyes narrowed as he tugged at his moustache. "I do," he said disdainfully.

***

Friday evening, Cale worked at the depot until it was time to creep through his neighbors' back yards to visit Claire. When she answered the back door, Claire allowed Cale a moment to admire her in the scant negligee she wore, to let his eyes dart from her piercing nipples to the jolting definition of her crotch displayed by the bright lights behind her. Then she spoke abruptly. "There are two things you must know, Cale. While Harley is out of town, he will be screwing any woman he can get his hands on. We have an open marriage, that's the fashion for faculty these days. He has his lovers and I have mine.

"The second is, if you choose to come in this door, you are going to screw me, you are going to screw me all night. And in the morning, I will fix you a nice breakfast, screw you one last time and then I'll never see you again. Would you like to come in, country boy?"

Late Saturday morning, Cale retreated to his shop, sat at his workbench and stared at crumpled red panties stuffed in his nail apron. In the passionate lust that had raced through him, Cale had felt a deep hunger for love and dedication. His heart was not dead. Not yet.

***

At the end of October, when the crew at the depot had stopped working for the day, Cale announced to Boss, "I've got to go home tonight but I'll be back tomorrow afternoon. I've got to help my brother Marsh bring in the last of the corn, and I know he'll ask me to carry the cripple goat. He always does. It's a family tradition."

"No problem," Boss replied. "But what's with the goat?"

Cale put his tools down and lit a cigarette. "It's a harvest tradition for some Highland Scots. We've got a dozen Scots families around Adluh so we keep up the ritual. According to legend, the Corn Spirit must live in corn. It moves easily from plant to plant but it can't cross open ground. You never know which field it is in.

"The spirit runs away from corn that is being cut, so the last sheaf from one field could have the Corn Spirit hiding in it. This last sheaf is called the goabbir bhacagh, the cripple goat. The cripple goat is carried quickly from one field to another field where the corn has not yet been cut so the Corn Spirit can move into the standing corn.

"The cripple goat from the very last field in the community to be cut is used to make cornbread, which all of the farm families eat. The Corn Spirit then lives in their bodies until they plant new cornfields in the spring. As they plant, the spirit moves back into the corn.

"The farmer receiving the last cripple goat of the season is deemed the laziest farmer around because his corn is last to be cut. So, the cripple goat ritual connects keeping the spirit alive with keeping up with your purpose."

"My people have rituals for the Corn Spirit, too," Dakota observed. "They believe that the Corn Spirit gives life, to the corn and to the people."

"But only if they keep the ritual, right?" Cale asked.

"Sure," Dakota agreed, "because ritual keeps the Spirit alive."

"See you tomorrow," Cale called as he walked up the hill to Grace House. He cranked his truck and started for Adluh.

***

Cale walked into the RuSam Grill as the suppertime crowd was thinning. His mother, Ruth, looked up as he came in. "My usual, please Momma," he called to her then continued to the back of the restaurant where his brother Marsh was waiting for him in the family booth.

"I guess I can cancel that golf cart order now," Marsh said with a wide grin as Cale sat across from him.

"You taking up golf, Construction Boy?"

"Not likely," Marsh answered with a chuckle. "I was just trying to figure out how we could carry the cripple goat if you didn't come back home in time."

"Well, I'm here, and I'll carry it. You cutting it in the morning?"

"Yep. At sunrise."

"Who gets it?"

"Hugh Campbell. He's just behind me getting his corn in."

"Hugh's not going to like getting the goat," Ruth observed as she put Cale's supper on the table.

"No man likes getting it, Momma, but that cripple goat is a real motivator," Marsh called to Ruth as she returned to the counter. He lit two cigarettes and passed one to Cale.

Marsh stared at his brother and decided it was time. "When I got sent over there, the war had just started. We did a lot of patrolling and very little shooting. Mostly we drank and played cards and talked about home. It hadn't gotten hot yet like it was for you. What happened to you over there?"

Cale shuddered and looked away. As he crushed his cigarette and slowly lit another, his eyes tightened with deliberation and his face was very grave.

"You can't tell, Marsh," Cale began cautiously. "Momma can't ever know. Nobody else can know."

Marsh nodded solemnly.

Cale touched his brother's arm and stared at him fiercely. "And we will never talk about this again. You can't even say you're sorry. I will tell you. And that will be it."

Tears wet Marsh's eyes. "Ok," he whispered.

Cale leaned forward and put his elbows on the table. He finished his cigarette and put his head in his hands. He shook for a moment then spoke, in a leaden voice.

"I was in Thailand. Naval Intelligence had a joint operation with Royal Thai commandos. I don't know how they knew we were there, but they were waiting for us. Chinese commandos guarding the package. I was supposed to separate if we were compromised. I took out the target and was trying to make it back to the extraction co-ordinates when I got hit. It was a through-and-through on the right side of my belly. That's when they caught me.

"After that, I wanted to die every day. I hated the sun for coming up because every morning after they had their tea, they paid me a visit. Every day they came to my bamboo cage to see how much I could take. Every day. Then something happened. They just left. Those Chinese troops had to get out of Thailand quickly and quietly. That's why they didn't shoot me. The Thai commandos picked me up and took me to the border but I had to get myself back to an American base."

Marsh turned away and wiped his eyes. He tried to think of his baseball team to avoid picturing his brother's suffering.

"That's why I have to stay in Saluda for a while," Cale explained. "I can't feel anything inside. I can't feel the land. I can't even feel the river. I can't--." His voice drowned in despair.

***

Early the next morning, Marsh cut the last corn from Matthew's fields, tied the stalks into a sheaf and gave the bundle to Cale. Cale bid farewell to his brother, drove to the Campbell's land, quickly tied the cripple goat to a fencepost by a cornfield, raced back to his truck and sped away. Cale knew that the pleasure of continuing an ancient tradition should have delighted him, but he felt only the urgency to get back to work.

"Did you get the goat delivered?" Boss asked as Cale came into the depot.

"Safe and sound," Cale replied.

"Did anybody see you do it?" Dakota asked.

"I don't think so, it was pretty early," Cale answered as he tied on his nail apron.

"The Corn Spirit lives," Dakota joked while he and Boss snapped a blue chalk line.

Late in the afternoon, the crew finished building the stud walls that defined the kitchen and the bathrooms. Cale was examining the blueprints when the front door suddenly flew open and two unsavory looking men burst into the depot and approached Cale.

"You got Big George's money, soldier boy?" the man wearing a red cap angrily demanded.

Cale stood up and moved towards the intruders. "I've got some of it. I need a few more days to get the rest."

"Big George wants his money now, friend," the smaller hatless man said menacingly.

92

Cale leaned against a sawhorse and put his right hand on his framing hammer. Dakota and Boss flanked him at the ends of the sawhorse. Dakota slightly opened the denim jacket he was wearing and Cale saw that his hunting knife hung from his belt. "He said I had a week to come up with it," Cale said sharply. "That week hasn't passed yet, friend."

"Look at that," the man in the red hat said, gesturing toward Dakota. "These damn hippies already got an Indian in here."

Boss removed his Fedora, placed it on top of a toolbox and stepped closer to Cale so he could reach a crowbar that leaned against the wall.

"This is private property, boys," Cale said slowly, "and I'm asking you to move along. Big George will get his money on time."

"We'll move when we're damned good and ready!" the hatless man screamed as he advanced towards Cale.

Cale grasped the hammer and tapped it against his leg. Boss brandished the crowbar. Dakota drew his knife.

The hatless man stopped. He pulled a pistol from his pocket and pointed the silvery barrel at Cale.

"Do it man! Waste me!" Cale shrieked.

Fear and confusion shown in the hatless man's eyes. The man in the red cap stepped back.

"Go ahead, tough guy," Cale taunted. "Splatter my brains. You'll be doing me a big favor. I can't do it myself. I can't ask my friends. But you're not my friend. You are just a piece of shit gutter rat. You could do it. One squeeze of the trigger. Come on, tough guy. End it for me."

The hatless man saw the deadly calm in Cale's face. "You're fucking crazy," he stammered. "Do you know that? Crazy as a loon. You got that week Big George promised. But you better have his money then. I'll tell you this, crazy boy, you won't play cards in this town again. Big George will make sure of that."

"Do it, gutter rat. It'll make you feel better. I promise. It always made me feel better, every time I pulled the trigger. Especially," Cale added with a sinister grin, "at close range."

"We'll be back to collect, you can count on that," the hatless man said as the strangers hurriedly backed out of the door.

Cale lowered the hammer and turned towards Boss and Dakota. "Sorry you had to see that," he muttered.

"They'll be back," Dakota said softly. "Can you get the money?"

Cale nodded. "I can borrow it from my brother."

Boss donned his Fedora. "That was a pretty heavy conversation, man. Did you mean the part about him killing you?"

Cale glanced at his friends. Their faces were open and frank and concerned. Boss' alarmed eyes studied him while Dakota looked at the floor, solemnly and patiently waiting. They deserved the truth.

"Almost. I feel pretty much dead anyway," explained Cale. "Sometimes, I don't even know myself. I don't feel things like I did before I went away." Cale lit a cigarette and sat on the sawhorse. "I don't really want to be dead, though. Not yet."

"It was like that for me when I first got back," Dakota said. "Compared to war, everything back home was trivial. Especially me."

Cale nodded his agreement.

"Everything I saw and everything I heard was about money or status or power," Dakota continued. "I didn't connect with it. I had just come from a place where everything was about living and dying. Back here, nothing seemed to be about anything that mattered. I almost went crazy."

Dakota hurled his knife across the room. The blade stuck in the wall. "Until I realized that it was the war that was trivial."

Cale put out his cigarette. "When you realized that, did you start to feel normal again?" he asked seriously.

Dakota laughed. "I didn't feel normal again until I met Boss and he told me about the Potlatch. When he said they were trying to build a place where people would live by their passions, not by their pocketbooks, I stopped feeling bad. When I went to live at the Potlatch and saw people trying to find the best of what was inside them and actually making a life out of what they had found, then I felt normal again. You should come out for a visit, man. I think you could relate. After you pay Big George, of course."

CHAPTER 7--PAINTED PONY

November began with dark skies and cold, wet winds that tore the remaining leaves from the blackened trees and drenched the dead foliage of coleus and the dying stalks of nasturtium and marigold. Cale knew that the following day would be the perfect day to hunt deer. The soft buzzing of his alarm clock woke Cale at four o'clock in the morning. By the faint starlight cast into his room from fires unthinkably remote, Cale dressed snugly in his warm hunting clothes, pulled on his boots, took his bow and quiver and quietly went outside to his truck.

A sliver of moon hung over the river like a shard of conscience, marking the frosty current as profoundly right, deeply good and essentially true. Cale wondered if any of the books Jack and Hank would study held a knowledge as rare as the river. He drove to the farm, past the dark house where his grandmother would soon rise and fill the kitchen with the smells of browning pancakes. He parked at the edge of Bride's Woods. He crept through the darkness to a stout sweet gum tree situated in a dense thicket on the banks of a narrow creek. He knew that, after feeding in the farm fields, deer should return to the thicket just at dawn.

Cale sat at the base of the sweet gum; he nestled his back against the rough bark and waited. At first light, when a hunter's eyes are almost free of darkness and the world is preciously indistinct, a hunter's mind is most clear because all is dreamed. In that rare moment, Cale saw cedar tree bears, redbud demons, sumac deer, ticking leaf rain, fog dread, briar despair and Broadus dead. In a distant jungle as fantastic as this looming wood, Broadus could die, could lay dying now, grieving, in his last moaning moments, the end of his imagination. Cale shuddered and tried to clear his mind of such wild thoughts.

The world brightened imperceptibly, becoming forest again. Cale sat motionless and listened intently as creatures revealed themselves in sound: a bird twittered and a single dry leaf shook; in jerky steps, a squirrel's claws whisked against rough bark; a rabbit moved nervously in the damp grass, swishing its fur against crumpled weeds; the hopping of tiny birds crackled in the bristly brush. Cale waited for the blurred movement of a horizontal line or the crisp fracturing of a fallen branch. He could see the smudged ribs of the forest but individual trees had not yet emerged. He silently nocked an arrow in the taut bow string.

The world was just slightly more illumed when Cale heard heavy footfalls in the shrouded forest. He turned his eyes toward the creeping sound but did not move his head. Two small does approached the creek, deftly stepped across it and passed into the thicket. Cale slowly brought his bow up into shooting position, waiting for the buck that would surely be trailing the does.

He loved the feel of the weapon in his hand and the sense of earnest purpose it gave him. With bow or rifle he could both sustain his life and defend it: in that fundamental skill of provenance and survival, Cale knew that a wedge of liberty lay between him and raw fate.

"I don't make war on deer," Cale thought as he waited for the buck to appear. "I don't conquer them or subdue them or rule them; I don't destroy their homes and break their spirits. When I leave the woods, the deer are the same as they always were--only their number is less until spring, when it will be more again. The deer are not changed, the deer are not less free.

"Broadus should not be in that jungle where his killing will slay spirits, will destroy families, homes. He should be back on the river, where killing removes but does not destroy."

Cale saw the buck as it approached the creek. It was a young buck with small antlers and it was very afraid. Twitching its tail and ears anxiously, the young buck studied the forest. Cale knew that the buck had not detected him but had picked up the scent of a large, aggressive buck. Compelled by the irresistible scent of the receptive does to enter the domain of a powerful foe, the young buck stood on the edge of the creek, nervously flicking its tail. Nose to the wind, the timid creature sniffed the dawn air for the musky smell of a mature rival. Suddenly, the young male bolted across the creek and disappeared into the brush where the does had vanished.

Keenly awake now, Cale sat dead still, awaiting the young buck's adversary. Birds and squirrels, silenced by the passing of the deer, began hopping and chirping again; crows whirled overhead in the strengthening sunlight and the land brightened into day. Cale sat in ambush until the sun rose above the tops of the trees. He stood, stretched his legs and stepped into the small creek and quietly walked downstream looking for signs of the threatening buck. He had traveled only a few hundred yards when he discovered why the small buck had been so fearful. Tracks of a heavy buck lay in the mud on either side of the water and, on the bank above the prints, was a large scrape, which the mature male had made to attract does. The young buck had smelled the power of his rival but, compelled by a more powerful instinct, had risked discovery and combat to pursue copulation with the does.

Cale did not approach the scrape but noted its location. He knew he could find it in the dark. Next, he identified a clear shooting lane and the exact spot where he would lie in wait. Satisfied, Cale returned to his truck. "Saturday afternoon," Cale thought as he drove toward the grill to get breakfast, "when that big buck makes his rounds to check his scrapes, he will fall and the little guy will be free to chase the honey pot to his heart's content."

***

On Saturday morning as the roommates were getting coffee, Jack proposed a meeting of the Three Pussketeers in the parlor of Grace House later that evening.

"Why not now?" Hank asked.

"Because, Longfellow," Jack retorted curtly, "I need to take care of something first. Besides, as soon as you finish your coffee, you will retreat to your tower to lament the human condition while perusing those titty magazines—as you do every Saturday—and Cale will head out somewheres with either a shotgun or a fishing pole."

Cale laughed. "I am going hunting in a few hours but what Jack means, Hank, is that there is still one wrinkle in his scheme that needs to be ironed out."

"All hands on deck after supper," Jack declared as he went out to the Bismarck. Jack raced the engine to give emphasis to his departure but he merely drove up Station Avenue and parked behind the old train depot. Cale had mentioned the previous evening that Dargan would be at the depot measuring the windows and seeing the inside of the renovated building from the street was exactly what Jack wanted to discuss with him. Jack whistled happily as he approached the door. The timing could not be better for his proposal.

***

After a disappointing supper in the cafeteria, Jack and Hank returned from the cafeteria and found Cale in the parlor carefully applying neatsfoot oil to his hunting boots. Hank made coffee while Jack rounded up the cups.

"Any luck?" Jack asked Cale as he put three mugs on the coffee table.

"By jing, sir," Cale responded emphatically, "I've got venison hanging in the meat processor's cooler—two hundred and five pounds on the hoof. But I can assure you," Cale added with a sinister tone, "no luck was involved."

Hank came in and poured the coffee. "Did you get him with a bow?"

"Yep," Cale replied, "and it was a mercy killing."

"How so?" Jack demanded.

Cale took a long drink of coffee. "I took out the dominant buck. Now the younger bucks have a chance to get some pussy. Eventually, a dominant male will emerge but until then many bucks will get a crack at some crack."

"That, my good fellow," Jack said sonorously, "is precisely the point of this meeting."

"What are you talking about, Jack?" Hank cried.

"The poetry reading was a good start," Jack said merrily, "but it's time for a greater adventure."

Cale nodded. "Do tell," he said in mockery of Jack.

Jack tugged on his moustache. "Well, we had a sampling of the woman flesh hereabouts with the poetry reading," he said.

"Maybe you did," Hank complained.

"What happened with that girl from the drama department you met that night?" Cale asked.

Hank sighed. "She was good for intellectual conversation and she was a pretty good dancer but she didn't want to jump in the sack. She didn't even want me to feel her up. I think she has a boyfriend back home."

"As I was saying," Jack continued sharply, "we need to reach a broader selection of delectable poontang." He took a pipe from one of his bulging pockets, tamped it, and lit it.

"How do you aim on doing that?" Cale asked as blue smoke drifted across Jack's deliberate countenance.

"Well," Jack muttered, "we need to create a permanent attraction, more of a fixed magnet for the womenfolk."

"You didn't just come up with this scheme," Hank said accusingly.

Jack scowled at him. "A man doesn't get ahead without studying on things. Doesn't get any pussy either."

"The scheme, Mad Jack, the scheme," Cale insisted.

Jack chuckled heartily and flashed a broad smile. "An art gallery, my fellow Pussketeers, an art gallery."

Hank and Cale were stunned into silence.

Jack stood and began to pace, slowly stroking his moustache. "I went down to the depot this morning and introduced myself to Dargan. Since he was thinking about windows, I figured he would entertain an idea about improving the street appeal of the place. He agreed with my notion--if you mates throw in with me."

"Five'll get you ten that this one is a doozy," Cale taunted.

"Dargan's got more space than he needs for the Colorado Café, and he knows he needs an additional attraction to bring folks over to his side of the street and get them away from the coffee shop and the bookstore," Jack continued. "So I said to him, 'Well, I'm a photographer and I've got two roommates of the artistic bent. We could put in enough of our work to have a gallery in your extra space. You build and paint the space and take a percentage of the profits for the rent. No profit, no rent. The fly in the ointment is that the gallery must be finished and stocked by Thanksgiving so we can cash in on Christmas shopping. We can get it started with our work and, if it takes off, you can have the Potlatch artists put in their stuff to raise the margin. Either way, you're giving people a reason to cross the street and frequent the cafe when it opens.'"

"Are you crazy?" Hank asked incredulously.

"Half of Halcyon thinks so, but this is a Jim Dandy idea," Jack countered. "It will cost us nothing. We might make a dollar. But we will surely be awash in winsome woman flesh as the redoubtable artistic captains of Station

101

Avenue. We will have the most thunderous beds in Saluda!"

"And let me guess," Cale suggested with a grin, "that this pudendum palace will be called Mad Jack's."

Jack grumbled to himself. "Name's not decided yet. What is important is that we've got to put stuff in it. Now I've got plenty of photographs to hang, and I thought if Hank could copy some more of his poems in calligraphy, and you, Cale, could make some small furniture, then we've got something."

Hank leaned forward. "Then we meet women!" he cried excitedly.

"Beaucoup women for the Pussketeers, would be my guess," Jack observed smugly.

"I'm in!" Hank exclaimed jubilantly. Then he added glumly, "I just hope my muse hasn't abandoned me."

"Cale?" asked Jack.

"I think it's a great idea, Jack," Cale said hesitantly, "but I don't know what I could put in. I took shop and drafting in high school. I can draw whatever it is I want to build. I had a workbench and a few tools at the farm, like I do in the garage here. I've only made utilitarian stuff. As I said at the diner when we formed the Pussketeers, I'm just a carpenter. The idea of being a cabinetmaker is very appealing, and it comes into my head now and then, but I'm not there yet. I can make anything I can draw, but I don't know a damn thing about designing real furniture."

"Well, I've got an idea about that too," Jack said.

"And what is that?" Cale asked cautiously.

"You make simple little things that the girls could put in their dorm rooms-- like stools, nightstands, bookshelves. Stuff you could make in your shop with cheap lumber. And then you just change the shape a little bit. Instead of everything being straight and square, you make parts of them curved or heart-shaped or curly-queued or something that girls like. And you paint them--wild colors, flowers and things. I can get you lots of paint from the art department."

"If I can fake being an artist then I'm in," Cale said with a laugh.

"You don't have to fake it, except at first," Jack sternly rejoined.

"What do you mean?" asked Cale.

"I can bring you all kinds of books from the library about furniture design and furniture building. You can teach yourself to make fine furniture. You've got the love for wood, can do drafting, and have a knack with tools. It's all in how you see things," lectured Jack.

"Do tell," Cale said sharply.

"Then let us put our hands together," Jack declared eagerly, "the Three Pussketeers vow to take up this quest to pursue pussy in quantity."

They joined hands and shook heartily, then withdrew in easy laughter.

"Ok, ok," Hank said urgently, "now what do we name this enterprise?"

"I've been studying on that too," Jack declared. "Seems to me it needs to be artsy-fartsy but girly enough not to scare off these skittish fillies. Needs to be a little hippie, but since this town may not be too partial to the hippies, it needs to just suggest a connection to the new age."

"I'm with you so far," said Cale.

"I'm thinking that the Painted Pony would be a good name. Fillies love horses. It's different enough to rub elbows with hippie, but cute enough not to be threatening."

"I like it," Hank said enthusiastically.

"You're a born marketeer, Jack. By me," Cale replied.

"Done!" Jack declared. "The Three Pussketeers will be the artful proprietors of the Painted Pony. We need to get a move on creating inventory so we'll have something for the shopping spree that will start after Thanksgiving."

Before going to work the next morning, Cale had coffee with Jack and Hank in the kitchen. Jack made a list of the furniture he needed from Cale for the initial stocking of the Painted Pony, and he promised to start filching paint from the art department. On his first break at work, Cale got permission from Boss to take as much scrap lumber as he needed. After supper, he built a small shelf above his workbench to hold the furniture encyclopedia and design books Jack had brought to him. On the kitchen table, Cale began making measured drawings of the bookcases, nightstands, tables and hanging shelves he would build for the gallery.

Working evenings in his crude shop in the garage, Cale began to fashion with hand tools the pieces specified on the drawings. Occasionally, while waiting for the kerosene heater to warm the drafty garage, he removed Claire's red panties from his nail apron, inhaled her scent, read from Jack's books on furniture design, and worked on a sketch for a writing desk he wanted to present to Jack as an improvement in the inventory.

Methodically, he joined the components he had made and set the assembled items aside. When the garage was warm enough for paint, he applied bold colors to the simple furniture. Cale hated everything he built. He despised using the fine woodworking tools he had inherited from his grandfather to create furniture that had no elegance of its own: no graceful lines, no difficult joints, no complex finish, no beauty in form or execution.

The gallery was framed and wired in a week and Dargan used his influence with the city government to get both the cafe and the gallery spaces inspected immediately and accepted. Dargan intended to have a gala opening for the cafe so he delayed the restaurant opening until spring.

The gallery walls were closed in and painted, but Boss stopped the crew from cleaning and finishing the floor.

"It will take a lot of time and work," Boss explained, "to get up the paint we've spilled. The floor is too dinged up to sand and finish it. Let's just get up the dirt and loose crud and then throw paint on it. Make crazy patterns. Let the colors run together.

"Intentionally throw the paint hard next to the walls so it splashes up on them. Then just let it dry. We'll use latex so we can walk barefooted on it. We can even leave a few footprints in the finished work, if we want to. We'll be messing up each other's patterns so we have to agree it's all in fun and a lazy way to finish the floor."

Dakota flashed a big grin and tapped Boss's Fedora. "Boss always has a plan. An arty floor for an art gallery. That's a trip!"

Cale laughed and patted Boss on the back. "I'm in Boss, but if we are going to do it right, we need to smoke up first--and we need to remember to work toward the door, man."

While Dakota rolled a couple of joints, Boss and Cale went to the hardware store and returned with gallon and quart cans of latex paint in several bright colors. As Boss opened the cans, they discussed the areas in which the gallon colors would be used and agreed that the quart colors should be tossed wherever the individual painter thought they looked best at that moment.

"We will call it the Sistine Floor," Dakota began as he lit a joint.

"The story of man giving birth to the human spirit," Cale added as he took a deep drag and passed the joint to Boss.

"And then trying to live like he had nothing to do with it," Boss concluded before he inhaled. Dakota ate the first roach and after the second joint had made the rounds, Boss swallowed the last one. As the marijuana took effect, they took off their shoes and stored them outside. They threw down the gallon colors of red, blue and orange then began walking through creation with the quart colors of black, silver, olive, turquoise and white.

Cale watched as Dakota studied the floor, carefully stepped to a particular spot then drizzled, hurled or poured paint on the floor. More focused than Cale had ever seen him, Boss seemed to stalk a specific place then pounce and deposit color like a bee visiting flowers. Cale could see that the others were directed by a vision, either something they saw in the multi-color splotches and spatters on the floor or something they glimpsed within.

As they studiously dashed paint, Cale suddenly became fearful. Some from the jungle were trying to come up through the floor! He had killed them, he had watched them die, but they were not dead. They were coming for revenge. Those who had died in daylight were not among them, but the ones that had perished under the moon were rattling with fury just beneath his feet.

Cale grabbed the quart of black paint. He could stop them. He scrutinized the floor: colors collided and mixed like pooling blood shaken by exploding mortar rounds across divulged organs and wet, seeping brains. Florid hands and feet, broken and twisted limbs, ripped torsos, and crushed skulls surrounded him, and he walked on the palette of war searching for the unvanquished. In a corner he saw one, young and brimming with innocence; then another, smiling in memory of his mother; then another, craving a stick of candy. Cale ran to the faces and erased them with black paint. The faces fled but they did not die-- they would not let him kill them again.

***

Broadus knew the instant the small party of Viet Cong ran for the outcropping in the valley below him that the guerillas were trapped. He had once seen a bear make the same mistake. The sun striking a boulder as it jutted out from the face of a rock wall had made that bear think a slab of granite was the opening to a cave. By the time that bear had discovered the mistake, it had been too late for the creature to escape the ferocious dogs snarling behind it.

When the frantic band of enemy soldiers realized their error, they dropped their rifles and raised their arms in surrender. Broadus shoved a fresh banana clip into the receiver of his M-16 as the platoon fell into line beside him. Now the VC were shouting but Broadus could not understand them. He just knew they were done fighting.

"Fire!" the sergeant screamed.

The Marines looked at each other.

"Gunny?" one of the men questioned.

Before the sergeant could reply, Broadus switched his weapon to fully automatic and sent rounds flying through the chest of one of the guerillas. The stricken warrior's body wriggled as if he were dancing and his fellow soldiers wailed in horror as the entire Marine squadron fired on them. The Viet Cong were cut down so rapidly that within moments the jungle was silent.

"Gervais!" the sergeant barked. "Go down there and get a body count. Just radio it in and leave their goddamned ears alone! Cottle, take the point. We're going upstream to that village where these Charlie bastards came from. Move!"

Broadus was glad he had the point. The head of the line was the most dangerous position when the squadron patrolled. He wouldn't have time to think about what he had just done—but he could feel it. And it was bad.

Broadus was not sorry that the enemy had laid down their arms and tried to surrender. Surrender was only an offer. It did not have to be accepted. The guerillas had chosen to engage in war and that was reason enough for him to kill them. Broadus was miserable because killing the enemy had been simple and meaningless. His naked act of war was beneath him. Extinguishing the soul of another did not touch his soul, did not make him less of an animal.

Broadus wept silently as he peered into the jungle and moved cautiously through the foliage. Cale had been right. There was no glory in war. There was no glory in anything except love and Broadus had never been touched by it. Even with his girlfriend, Bernice, desire and desperation were the only things that connected them. His loneliness endured. Broadus shuddered as he realized that he could die without ever escaping himself.

***

On the ides of November, while the three roommates were having coffee in the parlor of Grace House, Hank made a surprise announcement. "I'm getting a car!" he said proudly.

Jack and Cale were shocked. Hank did not have an income or a great relationship with his parents. They had not heard of any deaths in the family.

"Do tell," Jack prompted.

Hank began to laugh. "My dad has this gigantic old Buick station wagon. A huge brown job. It is beat to shit and he only uses it to haul junk. It gets about three miles to the gallon. I call it the Barge. But it's a car. I finally talked him into letting me use it. And he's bringing it up this weekend."

"Way to go, Hank," Cale declared.

"Dang if that don't beat all!" Jack exclaimed.

"Why?" Hank asked cautiously.

Jack scratched his beard. "Well, I've got this problem up the mountain and I've been studying on how to fix it. The Barge could be part of the answer."

"Do tell," Hank insisted sternly.

Jack fumbled for a pipe. "It's Aunt Rose. Sweetest woman God ever put in creation. But delicate as a honeycomb. She's worried to death about me being away in the flatland. Don't sit right with her 'cause she thinks I'm holed up in some boarding house with a bunch of blackguards. Keeps her in a tizzy, don't you see?"

Jack quickly scanned his roommates to see if he were making sufficient progress. Hank was inclining. Cale was not.

"Where do we, and the Barge, fit in?" Cale challenged.

"Evidence and providence," Jack retorted.

"What the hell are you talking about?" demanded Hank.

"Hold on to your galluses, Longfellow," Jack replied, "I've a simple proposition with no skullduggery. A road trip. I'll pay for the gas and the eats along the way. You and Cale meet Aunt Rose. Present evidence of your good character, as it were. Aunt Rose relaxes. Providence is that none of us had a vehicle that would hold the three of us comfortably—until the Barge arrived on the scene."

"It will take a lot of gas. The Barge is no gazelle," Hank cautioned.

Jack went in for the kill. "Did I mention that Aunt Rose is the best cook in the county, bar none? Her pies and preserves have won so many blue ribbons at the county fair there's no room to keep 'em in the house. 'Sides, Hank, you've been complaining about a hitch in your poetry giddyup, maybe a change of scene would be just the spark you need. Halcyon sits at the mouth of the Halcyon Valley, where the big mountains are. You can see 'em from Aunt Rose's table."

Jack turned to Cale. "Wouldn't hurt you none to get out of town for a day or two. It would really help me out to know that Aunt Rose was done fretting. I could put more focus on my photography."

Jack stopped. The pitch had been made. His cousin Odell, a horse trader of some repute in the Great Blue Mountains, had once told him, "You can't sell nobody twice. If they've taken the bait, shut up and let 'em chew on it. They'll come around and think it's of their own accord to boot."

Hank sought clarification. "You'll pay for all of the gas and for all the snacks we might want along the way?"

"Yep," Jack said. "Won't need no snacks when we get there. Aunt Rose will stuff us all as full as she can. I can taste those hot biscuits now, dripping with butter and the tangiest apricot preserves you ever put in your mouth."

"I'm willing to give it a try," Hank offered.

Cale scrutinized Jack. "I can't see the angle in it for Jack. But I know there is one. Jack and his money are not parted on humanitarian grounds."

Jack was prepared to close the deal. False confessions were usually undetectable. Jack filled his eyes with sincerity. "Look, mates. The truth is, I need to retrieve a large studio camera and some other equipment. It won't fit in the Bismarck. And Aunt Rose truly is worried sick about the denizens of Grace House."

Cale was satisfied. "By me," he said with a chuckle.

Hank's dad delivered the Barge on Friday evening, abruptly said farewell to his son, climbed behind the wheel of the sleek sedan Hank's mother had driven and, when Hank had kissed his mother goodbye, barreled out of the driveway. The roommates examined the enormous station wagon. "It's big enough for you to fuck all of the cheerleaders at the same time," Jack observed.

Hank grinned. "Just one will do for now. One would be gracious plenty, especially if she were dripping wet and letting me taste her tangy preserves." Cheerily, he added, "I don't expect she would taste like apricot."

"Some of them do," Jack grumbled. "Some of that nectar is divine."

The next morning, with Hank at the wheel, Jack beside him to navigate, and Cale in the rear seat, the roommates drove away in the Barge. The heavy automobile gained speed slowly as they followed the path of the Glory

River northward but the ride was so smooth that Cale was asleep before they got to the foothills. When the towering Blue Mountains came into view, Jack woke Cale and explained the lay of the land to his roommates.

"Halcyon sits on the very edge of the Halcyon Valley, just this side of the Eastern continental divide, so it's not in the valley itself. Once you pass through the town of Halcyon, you have to go over that front range and then you drop into the Halcyon Valley itself, the prettiest place there is."

Hank and Cale were pleasantly surprised by the tidy, old fashioned small town of Halcyon. "Another time," Jack commented as they passed through his hometown, "we'll take us a ride over the divide and into the Valley. Right now, I need to see about Aunt Rose. 'Sides, the Barge is a mite heavy to climb up the front range."

Jack directed Hank to a large white house on the outskirts of town. The two-story building sat on broad knoll above a large plantation of Christmas trees. Hank went up the long gravel drive and parked beside an old dusty pickup truck. "Well, I'll be a monkey's uncle," Jack cried when he recognized the antiquated vehicle.

"What is it?" asked Cale.

"Cousin Odell is here. It's a rare moment when he ventures back into civilization." Jack pointed towards a large garage where an old man and a middle-aged woman were standing beside a gray tractor. "But it's a stroke of luck, Cale. Cousin Odell is a master cabinetmaker and he makes everything by hand, the old way."

"Why, Jack," the woman called as the young men emerged from the Barge, "look who's here. It's Cousin Odell, in the flesh."

Jack quickly strode over to his aunt and gave her a hug and a kiss on the cheek. "Aunt Rose, Cousin Odell, I want to introduce you to my two roommates in the flatland. The feller with the long hair is Cale Haines—

cabinetmaker—and the feller with the big smile is Hank Kelley—poet."

Rose gleefully embraced Cale and Hank saying, "I'm tickled to meet both of you. Jack has told me so many good things about you and that grand old home you boys live in."

"Proud to know you," Odell said, offering his hand to each of the strangers."

"You got some kind of trouble with the tractor?" Jack asked pointedly.

"I just had it re-built," Rose said irritably, "and the dang thing won't run now. Cousin Odell happened by on his way back home and he can't get it to do a thing either. Let's go in the house now, Jack, we've got company."

"Is that a 9N?" Cale asked suddenly.

"Yes, it is," Odell said, puzzled that a college boy would know such a thing.

"I've got one of those back home," Cale explained. "My brother and I bought one after my grandfather died. We needed one with enough power to work the farm but small enough for my grandma to handle."

"You worked on 'em any?" Jack inquired hopefully.

"Yep. Had to. My grandma's plenty tough but she's not a mechanic," Cale replied.

"I 'spect Aunt Rose's got a fresh pie in the kitchen. Let's go in and jaw on this. Cale might be able to help us skin this cat," Jack proposed.

They gathered around the table in the small dining room and Rose served them pie and coffee. Odell explained the situation. "She won't crank and run. If you spray ether in the carburetor, she'll fire back through the carb and run for a few seconds."

"Is gas getting to the carburetor?" asked Cale.

Odell nodded. "Carb's got good vacuum when you put your hand over it. Compression measures about 95."

"That's where it should be. Is the distributor cap in the correct phase?" asked Cale.

"Yeah," Odell replied, "and best I can remember, the plug wires are on the cap right."

"The firing order," Cale explained, "is 1, 2, 4, 3. Number one is at the radiator. The rotor turns counterclockwise so 1 is top left, 2 is bottom left, 4 is bottom right and 3 is top right."

"Lordy, Cale knows his red belly Ford tractors, don't he Cousin Odell?" Rose marveled.

"Good thing, too. It's shore got me stumped," Odell said.

Rose regarded Hank and Cale. "You see, Cousin Odell is just trying to help a body out. He uses mules on his place. He don't mess with machines. More pie?"

Hank eagerly extended his plate.

"The timing's been checked and re-checked. And the old boy what rebuilt it said he pulled the check spring on the oil pump and got a good flow," Odell continued.

"How good is the spark?" asked Cale.

"She's got a new 6-volt battery and each plug is throwing a good blue spark," Odell answered.

"Could the exhaust be plugged up?" Cale inquired.

Odell shook his head. "Checked it myself. She's open."

Cale sipped his coffee pensively. "If she's got gas at the carb, then the fuel petcock is set right."

"Yep," Odell agreed.

"I know what I would try, if you haven't done it yet," Cale ventured.

"What is that?" asked Odell.

"I'd pull the plugs and squirt a little oil in each cylinder," Cale advised. "Maybe those new rings haven't seated yet and you're losing compression under fire. A little oil would fix that."

Odell stared at the young man. He was pleased with the good sense of this stranger, especially since Jack had brought him home from the flatland.

Rose stood up and gestured to the men not to rise. "You men enjoy your pie and coffee. I'm going to try Cale's little trick. Be back in a jiffy. Jack, freshen up that pot of coffee on the stove."

As Rose went out, Odell began to laugh. "Rose is just like my old woman, Acrilee. She don't stand on ceremony, she does for herself, and she speaks her mind. Jack, how did you get these boys to come back in the hills?"

"They didn't take much convincing, Cousin Odell," Jack answered. "Hank has been having a little trouble coming up with new poems so he took right away to a change of scenery."

"I 'spect keeping the mind stirred up is good for a poet. These mountains surely do stir up the mind," Odell remarked, "they surely do."

"Cale here is like a chicken on concrete," Jack declared.

Odell chuckled. "How is that?"

"Well," Jack explained slowly, "it's in the nature of a chicken to scratch. But a chicken on concrete just can't be satisfied with the results. Cale has a love for wood and working with wood—using nothing but hand tools, mind you."

Jack glanced at Cale and saw that he was not comfortable. Jack pressed on.

"He's making some cute furniture we are selling to college girls at our little gallery but I know he hates every bit of it. He wants to make fine furniture like you do, Cousin Odell. He's a good draftsman and can draw anything. Somehow he's got it into his head that he has to have some special design training before he can make the good stuff."

114

Cale blushed. Jack had ambushed him—but it was for a good cause. Odell saw Cale's discomfort.

"Wouldn't know about special training for furniture. I ain't never had no furniture training at all. Lordy, son. I hated everything I made for the first few years," Odell confided. "Seems like when you start any new thing, it ain't you right away. At first, it's just your ambition."

Odell fiddled with his fork and his eyes showed that he looked at the past. "Your excitement may be in it but your heart ain't in it at the beginning. Somewhere along the line, something happens that makes it yours, lets you put your spirit into your work. If you stay at it long enough, you get the problem I've got."

Suddenly, they heard the tractor fire up and run steadily. Rose's gleeful whoop rang through the yard up to the house.

"Hot damn, Cale, your idea worked!" Jack exclaimed.

"If I may ask, sir, what problem is that?" Cale inquired earnestly.

"Don't need no sir around here. Just Odell is fine. The problem for me, son, is that I've run out of inspiration. New things to build don't come to me anymore. That's natural, I guess, after all these years of having a head full of ideas. I guess the brain has to slow down or the body just won't quit."

Odell paused and stared at the mountains towering in the distance. His eyes were suddenly sad.

"I'm getting too old to do the physical work but I've got customers who have been with me for years. I need to let go of my shop but I'd like to ease away from it and steer my customers to a younger feller who still builds furniture by hand. Trouble is, ain't so many of that kind left in these parts."

"That feller will come along, Cousin Odell," Jack predicted. "Course living way out in the wilderness like you do adds a degree of difficulty."

"Do tell," Odell mused as Rose came into the house, bubbling with excitement because her tractor had been restored to working order by one of Jack's new friends from the flatland. Rose announced that she would prepare a special mouth-watering supper to mark the occasion.

Jack was pleased to see Rose happy and relaxed. He hoped to find himself in the same state someday soon. For the moment, he was in the company of family and good friends, and life was rich enough that he could enjoy it and briefly forget his war against the reptilian nature of the present age.

CHAPTER 8--THE POTLATCH

Cale rose before sunup on Thanksgiving morning and made the short journey to Adluh in time to have breakfast at home with his family. While Julia and Ruth cleared the dishes, Olivia beckoned Cale to walk with her outside. When no one questioned why they were going out in the cold, blustery weather, Cale realized that the rest of the family already knew what his grandmother would tell him.

"What is it, Grandma?" Cale asked as they crossed the brown grass in the back yard.

Olivia paused near a plum tree. "I'm not getting any younger," she said seriously.

"Yes, ma'am," Cale responded gently.

"I decided not to wait until I die to settle what's to happen to the farm." Olivia turned to Cale. She took his face into her hands and gazed at him lovingly. Then her eyes grew sad, she kissed his forehead, and continued walking.

"Your grandpa and I always wanted you to take over the farm. We knew how much you loved the land, the crops, the animals, and the river. You spent so much time with us, and you were so happy there, we always felt the farm was your real home."

"It still is my real home, Grandma. I just went to Saluda--."

Olivia shook her head. "This isn't about Saluda. I know the war hurt you bad, son. I know you can't feel things like you want to. That will take a while."

"What is it?" Cale asked fearfully.

117

Olivia gazed at her grandson and Cale saw deep remembrance in her eyes. "I had a medicine dream. In that dream I saw that the farm is not your home. It was a home for me and Matthew. Matthew found this place, built the house, and brought me here. Together, we made this place a farm. We put all of our hearts into this place and that is why it became our home. Matthew's been gone six years. When I am gone, the home that this place is, will go with me.

"I could give you the farm, Cale. But home is not a place. Home is the way you live your life, according to the truest things you know in your heart and mind. Home is where the spirit rests, not the body. Home is what your heart and mind love most deeply. Those things, when you know them, will lead you to a place. Maybe more than one. But each one will be home."

Cale lit a cigarette. He puffed it defiantly, as if its roiling blue smoke could repudiate the words that were coming.

"If you have the farm, you will never find home because you will not look for it. You will think the memory of me and Matthew is your home. But it is not. Your home is within you, within your spirited heart and your strong mind. I cannot take that home away from you the way the river took Matthew away from me.

"My own sons, your father and your uncle Buck, have never needed a home for their spirits. Their hearts and minds do not seek. That has been the sorrow of my life but it is the truth. I could not save the farm and save you, so I signed the farm over to them."

Cale stopped. His body contracted and bent. He winced and looked away from his grandmother. The wound in his belly ached. He choked the moan that rose in his throat. Hot tears laced his eyes as precious memories assailed him and the dream of his heart cracked and splintered and a canyon of despair opened in his mind.

118

Olivia approached him with a look of knowing kindness. He could see only love in her eyes, the love he had always seen. Cale could not understand the reason for her words but he knew the meaning of her eyes. He had always trusted those eyes because they had always looked upon him with love.

Cale let the old woman hug him as he trembled. Into her gentle embrace his sorrow erupted but he did not grieve the loss of the farm: he howled for the loss of himself when he had been forsaken in the jungle.

***

Hank opened the Painted Pony the day after Thanksgiving. He had been glad to have any excuse to leave his unhappy family celebration and return to Saluda. He soon discovered that, in the role of a salesman, it was easy to talk to pretty women and it was simple to see when they flirted with him. For the first time since he had been at college, he relaxed and had fun. The Painted Pony would be his salvation with women.

During December, Cale was busy in his shop crafting replacements for the items Jack and Hank had sold, studying books on design, and scrutinizing examples of fine cabinetry in a furniture encyclopedia. He glanced at the elegant highboys, secretaries, sideboards, gate-leg tables and Windsor chairs in the thick reference book. Not only were these historic pieces utilitarian, they were artistic: they captured beauty separately in their graceful lines, crisp angles, flowing grains, inlaid complements, and lustrous finishes; and jointly in the look of the furniture as a whole. Each work expressed some vision of its creator.

Cale's own work revealed nothing but Jack's contrived concepts. None of him went into the pieces he made for the gallery. He was deeply embarrassed that he had nothing inside to give to his work. He was pretending to be an artist, and he hated it. He didn't even like the designs he had made for the writing desk.

119

As Christmas approached, Dargan halted the work at the depot, so Cale accepted Dakota's invitation to visit the Potlatch for a planning meeting. On the afternoon of the winter solstice, Cale ventured into the frozen countryside searching for the abandoned farm. He easily found the brightly colored marker Dakota had described, a section of telephone pole which had been set into the ground where two gravel roads joined. The wooden column was painted with brilliant hues abstractly depicting visages of man and beast. He slowly followed the washboard ribbed lane and stopped the truck on a small rise where a break in the hardwood grove that lined the road allowed him to look down on the farmhouse and the fields of the Potlatch.

The Glory River bordered the farm on the east and he could see on its banks three yellow structures that looked like tents. Beyond the tents, the land plunged into a narrow, rocky canyon then rose up sharply and flattened into a small mesa. In the southwest corner of the farm was a lake from which a creek ran down to the river. On the far side of the lake stood four teepees, arranged in a ring. Beyond the teepees was a small red barn and a much larger rock barn. Past the bigger barn was an adobe house enclosed by a wall. A huge garden lay opposite the farmhouse, and the northern edge of the open fields was fringed by orchards. Small sheds and pens were scattered throughout the land.

He drove down the slope and parked beside a large sycamore tree in the front yard of the three-story farmhouse. The enormous house testified to the farm's past success, but Cale knew it had not been a fully working enterprise in many years. He surveyed the neglected farm and noted the vestiges that belied the history of its decay.

The fieldstone chimneys at each gable end of the center portion of the farmhouse were the remains of the original cabin, whose hall-and-parlor floor plan was unchanged. The brick foundation of the current kitchen indicated that it had been a separate building in the initial design, which still bore a stone foundation, and the narrow hallway which now led to it, Cale knew, had been a dog-trot, a breezeway that protected the main cabin from the frightful danger of fire in the separate kitchen.

The Flemish bond in the foundation of the huge rock barn with the silo suggested that the barn had been built in the days when the wind still whistled between the cabin and the kitchen. Because the rock barn had been built down the hill from the cabin, on the edge of the creek where a shallow trough diverted a thin stream of water into it, Cale reasoned that the original farmer had been a German and had housed his cattle in the barn. Just visible beneath the back steps coming off of the kitchen, was a concrete cap that Cale knew had sealed the original well. The rearward expansion of the house, when a hallway had been built to close in the breezeway and connect the cabin to an enlarged kitchen, was visible in the brick foundation that extended the original field stone base of the cabin.

The front section of the house had been added when the farm had been most prosperous, probably in the nineteen twenties, Cale surmised from the look of it. Established fields of timothy and lespedeza beyond old stone walls and hedgerows indicated to Cale the sudden expansion of acreage and he imagined that the proud farmer sitting on the broad planks of his new front porch was confident that he was the founder of a dynasty that would rule over this parcel of earth for generations to come. Cale knew that farmer had not heard the winds of disaster rustling in the account books of businesses in the great cities far away, and had been rocking peacefully on that spacious veranda when the Great Depression blew devastation across his lands and strangled his dream of prosperity.

The proximity of the grape arbors and the apple orchard to the farmhouse warned Cale of a sudden change

121

in the scope of farming operations. The running bond in the foundation of the small red barn near the house suggested that the smaller barn was built as the farm collapsed, and its simpler design, constructed of cheaper materials, had been meant to house a few mules, or goats, or sheep and a small amount of feed. The crudely fashioned shed attached to the red barn was so low that it would have housed only a basic red-belly tractor and a compact stake-bed truck used, Cale thought, by a tenant farmer in his struggle to make a living selling fruits, vegetables and eggs in the farmer's market, and a few pounds of tobacco at auction. The dilapidated chicken coop, along with the teetering rabbit cages, had been built by this last desperate farmer.

The tiny greenhouse attached to the other side of the red barn had probably come, Cale thought, when debt and blight had driven out the last tenant farmer and some doctor or lawyer had installed the glass and metal framework so that his wife could indulge herself in a hobby of growing flowers while the land eased itself out of the bonds of cultivation and slipped into wildness.

Cale felt a sense of regret at his deciphered history of the failed farm. "Maybe the farm will have a new life now", he thought, "even though the freaks are not farmers. These fallow fields, downed fences, empty barns, overgrown orchards, and brushy pastures should be put right. I don't know if these folks will be the ones to do it."

Cale suddenly imagined his grandfather plowing behind his two prized mules. Named for their quality in pulling the plow through unbroken earth, his grandfather trudged behind Silk and Sack, and bright green stalks of corn thrust themselves up from his footprints in the open earth, to be washed in the golden light of a never-setting sun.

As he approached the back door, Cale saw Dargan ringing the large farm bell which hung outside the back door of the farmhouse. Cale hurriedly walked up the steps and entered the large kitchen just as Dargan was settling himself at the head of a table where several others were assembled.

"Find a seat, Cale," Dargan called to him. "We're just about ready to start."

"I guess we should make sure that everybody knows everybody first," Boss said as Cale slid into a chair at the large table. "Cale is our carpenter in town. He's building the café and the shops for us in the depot and he will be helping us out at the farm too.

"Cale, you already know me and Dakota and, of course, Dargan. Dargan and his wife Meredith own the farm and run the show. They come and go and live where they please.

"Dakota runs the Lodgekeepers. His group is really into Native American culture and crafts, and they help out wherever they are needed. They live in the teepees out by Spirit Lake and they call their camp Paha Mata. You'll find them fishing in the lake and Ascension Creek most any old time. They keep their council fire burning continuously, and on special occasions, they make a huge bonfire on the top of Blue Mesa.

"I run the Reds. My group is really into alternative construction, especially geodesic design and earth-friendly techniques. We built all the camps, except Paha Mata. Dakota is a stickler for tradition. We live in this farmhouse, which we call the Kremlin. People come to me to handle the red tape--to organize work crews and to plan whatever needs doing. "

"Boss always has a plan," Dargan interjected with a chuckle and the members of the commune laughed.

Boss grinned, tipped his Fedora, turned to his right and nodded toward a young woman leaning on a cane. She smiled broadly and the lines around her mouth indicated she habitually bore a happy countenance. Her sharply chiseled, classically beautiful face was surrounded by long, silky red hair, and her sharp grey eyes overtly studied Cale.

"This bundle of tightly capped, but boundless, energy is Mama Lucy," Boss announced proudly. "She runs the Diggers, the group that feeds us all from their gardens and with their cooking. They live in the big adobe house and call their camp Mudville. Their compound is just on the other side of the Rock Barn.

"Don't let the cane fool you. Mama Lucy works harder than anybody. She's the first one up, every morning. She can't wait to get to her gigantic Physic garden. She loves the earth and this farm. Oh, yeah--" Boss put his arm around Mama Lucy--"she keeps company with me."

"Hello," Cale said softly to the scrutinizing woman.

Boss turned to his left and addressed an exotic looking young woman with dark hair and piercing dark eyes. "This intense, darkly mysterious woman is Sable. She was a nurse in Vietnam."

"What was your AO?" Cale asked suddenly.

Sable looked at Cale with sad eyes. "I Corps,", she answered quietly. "I worked at Da Nang."

Cale nodded slowly, glanced quickly at Dakota, then turned to Boss.

"The dude beside her"--Boss indicated a thin young man wearing a red beret--"is her old man, Jugs. His pots are as beautiful and strong as his opinions, which are legendary for their opposition to conventional wisdom and their impassioned expression."

"You only live once," Jugs declared, "if you live at all."

"Jugs runs the Gypsies," Boss continued, "they are the artists and artisans here. They live in the big yellow yurts and they call their camp the Shuttlepot. It's on the edge of the river across from Paradise Canyon."

"Pleased to meet you," Cale said.

"Likewise," Jugs responded.

Boss gestured towards a beautiful, black-haired young woman who stared at Cale with bright green eyes. "This painter extraordinaire is Bridget Chattan. She's one of the Gypsies but she is kind of a general counsel. Bridget helped to start a commune in the desert of New Mexico, so she knows the ropes. She lives here in the Kremlin."

Cale nodded to the lovely young woman.

"Now that that's settled," Dargan said, "we can get down to business. Of course, first things first." Dargan took two thick joints from his shirt pocket, lit them, and started them on their journey around the table. When the roaches had been eaten, he asked, "What you got, Boss?"

Boss leaned forward. "The plan is for the cafe to open in the spring, even though it could be opened sooner. But we won't have fresh food until the spring and nobody will attend a grand opening in bad weather. We can supply the cafe at first from the Physic garden, but we need field crops to support the food co-op Mama Lucy wants to get going. Luckily, Cale is not only a carpenter, dudes, he is a farmer who has a tractor."

"Far out!" cried Mama Lucy. "So could you turn the fields now and lay off rows in the spring?" she asked excitedly.

"It's too late to turn now unless we get a major thaw," Cale explained. "In the spring, I can disc it and lay off rows, no problem. What about fertilizing?"

Mama Lucy's eyes widened. "Oh, no, we're organic. We'll have to cut in compost and manure. That's why we have the cows and goats and chickens."

Cale shook his head. "That will have to wait till next fall. If you cut it in this spring, it will burn up your crop as it rots."

"I can dig it. I'm done," said Mama Lucy.

"What else?" asked Boss.

"Wait a minute! Wait a minute!" Mama Lucy cried. "I tripped out for a second. I need a room created in the

Red Barn for the co-op. Shelves to store stuff and a little office to deal with the co-op members and customers."

"As long as we're talking about the Red Barn," Jugs began, "remember, we already decided to keep Mama Lucy's goats and the other stock in the Rock Barn. I need some big windows in the loft to make studios for the artists and I need the stalls converted into workshops for the artisans. It's a hassle the way we're doing it now. If we are going to have retail shops in the depot, we've got to have the right places to make the art."

"Boss's head is spinning now, making plans, right Boss?" Dakota shouted.

The group laughed and then fell into a long silence. Finally, Dargan addressed the drowsing members. "I guess we're all cool with everything. I won't remember shit because this is bang-up weed, but I know Boss will have filed everything away in his plan-making brain."

Dargan's statement effectively adjourned the meeting, and Cale walked out onto the veranda and gazed at the farm. The Potlatch was much larger than Matthew's farm, and because it lay in the upper piedmont, its spacious fields rolled up gently from the Glory River, which was the farm's eastern boundary. The broad swath of these eastern fields was wooded only on its northern tip. Highway 611 ran along the farm's northern edge and separated the Potlatch from neighboring parcels of this rich piedmont land.

The Kremlin, the Rock Barn, and the Red Barn were clustered in the western region of the Potlatch, above Spirit Lake and Ascension Creek to the south. Sturdy fences separated the barnyards from the crop fields in the north and west and from the barns and living areas in the south. It seemed to Cale that the weathered buildings sat upon the soft hills and valleys of the Potlatch like buttons on a coat--sensible, rightful, providing an order that gave the whole thing meaning.

Dakota came out on the porch. "The Diggers are just starting supper in the kitchen. Want to walk down and see my camp, Paha Mata?"

"Sure, man," Cale answered and they headed toward the lake.

"I'm really glad you came out here," said Dakota, "we really needed to solve the problem of getting in the field crops."

"I'm glad to help," Cale replied.

As they came into the camp, Dakota stopped in front of a teepee that had been painted with large images of grass that had blue stalks and green leaves. "This is the Blue Grass Lodge, my lodge. I live here with my woman, Gretchen. She's around somewhere. You'll meet her later."

Dakota pulled back the flap to go in the teepee, then released it. "Got to do something before I go in." He tossed several pieces of stove wood onto a blaze that burned inside a stone-lined fire ring in the center of the camp. "This is our council fire," he explained. "It is our duty to keep it burning forever. It reminds us that the people in this camp live by the fire of their spirits. If we let the council fire go out, our people will go into the earth and become lizards."

Inside the teepee, a small fire was also burning. "This fire is for cooking and for heat--the council fire is for heart," said Dakota.

They sat on the skins that covered the floor. Cale noted the leather bags that hung from the lodge poles and the bow and quiver of arrows that lay against a large bundle of fur on the far side of the lodge. He took off his heavy coat.

"I've been thinking about your encounter when the dude drew the gun. How did you know he wouldn't shoot you?" Dakota pointedly asked.

Cale stared into the cooking fire. "He didn't have the eyes of a killer. I knew that punk wouldn't shoot me. He knew I would shoot him or cut his throat or do whatever it took to end his miserable existence. He saw the robot in me."

"Maybe but maybe not. The robot could be illusion."

Cale's eyes sharpened.

Dakota continued. "It's true. The government made both of us killers. Some guys can't take it. They need to think that the killer isn't really them. But it is."

"Hence the robot," Cale surmised.

"Yes. Most guys do the super macho thing but all that means is that they want you to believe that they are softer inside, hence they are not really--".

Cale exhaled heavily. "A killer."

"I come from a long line of warriors. A warrior's job is to protect the sacred life of the people. The dead have no sacred life so a warrior preserves the heart of the people by fighting enemies. His method is killing but his purpose is to protect the thing the people love most dearly: the spirit inside them that they can share in their traditions.

"The council fire of Paha Mata is a ritual that proclaims that we are people who honor the spirit inside us. I believe you have this honor also, killer."

"I did before the war. Now I can't touch life and it can't touch me," Cale exclaimed.

"And it's painful--right?" demanded Dakota.

Cale's eyes sank. "Yes," he mumbled. When he looked up, Dakota was staring at him fiercely.

"A robot would not feel your pain but a warrior would. You killed them as I did, believing it was for good. They would have killed you."

Cale beat the ground with his fist. His face was twisted and his eyes were pained. "Not all of them," he cried.

Dakota stood. "Let the dead ones go, man. Your sorrow cannot help them. Letting yourself live again will help us all," Dakota said gravely. They gazed at the fire for a while then Dakota said, "Let's go eat."

Before they could leave the camp, a troupe of hooded figures, clad in capes emblazoned with strange geometric shapes, gathered around the council fire. The strangers danced slowly around the flames, chanting unintelligible sounds to the sky. Then they stopped and said in unison, "We seek from this fire the rebirth of the sun."

One figure stepped toward Cale and Dakota, saying, "We are the magi of mountain and leaf, of soil and stone, of water and wood, of fire, of air, of bloom and ice. We collect ourselves in the sacred oaks, we spin dreams in mistletoe, we drive blood into the holly berry."

A second caped being pronounced, "The rainbow wraps ribbons of truth across the sky. Water seeps into pools, gelid as the eye. Yellow spiders crawl across emerald patches of fog. Ever since, ever again, ever more, the world glitters and rustles."

The third oracle proclaimed, "Silver triangles float in the night. Golden drums crack and splinter. Pearled birds fall from the sky. Pustules of lava ooze the crimson tide. The north wind has no face. The east sea is without bottom. The southern wall crumbles. The western gate stands ajar."

The fourth herald declared, "Words of tongue unravel. Bowels embrace the poet's eyes. Seagulls assume algebra. Dolphins prefer genocide. Fountains of cream drown gabled houses. Shards of death pick their teeth restlessly."

The magi turned to face each other, clasping their hands like the spokes of a wheel. Together they called, "Come the sun, the leaf regains the root."

The magi suddenly broke apart and ran away from the fire, disappearing into the darkening fields. Cale and Dakota stared at the crackling flames.

"What the hell was that?" Cale asked.

Dakota laughed. "Must be some shit the Gypsies are doing for the solstice. Only in Paha Mata are all traditions sacred."

When they arrived at the Kremlin, Dakota went in but Cale lit a cigarette and lingered on the porch. He gazed at the farm. It seemed so soft in the evening light, as if embroidered on an ancient tapestry, capturing for all time some fundamental ritual of human society.

He thought of Dakota's words and Olivia's words, of the lives he had taken in the war, and of the life in Adluh he had lost.

Suddenly, Bridget approached him on the veranda with a warm smile. "The farm is beautiful, isn't it?

Without looking at her Cale replied, "Yes. It reminds me of a farm I once loved very much." Facing her he asked, "Have you painted any of it?"

"No. Not yet. I might one day. I'm working on other stuff. If you want to see it, I'll show you my work after supper."

Cale thought of Claire. Bridget was as beautiful as Claire but Bridget had honest, intelligent eyes. "Thanks," he stammered as they went in the kitchen, "I would like to see your art."

"Supper is pretty basic tonight," Mama Lucy announced as they came into the warm, fragrant room. "We've got a stew of root vegetables, some fabulous sourdough bread, and some leftover beef short ribs for the carnivores. Even though it's a week night, we do have dessert. Sable mixed up a big batch of her magic brownies. The tea is all gone. Water will have to do until Boss trades some more of our honey. When we get the co-op going, we'll have better food. Dig in."

Cale and Bridget ate at a table with Boss and Mama Lucy. Dakota grinned at Cale when he saw him trailing Bridget out of the kitchen with a handful of brownies. They went upstairs to Bridget's room and sat on the floor beside a foot locker that served as a coffee table.

"I'm a military brat turned painter," said Bridget as she munched on a brownie, "so I've lived a lot of places without putting down any roots. Fortunately, you can take art classes almost anywhere." Noticing the pack of Luckies in Cale's shirt pocket, she tossed a mayonnaise jar lid to him saying, "Smoke 'em if you got 'em."

Cale finished the brownie he was eating and lit a cigarette. "I'm a half-assed farm kid turned soldier who has never been anywhere except the war. I just got back. Well, physically I'm back.

"The roots I put down my whole life on my grandfather's farm have just been ripped up. You can't take classes anywhere for what I need to learn."

Bridget scrutinized Cale. He was handsome and in good shape and could make conversation. "What is it that you need to learn?" she challenged, expecting to hear words awkwardly contrived to begin the delicate task of seducing her.

"To let go of the ones I killed in the war," Cale answered quickly.

When he looked at her, Bridget saw his beleaguered sincerity. She thought of her family and her experience in New Mexico. "We all need to let go of something," she said darkly. Gesturing toward a large easel, Bridget's eyes brightened and she said, "This is what I'm working on now. It's a study for a portrait of a scrimshander."

Cale regarded the charcoal sketches that clearly defined several views of hands and shoulders but left the face in simple outline.

"Somebody you know?" asked Cale.

"No, just somebody I imagine. I have always been fascinated by scrimshaw, ever since I tagged along with my parents in the antique stores of Frederick, Maryland. As a little girl, I loved the ivory itself because it was the tooth or

131

the bone of a whale. When I got older, I could see the wild adventure of the designs--big ships sailing on the open ocean, fearsome whales attacking their bold hunters, bare-breasted mermaids and sea serpents--and loved scrimshaw for that.

"But when I became an artist myself, and began to sketch and paint, I was attracted to the scrimshander's technique. Now, I'm focused on the meaning of the scrimshander himself, not his work."

"The meaning of the scrimshander?" Cale inquired.

"Yes. I got the idea when I was reading about the history of hunting whales," Bridget excitedly explained. "A whaling ship was like a laboratory of society. Men from many walks of life signed up on whaling ships to make their fortunes and were sent on voyages of three or four years. They were alone at sea, and were ruled by sun and wind and appetite. They would have lived like animals.

"Except for the scrimshander. The images scratched on bits of bone didn't just pass time or record history. Because they were art, were beautiful, they rose above mere experience and reminded the crew that experience should have meaning. The crew, who lived so close to raw nature, depended on the scrimshander's work to remind them that they were, in essence, above the brute."

"I never knew that artists did that much thinking about their work," Cale said in amazement.

Bridget slid a little closer to the door. "That may be true, if you don't intend for your work to mean anything," she replied. "If you just want a pleasing design or something that looks pretty, you don't need to think about that. But if you want your work to move people, to show them something significant about being human, you sure as hell have to think about that."

Cale nodded solemnly. He was beginning to feel the pot. He glanced at Bridget. Her eyes were glistening and her face was thoughtful and happy. She was gorgeous, talented and purposeful. He was glad to be with her, to hear her talk about the meaning her life had. It made him feel as if he might speak that way again someday. "Did you always want to be a painter?"

"Not until I was a teenager and my father was assigned to Amsterdam. We kept a summer house on the coast of the North Sea at Noordwijk aan Zee. Noordwijk was a typical resort town but we had a really cool old house high up on the dunes near the water tower. It was on Doublemanduin Street. Even though it was the highest house in the town, you could not see the ocean from any window in the house. So I went down to the beach every day. In the hot weather it was packed with beach goers."

While Cale lit another cigarette, Bridget removed her shoes. She touched Cale's shoulder softly as she leaned to toss her desert boots into a corner.

"In the cold months," Bridget continued, "we did not go to the coast. But in May, we would open the summer house. The weather was changing then--calm mornings and afternoons with scattered showers. But the evenings, when the sun dropped towards the sea, the winds would begin. They started fresh and stiff but were not strong enough to drive people off of the beach.

"But one day, as the sky reddened, the wind became a gale and turned the people away from the blowing foam and the crashing surf. They scampered up the boardwalks and filled the cafés on Konigen Wilhelmenia Boulevard to watch the wind whip the grasses atop the dunes. I stayed on the beach then, that first time. Something told me to stand in the face of the howling wind and watch the furious North Sea.

"Suddenly the sun dropped below the thick cloud bank that the wind was piling up against the coast. A vast golden light broke across the sky, the sea, and me. It was the most beautiful, clear light I had ever seen. I could see the black line of cargo ships steaming towards Rotterdam and the small fishing boats desperately trying to cut into the massive swells and come into the wind. I began to shiver, but I stood facing that terrible wind and that enchanting light."

Cale touched her hand softly and Bridget knew he was as much enthused by the marijuana as she was. She stroked his palm with one finger and smiled. Cale waited for her words.

"At first, I saw only the struggle for existence in the battling fishing boats near at hand. As I looked farther out, I saw the earnestness of existence in the ships plying for the harbor. Farther out, where the sea met the sky, I saw the incredible beauty of life--I felt like I was going to explode with the sheer power of comprehending such beauty. And the wind, the blessed wind, told me that all living should have the power of this moment. That life is a serious thing because we have such a capacity to know beauty and there is so much beauty in the world. It told me that I must live with the wind, I must let my heart blow a gale into all things. Because one day I would be gone and my wind would forever cease."

Cale's gaze looked past her for a moment. Bridget paused for him to return to the present.

"When I turned to look at the cafés on the boulevard, I realized that most people flee the gale of life, fear howling beauty, and deny what is so fundamentally human and precious. At that moment, I knew that painting would be my wind. When I was actually painting, and when I was looking at the world for things I wanted to paint, capturing beauty in color would be my gale. Even if my painting was poor, painting would connect me to that seriousness of mind that tends to the power of the spirit, that constantly connects to the truth of beauty. I began to paint in Amsterdam, but I became a painter in Noordwijk."

Bridget looked at Cale. She saw his desire for her and she saw that he understood what she had said about becoming an artist. She saw also a darkness that he struggled with, a sorrow that lived in the edges of his eyes. She hoped he would tell her later. And it had been a damn long time. Bridget stretched her leg toward the door and kicked it shut.

When Cale kissed her, Bridget felt his tenderness and something inside her collapsed. She suddenly needed to feel that gentleness all over her body, to stop running for an instant, to be sought, to succor, to just be--in a moment of beauty and pleasure with a man who could actually see her mind. Bridget stood up, then sat on the bed and took off her blouse and bra.

"I'm on the pill," she whispered as she showed herself to him.

Cale was stunned by her full breasts and urgently erect pink nipples. He began to undress as she removed her jeans and panties. His body rippled with excitement and his mind rang with the clamor of lust to seize and penetrate, to stroke and soothe, to touch and excite, to join and expel.

Cale and Bridget made love as the stars glittered above the farmhouse in a dazzling spray of light eternal. When sated, they wrapped themselves in a heavy blanket and lay in entangled embrace. Sometime in the night, Cale awoke as a thunderous crash rang from Spirit Lake. He looked towards the lake and watched as the silvered water heaved and bubbled in eruption and a huge stallion, gleaming in iridescent rainbow colors, emerged from the waters and soared into the sky, showering the land with holly leaves that flew as glistening green sparks from its golden hooves.

***

The next morning, Cale helped Mama Lucy and the Diggers serve breakfast while Bridget slept. Over lunch, he discussed his strange dream with Bridget. "It would be easy to say that the pot caused that dream," she advised, "but I think, in the back of your mind, you think you are trying to emerge from something that has been holding you back. You want to show your true colors, which are dazzling and brilliant--not camo and olive drab as they had to be during the war."

"I guess that makes some kind of sense," Cale conceded, "but I can't think about it now. It's almost Christmas. My favorite time of the year. That's when my people, the Celts, celebrated their inner wind. They honored it with fire. The fire on the hill proclaimed the fire within.

"Merry Christmas, Bridget. I'll be back when the new year begins. Till then, I'll damn sure be seeing you in my dreams."

Cale kissed Bridget, lingered in her embrace, then went to his truck. He drove to the top of the hill overlooking the farm and stopped. He saw Dakota adding wood to the council fire in Paha Mata. That simple ritual connected his new friend to a devoted life in that place. Cale suddenly understood Dakota's love for the traditions of his people and saw that Dakota's reverence for his culture would be the center of his life no matter where he chose to spend his days.

Now Cale knew why his grandmother had denied him the farm. She had given the place to her sons in spite of Cale's love for Matthew's land because she knew Cale had a greater love to give some other life. As he pulled onto the highway and started towards Adluh, Cale felt a splintering shiver and a sharp crack deep in his icy soul.

***

Broadus saw the sergeant's boot hesitate as it hit the trip wire. The explosion ripped the sergeant's body apart and hurled Broadus off the trail. Tumbling through the bracken down the side of a steep ravine, Broadus heard withering fire from heavy caliber enemy guns. As he slammed to a halt at the bottom of the gully, Broadus anxiously listened for return fire. There was none. He

136

realized that his entire platoon had been bushwhacked by the North Vietnamese Army.

Knowing that the victorious killers would now pick over the bodies of the dead to seize weapons, valuables and baubles, Broadus bolted for a patch of thick jungle a few hundred yards ahead. Quickly reaching good cover, Broadus concealed himself and watched his back trail. If they were coming for him, they would come soon.

Broadus felt no pain, could not see, smell or taste blood and had a relatively calm mind. He was sure he had not been hit by rounds or shrapnel. He saw no movement, heard no disturbance and could not smell cigarette smoke. Broadus was suddenly thirsty but he dared not touch his canteen. He needed to watch for the enemy and he needed to think.

The gunfire had been so intense and had been delivered by so many heavy caliber guns, Broadus suspected his platoon had stumbled upon an NVA artillery battery. "If that's true," he thought, "they will hunt me down if they know that I'm missing."

Half an hour later, Broadus relaxed his watch. The NVA didn't seem to know that he had eluded the massacre. Broadus shivered. He didn't know where he was. To discourage desertion, the sergeant had kept all the maps in his pack. Those charts had been destroyed by the landmine or seized by the enemy.

Broadus' platoon had been away from their firebase for four days, and had twisted and turned through the countryside so many times, he had no idea where he was. There were no landmarks to help him reckon direction. The jungle was the same no matter which way he turned.

Panic knotted his gut. Broadus was prepared to fight against overwhelming odds. He was fearful of being captured. He dreaded dying alone. He was terrified of being lost. Night quickly settled over the jungle and unseen scurrying began.

Broadus forgot about the enemy. His frenzied thoughts were only of the darkness he had known all of his life. With no love offered to him from his drunken mother or absentee father, he had lived in the cold shadow of bestiality. He knew hunger and thirst, he knew fear and pain, he knew longing for tenderness, and he knew the touch of a woman's body but not the succor of a woman's heart. Privation had taught him that love let humans belong to each other and escape the isolation of their wildness.

Being loved was all he had ever truly wanted. Crouched beyond mercy within the unknowing jungle, Broadus grimly understood that he would die as he had lived. By the time the moon rose, he was broken.

CHAPTER 9--TOENAIL HILL

Cale thought of nothing but Bridget as he drove southward through the piedmont. Remembering his every exciting moment with her, he ignored the barren aspect December had cast upon the country through which he passed. Forests were mere skeletons of black trees, dimly speckled with dark evergreens. Littered with stubble and their soil broken and turned up to the coming frosts, the reddish brown fields seemed bleak and discarded. Garden patches flanking dreary shotgun houses were bare, having been stripped of their cabbages, broccoli, kale and onions. Gone from doorsteps and tractor tire flowerbeds were the last of the marigolds, coleus and impatiens. Against the diminished, dusky landscape, the colored illumination of Christmas lights seemed frail, inadequate and sad.

The land lay in darkness before he reached the Red Bank country, so Cale sped past his grandfather's farm, glancing only briefly at the lighted kitchen window where he knew his grandmother was making her Christmas cake. At the base of Toenail Hill, Cale pulled over, switched his headlights to high beam, grabbed a shotgun, stepped out into the cold night and fired. Retrieving his prize, he continued to his father's house. As he approached the back door, the sweet aroma of baking cookies, vanilla and fresh pine filled his nostrils. Ruth's happy smile greeted him as Cale went into the kitchen.

"Hi, honey. I'm glad you're home," Ruth said warmly as she slipped off her oven mitts and hugged him.

"Hi, Momma. Merry Christmas," Cale said. "I brought you some mistletoe."

"Thanks, honey. I can sure use it. You know, Matthew always brought me some. He always told me that you can't carry the cripple goat and then forget the mistletoe."

"Grandpa was right. How's Julia?"

"Oh, she's fine," Ruth declared cheerily, "and being pregnant--even though she will have no husband to help her--sure has worked a miracle on Julia."

Cale peeked into the oven and saw a sheet of sugar cookies just about to brown. "How so, Momma?"

"Well, she just seems so much more settled," Ruth explained. "She doesn't get mad about things anymore. I know she gets lonely at times, but in an odd way, she seems happy. I think she has some sense of purpose now."

Ruth suddenly flew past Cale; exclaiming, "Oh!" she snatched the cookie sheet from the oven. "I can't be jabbering too much when I'm baking." Ruth slid the cookie sheet onto a cooling rack and took Cale by the arm. "Try not to get too upset with your father this time, son. Olivia gave the farm to him. It just wasn't meant to be for you to have Matthew's land."

"I know, Momma," Cale said reassuringly.

"Hello Rembrandt," Julia said to her brother as she came into the kitchen with a laundry basket, "so what's it like having a gallery and being an artiste?"

Cale shook his head. "I'm not an artist. I'm just making some silly furniture for the college girls to put in their dorm rooms."

"Sounds like you hate it," Julia observed. "You always loved working with wood before. You've had some kind of workshop since you were a boy."

Cale took the hamper from Julia and put it on the floor. "Yeah, but I've never made real furniture. And I'm sure as hell not making it now either."

"I'll bet you could," Julia advised. "Grandpa Matthew was a cabinetmaker before World War I. After he

140

saw the farms in southern France, how everything was used to do something else with nothing going to waste, and witnessed the love those farmers had for their animals and their land, he fell in love with farming. He was born a city boy, you know."

Cale nodded. "Yeah, I know. So that's why he had all those fine woodworking tools in the workshop in the barn."

Julia cocked her head. "Yep. Didn't grandma give those tools to you?"

"Yeah. But grandpa never told me about being a cabinetmaker," Cale complained.

Julia thought for a moment. "He never told me either. I was looking for a thimble for grandma one time and under her sewing box, I saw a picture of him in his shop. She told me the story then. And she said grandpa had learned cabinetmaking in the orphanage so he didn't like to talk about it. But farming he had chosen because he fell in love with the idea of it in France, and he couldn't stop talking about that.

"So, quit bellyaching about the stuff you're making for Jack. You've got it in your blood to be an artiste, Rembrandt. Not me. I'm in secretarial school. After the baby is born, I'll be helping daddy with Glory Bend."

"What's Glory Bend?"

"That's what he calls the development he and Uncle Buck are going to build on grandpa's land. He's got a fancy model."

"What model?" Sam asked as he brought an empty mug into the kitchen. Ruth immediately took the cup and filled it with hot coffee.

"Glory Bend, Daddy. I was just telling Cale he should see your model," Julia replied.

"Hello, Cale," Sam said cautiously to his son. "I don't want to fuss with you about the farm this close to Christmas, Cale," Sam said firmly.

141

"I've had my say on that, Pop, so it doesn't matter to me anymore," Cale retorted sharply.

Sam relaxed and took a sip of coffee. "In that case, would you like to see the model?"

Cale nodded.

"I had to take my old couch out so I could get the model in here," Sam explained as Cale followed him to his office. "Marsh made a stand to put it on. It takes up near the whole of the back wall," Sam said proudly as he directed Cale towards the large sheet of plywood upon which the Glory Bend housing and resort development had been created to scale.

Cale marveled at the detail of the large boathouse and the precision of the pilings of the docks; the arched roof of the huge restaurant and the facades of the row of shops that ran along the river; the Byzantine inscription of winding streets and spidery cul-de-sacs, which hosted tiny replicas of expensive homes and condominiums rendered in painted balsa wood; the small park with its miniature trees; the Georgian club house with attending tennis courts at the foot of Toenail Hill; and an expansive golf course sweeping against the edge of Bride's Woods and enclosed on one side by Swede's Pasture.

Sam took a deep breath before he spoke. "Isn't she a beaut', son? It's like a whole town. People will live there, play there, shop, go boating, eat at the restaurant, live a pleasurable life, passing their time with tennis and golf. Right there, between those two trees, is the sales office and that big house, the really big one on the cul-de-sac, smack dab in the middle of it all, is your momma's dream house. Glory Bend will be the home place of generation after generation.

"Just imagine, Cale, people will be born in Glory Bend, they'll live their whole lives there and they'll die there. They'll pass their lives in a place we created, a place that wasn't there before. Me and your momma will go in there and we'll live our last days there. We'll go out of this earth in Glory Bend."

Cale nodded. "It is incredible, Pop," Cale declared.

"It is at that, son, it is at that," Sam boasted. "When it's done, your land will be worth a bundle. Subdividing Swede's Pasture would give you at least a dozen building lots right on the golf course. Marsh wouldn't let me do it any other way. Since Momma gave me the farm, he thought you would want to get another piece of land. Selling Swede's Pasture would give you the money to do it."

Marsh arrived and went into the office. "Hello Construction Boy," Cale called to his brother, "we were just talking about you."

"Hello, Saluda Boy. What were you accusing me of?"

"Trying to make me rich. Pop was just telling me how, thanks to you, I could get a bundle for Swede's Pasture."

"That's no bull, Cale. We're still grading and haven't put in the first foundation but already land prices are going up."

"I need a smoke. Let's take a walk, big brother," Cale suggested. "It smells like snow today. Maybe we'll have a white Christmas."

They lit up when they reached the garage and Cale said solemnly, "Grandpa's farm was the happiest place I ever knew. I never thought I would have to watch it go away."

"I know it's a hell of a blow, coming at you like that just when you got home from the war. But you know, Grandma is usually right in the things she does," Marsh reasoned.

Cale stared at the garage. Inside was his father's grey sedan, the vehicle that, like everything else in his father's life, was the hallmark of ordinary. No style, no beauty, no specialness of purpose—the car could have been

143

his father's body, a frame for ferrying purposelessness from mundane event to mundane event until the need for transport ceased. That gleaming automobile embodied the futility that had driven him from his father's house to the magical spell of his grandparents' farm.

"I know," Cale said, "it's just always been my dream to make my home there, to keep Matthew's cornfields going, to maybe pass the farm on to my own sons one day. The farm has always been such a special place."

"Maybe," Marsh replied, "but maybe it's a regular place where very special people lived, and one of them still does. How are you doing on getting your insides unlocked?"

"I haven't made any real progress with that," Cale answered, "but I have met a girl."

"So you've given up banging faculty wives?" Marsh rejoined.

"Let's don't jump to conclusions, Construction Boy."

"Tell me about this girl."

"Her name's Bridget. She's an artist--a painter. I met her at the Potlatch a few days ago."

"And," Marsh prompted.

"And I like her. She's beautiful. She's talented. She's very smart. I think she would understand anything I say."

"Even the part about the war?"

Cale looked through the window into the living room where an artificial aluminum Christmas tree glowed with gaudy blue lights. When he had first been shot, and later when the beatings and the cuttings began, he had tried to picture that tree, as if its image could deliver him from hell.

"I'll never tell her," he declared.

"Does she like you?"

"I think so."

"Have you had her in the sack?"

Cale faced his brother and grinned. "Yep."

"And you still don't know if she likes you?"

"We did a little pot. That blurs the lines a hair."

"So what are you going to do?"

"I'm going to see her again. After Christmas."

Marsh thought about his own troubled marriage. "Well one thing's for sure, Saluda Boy, a woman will either help you get your insides straightened out, or she'll fuck 'em up worse than they are now. Women try to fix the men they love, and they try to hurt the men they used to love."

***

The promise of snow that Cale had smelled earlier arrived on Christmas morning as a chilling rain which fell heavily across the land. Cale pulled on his coat and drove to the farm to get Olivia and take her to his father's house for the holiday celebration. While Olivia was getting ready, Cale walked across the freshly exposed red soil that had been revealed when the grading equipment ripped away the dark, loamy earth Matthew had spent a lifetime to develop in his cornfields.

On the top of Toenail Hill, he cut sprigs of holly from the large tree, and tenderly placed them on the grave of his grandfather. From his pocket, he took a small branch of mistletoe and put it with the holly. Cale watched the drenching rain leach the red ground in streaming flows of clay, and it seemed that the blood of Matthew was washing into the river from the ravaged land so his grandfather's spirit could never be trapped in Glory Bend. Like the cripple goat, Matthew would live in new fields of corn.

When Cale and Olivia returned to Sam's house, they found a note on the front door: AT HOSPITAL. JULIA'S BABY IS COMING! Olivia kissed her grandson on the cheek. "Merry Christmas, Cale. You're going to be an uncle! Let's go!"

145

As they hurried to the hospital, the rain became a heavy snow. The Red Bank country was enveloped in white and the festive lights of the season shone more clearly when a weary Julia kissed her newborn son on the forehead and spoke to the family members gathered around her.

"This is my son, born on a day of purpose, a day when we make a special beauty in our homes and hearts, to be shared by all. Because I wish for my son a mind that has no bounds and a heart that breaks no bonds, I have given him a special name. I hope you will all love him as much as I do. Say hello to Skye Matthew Haines."

***

When the sun came up, Broadus knew that this would be the last day that he lived. He had recovered from shock just after sundown when the pain from his injury had suddenly burst into his consciousness. His left thigh had felt like it was on fire and when he had tried to touch it, his fingers had been wet by his own blood. His fingertips had felt the shrapnel around which the blood seeped steadily.

When the moon had risen bright and clear, his pain had subsided. He had known then that he would perish. When the sergeant had been killed and his platoon had been ambushed, he had been relieved that the enemy did not pursue him. When he had realized that he was lost and alone, he had been terrified. With the dawn of his last day, Broadus now felt an odd calm.

Since there was no longer any need to be found, he was not lost. Since he would soon be dead, he would not suffer privation or capture. Because he was about to leave all humanity, being alone had no meaning so he was no longer alone. He just had no company for the moment.

Broadus was sitting on the ground with his back against a tree. His back ached but he could no longer feel his legs. Broadus opened his canteen and drank the warm, metallic tasting water. He lit a cigarette and stared blankly at the jungle.

"Why did I even have a life?" he wondered. "Every human born is an animal that is scratching to get outside of itself, to connect to something that can raise it up from the beast so its life will mean something. Shit, what does my life mean? I am eligible to die.

"I never knew my daddy and my momma was always at the mill or getting drunk so she could forget she had to work in the mill. Nobody never had no time for me. I never learned that my life should mean something. All I ever knew was to run from the darkness."

The jungle came alive with movement. Broadus listened but he did not care what scurried or crawled or walked or slithered around him. He had a full clip.

"How could I want love so much when I didn't even know what it was? The lack of it, that gnawing sorrow that never let go, that's how I knew it. I knew it as the light that should drive away the dark loneliness. I heard it as women singing in their gardens while they picked fresh flowers. I saw it in old movies when a guy hugged his girl so tight he could have broken her in two. I knew about it. I knew it wasn't going to shine on me. But why?"

Broadus spied clumps of purplish berries hanging from a vine. He marveled that he had absolutely no hunger. He drank more water.

"My last day. It is not special. That's how it should be. Like all the rest. Desperate. Lonely. I don't think I'll even make it until sunset. I hope I do. That would be a proper time to die. When the day is dying and throwing its full glory up into the sky for all to see.

"Glory. I never got that either. Wouldn't have needed it, if love had shined on me."

Broadus suddenly felt very sick. He wished he had not drunk the water. Chills rippled through his body. He turned on his side and vomited violently. He felt blood begin to ooze from his leg. He was too tired to stop the flow again.

Broadus tried to smoke another cigarette but his hands could not grasp the lighter. Now he felt very cold inside. Then she touched him and her hand was warm and soft and soothing. His mother's face looked haggard and her cheek was bruised but her eyes were shimmering. She was looking upon him with love, with gracious acceptance, with tender kindness, with welcoming affection.

Belonging suddenly warmed him, settled his sickness and let him flow out of himself into an expansive peace, a spacious luxury of being he had never known. Broadus felt radiantly human. He saw a golden light in his mother's gaze and his darkness—

A buzzing fly landed on the eyelid. Undisturbed, it began to feed.

CHAPTER 10--SNAKE MAN

Shortly after the old calendars were taken down and shiny new almanacs for 1972 were hung with hope for a better year, a furious winter storm swept across the piedmont and covered Saluda and the Red Bank country with deep snow. Arriving at the commune an hour after sunup, Cale paused in wonder at the white mantle covering the Potlatch. The gently sloping swales of the barnyards, the Physic garden and the broad flanks of the crop fields seemed to be quietly resting in peace. The alabaster shroud that lay over the farm was unmarked by hoof or shoe prints and that purity rang unabated through the camps of Paha Mata, Mudville, and the Shuttlepot.

Cale slipped into the kitchen of the Kremlin, quietly brewed a pot of coffee, and trudged through the icy wind and crunchy snow to the Blue Grass lodge in Paha Mata. Dakota stood before a blazing council fire.

"Want some coffee?" Cale asked as Dakota waved a greeting.

"Sure, man. I'll get some cups. It's about time for Jugs and Boss to mosey down to the fire."

Cale put the coffee pot on the edge of the fire as Dakota disappeared into his lodge. While Dakota retrieved the mugs, Cale saw a figure emerge from a yurt in the Shuttlepot and wave toward the Kremlin.

Dakota returned with four blue enameled cups as Jugs reached the fire and Boss was approaching.

"Cold enough for you?" Jugs hailed as he accepted a steaming cup of coffee.

Dakota nodded but Cale shook his head. "No, it's not," said Cale, "but it will be in February."

Boss grinned. "They say we've already set a record for snow, with plenty more to come, and that this could end up being the coldest winter on record. Unfortunately, our next projects will put us partly in the cold. We have to make lofts in the Red Barn for the artists and workshops down below for the artisans."

"All we have to do," Boss explained, "is to cut openings to install the six big windows I bought, put up partial walls to give each artist some privacy, and install some big-ass fans in each gable to cool it--after Dakota runs the juice up to the Red Barn. I'm not sure how we are going to heat it."

"It seems to me," Cale suggested, "we'll have to heat the loft and the workshops the same way--kerosene heaters. We put down fireproof mats for the heaters to sit on and let it go at that. There's no efficient way to heat a barn. Anyone who needs even heat for the paint on their work to dry will just have to bring that piece in the Kremlin at night. We have several months before we have to worry about cooling the place."

"This coffee has warmed us up, so let's get going," Boss prompted.

The first broad section of barn wall that they removed was taller than any of them and gave them a grand view of Spirit Lake. A broad shaft of sunshine now penetrated the dark loft. When they broke for lunch, Bridget was waiting for Cale in the spacious dining room of the Kremlin. "You'll have your studio in a couple of weeks," Cale said happily as he sat beside her.

"Great," commented Bridget, "I can't wait to be able to work in ample light. We've got salad, squash casserole and sourdough bread for lunch. Would you like for me to fix you a plate?"

"Thanks," Cale agreed.

Before Bridget returned, Gretchen stepped in from the kitchen and called to Cale, "Your roommate Jack is on the phone."

Cale walked into the hall and picked up the receiver that was lying on the telephone table. "Hey Jack, what new trinket do you need for the Painted Pony?"

There was gravity in Jack's voice. "Your brother Marsh called the house. He said your friend Broadus is missing in action."

"Thanks for letting me know," Cale answered despondently.

When Bridget returned with the food, Cale told her the sad news. He put his head in his hands and stared at his plate. "That poor son of a bitch," he muttered. "He's not going to have a chance."

"I'm sorry," Bridget said softly.

"Me too," Cale whispered.

Cale barely touched his food and said only a few more words before he went back to the barn. When he got back to the loft, Dakota immediately saw the sadness in his face.

"What's wrong, man?" Dakota asked.

Cale's eyes grew distant. "My friend Broadus is missing in action."

"Shit!" Dakota exclaimed. "What is his AO?"

"Same as yours--I Corps."

Dakota touched Cale on the arm. "Hey, man, I'm really sorry for your friend. I hope he makes it back ok."

They cut and framed two more large openings before calling it a day. Cale did not return to Grace House. He drove to a nearby beer joint on 611. Vivid memories of his own misery in the jungle filled his mind as he began to drink. He sat alone at the end of the bar and spoke to no one--he just drank.

"Broadus is a tough customer in a mill town brawl," he thought, "but his life has never been in danger. His wild

151

behavior is only an exaggeration trying to soothe his hurt. He never knew his father. His momma worked long hours in the mill and was so beat when she came home, she had no time for him.

"At school, he didn't join any clubs. As big and strong as he was, the ape didn't even try out for a single team. No father to hunt and fish with and tell him about the things a man has to think about, to encourage him to face his fears, to tell him about girls, to help him make sense of his feelings; no mother to make his birthday special, to read stories to him, to let him help her make Christmas cookies, to cheer for him when he couldn't cheer for himself, to patch him up when he was scared and hurting."

Cale ate a handful of stale peanuts. He had not thought about Broadus much since his friend had joined the Marines. He guessed he had been trying to protect himself against this day.

"Broadus never knew what being a part of something was. His quest for glory was a desperate cry against being alone. He wanted to share in the meaning that other people had in their lives because they belonged to others."

Tears welled in Cale's eyes. "Broadus is a lost warrior. Lost to his comrades and lost to himself. He is what he is most scared of: being all alone. He is not just alone, he is apart from all belonging, where life is not precious. Lost warriors never make it out of the jungle alive. They don't have a reason to live."

As he drained his last beer, Cale thought, "I don't know which is worse, to die over there or to come back dead like me." He stumbled out to his truck and headed to the Potlatch. He parked where Bridget couldn't see him from her bedroom window then staggered over to the Red Barn. Clumsily, he climbed the ladder to the loft and lay down on the floor.

He waited for his head to stop spinning then rolled over to the opening that faced the Kremlin. He pulled himself up and stood in the empty space. He could see the light in Bridget's window and he knew that she was painting, that she was putting her passion into her life. She was so beautiful. She knew so much about life. He wanted her so badly but he feared that a woman like that couldn't care for a man with a frozen heart.

"Before the war," he mumbled, "I had a man's heart. I loved life. I loved the beauty in the land, in exquisite things, in the kindness and affection people can show each other. I loved all that and I could feel my love for it. Now I can't love anything. I have the heart of a snake. They'll find Broadus. He'll come home and finally belong. He will not come back as a snake."

Cale stared at the faithful glow beaming from Bridget's window. Suddenly, he screamed into the night, "I am not a snake! I will not live as a snake! I am a man! If I cannot live as a man--!" He stopped. Below him a drum was beating slowly. He reeled sideways, peering into the darkness. He grasped the edge of the window opening to steady himself. Then he heard a strange chanting.

"Broadus! Is that you? Are you already dead?" Cale shouted. He teetered and his body swung out into the night air. The drumming and chanting grew louder.

"I sing the death song of the lost warrior," answered the voice.

"Then sing for Broadus," Cale entreated sadly.

"No, Snake Man. I sing for you. You are the warrior whose heart is lost."

Cale straightened and stared at Bridget's window. Suddenly he was grasped from behind and pulled to the floor. Instinctively, he kicked and punched furiously.

"Cale! It's me! Boss! Boss!"

Cale stopped struggling as Dakota rushed up the stairs and into the loft. "You're drunk man!" Dakota cried.

"Me and Boss are going to take you to the Kremlin to sleep it off."

"No," Cale protested. "Please don't let Bridget see me like this."

"Ok, man," Dakota assured him, "we'll take you to my lodge. You can sleep it off in Paha Mata."

Slowly they eased Cale down the stairs and carried him to the Blue Grass lodge. While Boss settled Cale against a backrest, Dakota whispered to Gretchen and she ran out.

"You get some sleep now," Boss chided, "we got a lot of work to do in the morning."

"Ok, ok," Cale mumbled, "Boss always has a plan."

Cale was asleep when Gretchen returned with Bridget. "What happened?" Bridget asked softly.

Dakota laughed. "It's ok. You can talk. He's out cold."

"Is this because of Broadus?" Bridget inquired.

"That's what got it started," Dakota began, "but that's not why he was standing in that opening in the loft."

Bridget's eyes flashed with alarm. "Do you think he was going to jump?"

Dakota shook his head. "I don't think so but the fool could have fallen. I saw him when he drove in and staggered to the Red Barn so I ran to get Boss. By the time we got back, he was already standing in that big opening. I distracted him with my drum while Boss sneaked up behind him.

"He was staring at your window, Bridget. He was complaining that his heart doesn't feel things like it did before the war. He got hurt bad over there. He was captured. He won't say what they did to him but he said that when he got out of the war, his heart was cold and dead inside."

Dakota stared intently at Bridget. "Now he has something he really wants to care about but his spirit is crippled by very dark memories of the jungle. He wants to care about you, Bridget."

Bridget looked startled and a little embarrassed.

"When I came home," Dakota counseled, "I went through what he's going through, only he's got it tougher. Nobody captured me."

"What did you do to recover?" asked Bridget.

Dakota thought for a moment. "I tried to focus on the fact that I was the same person I had been. That my spirit had experienced a great shock. That I was still me inside but it would take some time to feel like me again. That life in war and life back home were different, but I was still the same."

"How long did it take for you to get past the shock?" asked Bridget.

"I don't know," Dakota insisted, "because it comes in many separated moments. Like thawing. One spot gets warmer, then another spot, then the ice falls away. Cale's despair is really just impatience to get his feelings back. The part of him that cares for you, Bridget, knows he's the same passionate guy he was before the war. He's in a big hurry for the rest of him to get free of the war."

"Come on, Bridget," Gretchen said gently, "let's go back to the house. He's going to sleep for a long time and Boss and Dakota will watch out for him"

Bridget's concerned eyes glanced at Dakota. Dakota nodded, and Bridget left with Gretchen. "Do you think we'll have to keep watching him?" Boss asked Dakota.

"I don't think so, Boss. The news about his friend was bound to stir up some very bad memories. But I think those memories, rising up fast out of the dark places where he tried to put them, probably lost a little bit of their grip on his heart."

***

The next afternoon, Cale appeared in the loft as Boss and Dakota were installing a window. "You might

155

need a carpenter to help with that, if you want the windows to fit," Cale said quietly.

"Know where we can find a sober one?" Dakota chided.

"Thanks for last night," Cale said sincerely. "It's nice to have real friends."

"Quit your blabbering and drive some nails," Boss rejoined.

When his crew knocked off for the day, Cale found Bridget sitting on the tailgate of his truck. "Feeling better?" she asked with a strained smile.

Cale looked at her. The question had been sincere. "Yes," he said quietly, "I think I got something out of my system. I'm not sure what it was, but I feel like I let go of something."

"Are you going to have supper with us or are you going to town?"

Cale took her hand. "If you'll let me, I'd like to take you to supper. I know this little diner on 611."

Bridget kissed him lightly on the lips. "Sure thing, Snake Man."

CHAPTER 11--XANADU

The ice storms of February glazed the piedmont in a glistening chrysalis that encased the forest and covered the woodpiles in Paha Mata and the Shuttlepot. After helping Dakota struggle to free sticks of wood for the council fire, Jugs suddenly bolted into the Red Barn and turned up the heat on the kerosene stove that heated his workshop. When his space had warmed enough, he wedged several huge blocks of clay and then began working at the kick wheel.

In the early afternoon, Jugs left his studio and went into the kitchen of the Kremlin. Boss, Mama Lucy, Cale, Bridget, Dakota, Gretchen and Sable were seated at the large table. Sable rose when Jugs came in, went to the electric stove, filled a large bowl from a pot on the front burner and placed the steaming dish on the table in front of him.

"We've got white bean soup with smoked ham today," Sable said to Jugs as she sat beside him.

"It smells great!" Jugs cried as he broke a piece of bread from the loaf in the center of the table.

"How are we doing on groceries?" Gretchen asked.

"We're starting to get a little low," replied Bridget casually, "we're going to need a few things soon. I've got a list for the next person who goes into town."

Jugs hurriedly wiped his mouth and said, "I'll be going into town as soon as the roads are clear. I need to pick up some fire bricks to reline my kiln. The lofts must be done, Boss. Nobody is working upstairs in the Red Barn."

Bridget's eyes widened. She stared at Cale. He nodded. "When were you going to tell me, Snake Man?" she demanded.

Cale smiled. "As soon as I finish eating, darlin'."

Immediately after lunch, Cale helped Bridget move her work into the loft of the Red Barn. She put her kerosene heater by the window that faced Spirit Lake. While she worked at her easel in the loft, Cale and his crew framed additional workshops on the ground floor. When they knocked off, Cale and Bridget went into the kitchen.

"I'm having a hell of a time with something I'm working on," Cale told her.

"What are you trying to do?" asked Bridget.

"Design a writing desk. I'd like to raise the level of the furniture we're offering at the gallery. I've been reading books on design that Jack brought me and I've been looking at pictures of other desks, but every one of my sketches stinks."

"Why do you think that is?"

Cale tapped his finger on a salt shaker. "Because I don't know anything about design."

Bridget looked doubtful. "That's the easy answer. What's the hard answer?" she insisted.

Cale frowned. "I don't know. That's why I'm talking to you."

"It's like this old sergeant used to tell me about running the table in nine ball. You see the shots or you don't. Design comes in two forms: the big picture and the small details. Before you can do either, you have to picture the thing itself in your head. You could always copy one of the desks you have seen."

Cale shook his head.

"Then your problem," Bridget added, "is creation, not design. After supper, I want to show you one of my special creations."

"Sure," Cale agreed.

158

After eating the evening meal with Dakota and Gretchen, Bridget scrambled to her room ahead of Cale and was dragging a steamer trunk from her closet when Cale entered her bedroom. She gestured for Cale to close the door behind him.

Cale swung the heavy door until the latch snapped into the jamb, then eagerly turned to Bridget, who was now seated on the large wooden trunk and regarding him with serious, yet nervous, eyes.

"I have never told you about this," she began hesitantly, "because I have never shared this with anyone. Maybe I shouldn't share it now but I think if anyone will understand this, you will."

Bridget looked at Cale tenderly for a moment then let her eyes fall away from him. "This trunk belonged to my great-grandfather, Angus Chattan. He left Scotland in the early eighteen hundreds with his family and settled in Delaware. I don't know much about him really, except that he was an itinerant sign painter. My grandfather, Donald Chattan, says that some of Angus' signs are still hanging in little towns in the country. He also says that Bannock, my father, should take me to see those signs one of these days."

Cale sat on the bed and lit a cigarette. He took from Bridget's nightstand the jar lid he had grown accustomed to using as an ashtray. "There are many things a father should do," he said gravely.

Bridget nodded her agreement. "I got the trunk because I used to play with it when I was a kid and my grandmother finally got tired of hauling it around from one duty station to the next. My grandfather was a career military man just like my dad. When I got it, it had Angus' paint box and some old cigar boxes in it, along with some yellowed newspapers, tied up in a bundle. I didn't use it for anything at first. I just oiled it and polished it and enjoyed looking at it.

Bridget paused and gently rubbed the lid of the trunk. "Like I said, my father was a military man, so we were always moving. Leveraging your circumstances is what my father calls giving up all of your friends. Bargaining for a better position is how he describes the moving truck backing up to the door and sucking out all of the artifacts of your life in that place and spitting them out in another place."

Cale stared affectionately at Bridget. He felt the need to say something, but the sincerity and intensity of Bridget's countenance silenced him.

"Every time he got a new duty station, he would gather the family together and explain the new deal, would list the things we would have to give up--which mattered a lot to the kids--and the things we would get--which only meant something to my parents.

"Vague things like money, rank and prestige were always traded away for my specific friend who had a distinct face and discrete gaps in her definitely misaligned teeth or my specific homeroom with a distinct shit-green paint job and a definite teacher or my specific house with a distinct room that was definitely mine."

Agitated, Bridget bit her lip and turned away from the chest. "I would be lying if I said I got used to it. Abandonment teaches abandonment, so I stopped putting my mark on anything, stopped making anything mine. Except for the trunk. It was mine. It had been given to me and, unlike my parents' values, it was non-negotiable. I thought I was doing all right with my aloofness, that I was coping with the constant uprooting, until we moved out of the country."

Bridget paused and stared at the floor. She stiffened her legs slightly, as if trying to block an onslaught of memory.

"The move to the Netherlands was a terrible shock, but it was also something of a compass for me--the way the river was for you," Bridget observed.

Cale extinguished his cigarette. "How so?"

"Once I realized that I was a painter, in that gale at Noordwijk," Bridget continued, "life away from home became easier. Before that, I had just been hanging out in Dam Square with all of the dope heads, or wandering through the University listening to the students pontificate about the evils of the world, which the world so deserved to suffer because the world outside their own quarter was ignorant and, though none would say so, it was probably meant to be that way.

"We lived just beside the University on what was the shortest, quietest, most beautiful street in Amsterdam-- Ververstraat. I have a painting of it somewhere--not a good one. I used to set up my easel on the little bridge at the end of our street. I would cross the canal and set it up on the far side of the bridge near the cafés so the students would have to pass me on their way to get drunk.

"I didn't spend a lot of time in the museums, but I did take the tram down to Museumplein once in a while and spend the day looking at paintings. I was most fascinated by the portraits. For me there were two kinds of portraits: the story of a face and the story of a land. Rembrandt really had the face thing going and Van Gogh had the land thing going."

Cale stood and looked out her window at the studio in the Red Barn where Bridget now did her work. He thought of his own desire to create, to do substantial work. "So what did you have going?" he asked.

Bridget looked away from him. "I guess that was my way of going to art school--and it still is, I guess. Anyway, after two years in Amsterdam, my father's duties with NATO ended and he was reassigned to the States and we moved back to our house in Maryland. And that's when

I told my father I wasn't moving again. He managed to hold his career ambitions in check long enough for me to graduate from high school and do a year of college at Georgetown.

"Then a slot became available in California and the negotiations started again. This is what we'll have to give up, this is what we will get and it will be a net gain for the family. I told him I wasn't buying it, so when they packed up and moved out west, I finished the term at Georgetown and bought a bus ticket and headed for the Potlatch."

"So it was your father's pursuit of a career that landed you on our doorstep?" Cale suggested.

"Hell no!" Bridget cried irritably. "My father's ambition just put me on a separate path. I brought myself to the Potlatch!"

"I'm sorry," Cale explained. "I didn't mean anything except that it caused a break."

"I know," Bridget said with a frown, "but the break came a long time ago and it caused me to create the thing inside this trunk. The break was learning that my parents saw everything as negotiable for greater comfort and prestige, that they saw no enduring value in anything, that they always leave everything behind and move on to something else, which in turn will be abandoned.

"I was thinking about this the night before we left the country as I lay in my bed, surrounded by cardboard boxes that would be loaded onto a moving van in the morning and shipped to Amsterdam. I looked into the sky and imagined that my parents were driving a starship, The Departure, and that, although there were trillions of stars in the universe, they would find a way to touch and then leave them all. Suddenly, I saw the one thing that could never be abandoned, even if you could travel a million times faster than light, there was one thing The Departure could not leave behind. Infinity."

Bridget laughed painfully. "I jumped out of bed, flipped on the light, and opened my beautiful steamer trunk. I took out my grandfather's paint box, the cigar boxes and the bundle of newspapers. I was still marveling about infinity as I loosened the string around the papers. I had always thought that these were just old papers that my grandfather had saved because they had stories about his work but as I peeled them apart, I found a small collection of miniatures. There was an exquisite tea set, an oriental rug and a glass chandelier. Slowly, I realized why all of these things had been together in the trunk."

Cale rose and put his arm around Bridget's shoulder. "Why?" he asked tenderly.

Bridget smiled at Cale. "My grandfather was going to make a dollhouse for my grandmother. He was going to paint the inside of the trunk and tack the cigar boxes to the sides of the chest to make multiple rooms--one part of the box for the floor and one part for the ceiling. He had started gathering the miniature furnishings when he died.

"My mind exploded then. I decided that I would make, not a dollhouse, but a space house. I would make the little rooms and furnish them but I would paint the inside of the trunk to look like infinity, so that my little house could never be left behind. I was up until dawn, working on the design.

"Once we got settled in Amsterdam, I painted the inside of the trunk and gave it a name--Infinitus. I used my allowance to buy some really beautiful miniatures, and I made several rooms. I have saved space for two more rooms, which I will finish someday when I have my own home. Anyway, that's the story. And you're the first person to see my masterpiece."

Bridget abruptly stood up and opened the trunk.

Cale was astonished by the painting he beheld inside the trunk lid: on a deep blue field of sky in the center were brilliant reeling galaxies and comets; outward, in all four directions, the solar system, in dazzlingly cool colors appeared in varying aspect and angle; moving from glittering night towards opalescent day, the planets gave way to vivid earthrise, then stunning moonrise, then glorious streaming sunrise at the edge.

"It is absolutely beautiful," cried Cale as he stared in wonderment at Bridget.

"Come see the little rooms," Bridget pleaded with a blush.

Cale hugged her and glanced inside the trunk. There he saw a miniature drawing room, attic, and living room.

"It is so incredible. Why do you keep it hidden?" Cale asked urgently.

"Because it's not a work of art--it's still a work of heart. One day, when I'm not so close to it, when I don't need to and don't want to tell the story of it, then I'll show it. I just wanted you to see it so you'll know something more about what goes on inside my head," Bridget insisted.

"And when you finally have a home, then you'll finish Infinitus, right?" Cale asked.

Bridget nodded.

"Well," Cale began with a sly smile," how will you know when you've found home? How will you recognize it?"

Bridget closed Infinitus. "That's easy, Snake Man. That place will make me dream about it. That's how I will know that it's home," she said with a smile.

Cale took Bridget into his arms. They looked intently into each other's eyes and saw their own story, their own hearts, their own minds. The separateness between them cleaved slightly, and they felt united in spirit and desire. They kissed deeply, and in that moment, a bridge of sorrow and joy, newly girded by affection and hopeful trust, joined between them.

"Fear of abandonment is my demon," Bridget said sorrowfully. "It is real and it is powerful and I will have to

164

go back to New Mexico soon to defeat it." Bridget bravely tried to smile but could not: the memory of Dakota's grim words about Cale's experience in the war would not let her spirit rise.

Bridget began to cry. "I know your demon is a thousand times worse than mine. I know it comes from the war, and I know it is terrible and I know it hurt you so bad—," Bridget sobbed loudly and pulled away when Cale tried to hold her. "We connect. Even though I don't want to and right now you don't know how to. I feel the connection, Cale," she cried, "but I can't stop your torment. And you can't stop mine."

Cale gently touched her shoulders. "We do connect, Bridget. My insides are still cold, and I can't feel things like I did before. But I know we have a connection, Bridget. I know."

Bridget hugged Cale and kissed him on the neck. "You go back to your shop now. Try to see the big picture, see that writing desk standing in some great author's study. See it and then give it form."

When he returned to his shop, Cale studied the sketches he had made for the writing desk. All of them were boxy, as if all he had done was put a wide top on a bookshelf. Glancing through the furniture encyclopedia, he saw several beautiful desks that he knew he could copy but imitation was not his goal. Bridget was right: he had a creation problem.

Cale didn't have an idea for the desk he wanted to build. He couldn't see it and he couldn't feel it. He was being guided purely by function: a desk needed a frame, drawers, and a top. He could only think of it as boxes with a wide top. He thought about Matthew. His grandfather had learned cabinet making in the orphanage as a means of survival. Matthew didn't have a love of wood, so he had easily given up building furniture when he had discovered what he truly loved: husbandry.

Cale had always enjoyed making things with wood. Carpentry satisfied that passion somewhat but he was always following someone else's plan. Even in making things for the Painted Pony, he was complying with Jack's directions. Suddenly, he realized that his contempt for the furniture he had made for the gallery was actually two things: he wanted the result to be beautiful and he wanted the concept to be his. He had no trouble making boxes but he did not know how to make an idea.

Cale chose one of his sketches that he despised the least and began to build the writing desk. While the piece was slowly cut and assembled in his shop at Grace House, Cale's crew finished the workshops in the Red Barn. Cale was sitting by the council fire, smoking and chatting with Dakota, when Boss ambled down the hill from the Kremlin to Paha Mata.

Boss rubbed his hands together above the flames. "Great job in the Red Barn, dudes. Jugs is happy to have better spaces for his people to do their work. Of course, you never get something for nothing from Jugs, so now he wants a place in the depot to sell the work of his artisans. The artists already have the Painted Pony for their wares. So Dargan wants to frame in half of the remaining space for a head shop. The plan is this. We just basically have to put in a door onto Station Avenue, a few non-load-bearing walls and some built-in display shelves and closet rods. People can go to the gallery, or the café after it opens, to pee."

"What name has Jugs given to his head shop?" asked Dakota.

Boss lit a joint in the fire, took a hit, and passed it to Dakota. "Xanadu."

Cale laughed. "One man's head shop is another man's pleasure palace."

***

166

Just after Valentine's Day, construction started on Xanadu and Cale was ready to finish the writing desk. He cranked up the kerosene heater and carefully sanded the uncomplicated surfaces. Once the garage was warm, he applied a light mahogany stain and left the desk to dry. After several days of applying multiple coats of varnish and polishing the piece with wax, Cale presented the writing desk to Jack.

Jack tugged on his moustache as he scrutinized the piece. "She's definitely well built, mate," Jack said hesitantly, "but she doesn't have enough sail. The furniture we've got in the gallery now is not art. It's utilitarian pop. And it sells. I'm in favor of raising the bar in the gallery because that'll give us a lot more profit. This piece ain't pop but it's more functional than artistic. Sorry, mate, I just can't use it."

Cale frowned but he was not crestfallen. He didn't like the desk either.

"I could use it," Hank said quietly.

Cale smiled. "Longfellow, the desk is yours, free of charge."

***

The second week in March, the first crocus blossoms appeared in the piedmont. Delicate purple petals surrounded the yellow and orange centers of the flowers that presented the first bit of color on the brown banks of the Glory River. Jugs and Sable drove their old van into town and began filling Xanadu with merchandise from the Potlatch.

"Naturally," Jugs said to Cale said with a grin, "my bongs will be displayed in the windows."

"Of course," Cale agreed. "The question is, is this space ok? We could only fit two small islands in here for the jewelry because of the changing room."

Jugs turned to Sable and touched his red beret. "This will work for us, Cale," Sable confirmed. "We've got

167

more clothes than anything else. Boss has a friend who has a friend who gets this stuff from India real cheap. Most of the Gypsies' stuff will go in the gallery."

"It's a great space, man, thanks." Jugs said. "Oh, Boss said to let you know that Dargan would like you to drive out to the Potlatch this afternoon. I smell another project."

When Cale arrived at the Kremlin, he found Mama Lucy in the kitchen putting bread in the oven. "Is Dargan around?"

Mama Lucy thought for a moment. "I think he went with Boss to Paha Mata."

"Thanks," Cale replied. "Oh, my brother will be bringing my tractor up in a few days, and I'll turn the crop fields and lay off rows."

Mama Lucy limped across the kitchen and hugged him excitedly. "It's been a long winter. We've already planted the early stuff in the Physic garden but the Diggers can't wait to play in the big dirt!"

Cale stopped by the Red Barn and found Bridget in her studio in the loft. "Hey, Baby," she said softly as she kissed him on the cheek.

"Are you going to be working tonight?" Cale asked.

Bridget seductively tilted her hips towards him. "That depends. Are you going to be around?"

Cale nodded. "I've got to see Dargan about something, so I thought I'd stay for supper."

Bridget smiled. "In that case, I'm not working tonight. Anyway, I have a surprise for you."

"See you at supper," Cale called as he hurried down the stairs and walked rapidly to Paha Mata. Gretchen was sitting by the council fire, doing beadwork on a leather dress. She pointed to Dakota's lodge. "Heap big powwow."

Cale opened the flap and entered the Blue Grass lodge. Dargan and Boss were sitting with Dakota.

"Glad you could make it, man," Dargan said quietly.

"What's going on?" Cale asked as he sat.

"We're kicking around the next project," Boss began. "The thing is, it has nothing to do with the Potlatch or the depot but it could make enough money to make the Potlatch secure for a while."

"So what is it?" Cale inquired.

"The plan is for Dargan to buy some old houses in your neighborhood, renovate them and sell them. The question is, which way is that neighborhood headed, up or down?" explained Dakota.

"Since you live there," Dargan said, "we wanted to know what you think."

Cale thought for a moment of the once grand homes in College Hill. "There are a lot of great houses. It would be wonderful to see them returned to their former glory. But they've been neglected and they've been turned into student housing. You'd have to pick a block where the side streets have lots of trees, buy several big houses on that block, and fix them up at the same time. That way, you could sell them to faculty members and start the trend towards a restored neighborhood."

"That's what I thought," Dargan declared. "I guess I'll poke around College Hill and see what I can find."

***

After supper, Cale followed Bridget up to her room. She pointed to an easel draped with a large towel. "I did this for you," she said cheerfully and removed the towel.

Cale saw a marvelous painting of a scrimshander carving a whale's tooth and all around him an empty blue sea. The artisan's face was Cale. "It's amazing, Bridget! Thank you. But why did you give the scrimshander my face?"

"Do you remember what I told you about the meaning of the scrimshander?"

169

Cale nodded.

Bridget kissed him lightly. "Well, that's how I see you. I don't know what your ship is, or where it's headed, but I know that you are the scrimshander on board. I think you want to capture beauty with your hands because your heart sees so much beauty in the world."

"I don't know about that," Cale said dejectedly. "I finished the writing desk the other day and showed it to Jack. He rejected it. He said it had no art about it. Hank took it as a gesture of mercy."

"It's a start, Baby. My first paintings were terrible. All I had then was the desire to paint. It took a while for me to find what it was inside of me that wanted to come out in my work. Yours will come."

Cale sat on the bed and put his head in his hands. "I don't know, Bridget. Nothing's trying to come out of me, at least nothing beautiful. Anything I do, I'm forcing it. All I know is, I would love to make things with wood that weren't ugly or silly or just functional."

Bridget sat on his lap and kissed his neck. "Then you will, Baby, you will. You can start by making love to me."

They joined tenderly, then passionately, then furiously. When they were satisfied, Cale mumbled, "I'll tell you one more thing I know."

Bridget kissed his shoulder. "What's that, Snake Man?"

"I want to take you to Asheville. It's a beautiful drive from here and it's a quiet town. They have one or two art galleries and antique shops. There's a new spot for live music. Taking you there would be like taking you on a proper date. Don't get me wrong, our passionate, improper dates are my favorite. But still, a fellow likes to take his girl on a proper date every now and again."

Cale quickly fell asleep. Bridget thought about Cale's growing affection for her. Then she remembered

New Mexico, stared into the darkness, and lay trembling with fear until the moon went down behind Blue Mesa.

***

Two days later, Marsh arrived at the Potlatch in his flatbed truck, unloaded a tractor, and parked it beside the Rock Barn as Boss requested.

"Cale will be glad to see this tractor. Thanks for helping out," Boss said as Marsh departed.

The following Saturday, Cale rose early, had breakfast at the 611 Diner, drove to the Potlatch and began turning the crop fields. As he ploughed, Cale decided to put the writing desk project aside for a while and just enjoy his relationship with Bridget. He had feelings for her that did more than just excite him: he was satisfied and calmed just being in her presence. Her body pleasured him greatly but her quick and tender mind soothed him, combed away, with feminine understanding, some of his restlessness.

When Cale went into the Kremlin for lunch, Mama Lucy embraced him. "Thank you," she said quietly. Cale sat with Jugs while Mama Lucy fixed plates for them.

"Spring must really be coming, man. I saw you out there plowing," said Jugs.

"Yep," Cale replied. "It's here. How's the new kiln?"

"Don't know yet," Jugs responded. "I've only had a few low fires in it so far. Does Bridget know you're here?"

Cale took the plate Mama Lucy offered. "I don't think so. She can't see the fields from her studio. Besides, I don't have any will power around her. If I see her, I won't get any work done."

Jugs grinned. "Everybody around here thinks you and Bridget are getting heavy. Dakota told me that Bridget is definitely your medicine."

Cale put down his fork and leaned towards Jugs. "Dakota is a very smart dude. Did he happen to say that he

171

thought I was Bridget's medicine?" he asked softly, as if afraid of the answer.

Jugs grimaced. "Not exactly. He did tell me that your shadow and her shadow will be removed by the same sun but on different days. The dude is one of my best friends but I don't understand half of what he says—even when he's not stoned. All I know is that he has a spooky way of being right about a lot of things."

After lunch, Cale returned to the fields and worked until dark. When he went to the Kremlin and walked into the kitchen, Bridget was shocked. "Hey, Baby," she cried. "I didn't know you were here."

"He's been here all day," Mama Lucy said proudly. "He's getting the fields ready for planting."

"I didn't want to disturb your work," Cale said quietly to Bridget.

"Crap. I do have to work tonight, Baby. I'm into to something I can't put down. Sorry," Bridget explained.

"That's ok. We didn't have plans. The plowing couldn't wait. Spring is coming fast. But we're still on for next Friday, right?"

"Absolutely," Bridget said brightly. "You come here for lunch and then we'll head out for Asheville. We can make it before dark. Are you done with the plowing?"

"No," Cale replied. "I'll be back tomorrow to lay off the rows."

Cale took Bridget's hand and they walked out on the porch. She kissed him tenderly. "Since I know you're coming, Baby, I'll make time for an improper date tomorrow night."

***

Cale and Bridget arrived in Asheville late in the afternoon on Friday. Cale parked on a side street near the Downtowner Motor Inn. "You just sit tight," Cale instructed Bridget. "I'll get us a room. I'll have to say we're married. But don't worry. These mountain boys don't

172

always wear wedding bands and this establishment doesn't look at you too closely."

After checking them in to the motel, Cale took Bridget for a walk downtown. "The mountains are beautiful," Bridget said as they strolled through Pack Square.

"Yep," Cale replied, "I've always loved the mountains. I haven't been in them much, but when I am, I hate to leave. When I am removed from my life in the lowlands, I realize that I don't want to go back. Of course I always do. That's where I live."

"Maybe you won't live in the piedmont forever," Bridget suggested.

"Maybe", Cale replied, "but I love being on the river."

Bridget stopped to watch the sun dropping behind the ridges that ringed the city. Clouds rumpled the sky like a red silk quilt. "Doesn't the river start somewhere in the mountains?" she asked.

Cale drew Bridget to him and kissed her. He held her tightly as he said, "Yes. So I guess it is possible to be on the river and in the mountains. But I don't know how I could ever do that."

Bridget kissed him on the tip of his nose. "You don't have to know how, Snake Man, you just have to know it is possible and that you want it. I'm beginning to want some supper."

"Lucky for you, I just happen to know about a place on Walnut Street, a few blocks from here. They feature good Southern cuisine and they have white tablecloths."

"I do declare, sir, your preparedness is quite comforting to a lady amidst strange surroundings."

"Madam, you are not only under my guidance for the duration of this proper date, you are under my protection as well."

"Kind sir," Bridget said as she bowed deeply, "as long as I am under you,"—Bridget arched her back quickly but brought her head up slowly, saying, "I have the utmost confidence I shall be satisfied, granting history to be instructive in this matter of delicacies."

"Indeed, that would be the case, Madam, wrought equally well for me as for you. May I take your arm?"

Arm in arm, Cale and Bridget strode synchronously to the warm, fragrant dining room of a small restaurant that sheltered them from the rapidly chilling night air. "We are in the mountains after all," Bridget remarked as she unfolded a crisp white napkin in her lap, "and spring has barely begun. The plantation has yet to flower."

Cale chuckled. "But it will. Ever since I plowed and laid off rows, Mama Lucy has been raring to get seed in the ground. The Potlatch will be in full bloom soon."

Bridget and Cale dined on quail with Cumberland sauce, sweet potatoes, and collards. "I guess it's no secret that we're stuck on each other," Bridget said coyly as she studied the dessert menu.

"I believe the exact scuttlebutt I got from the Potlatch is that we are beginning to get heavy," Cale answered cautiously. Bridget's tone had been a baiting one that women use when they don't want to come straight at a subject.

Bridget clasped her hands together on the table. "Heavy is just what I don't want our relationship to become. Heavy in the sense of a burden, I mean. I know I have feelings for you and I know you have feelings for me. I absolutely know that you get me, and I'm beginning to think that I get you—as you unfold yourself to me."

Cale put his hands atop hers. "But?"

Bridget gently caressed Cale's palms. She felt the new calluses that had come up since he had started working the fields. Those firm lumps gave her confidence. Cale honestly turned himself to the task at hand. Bridget smiled.

As much as he could, Bridget believed Cale would trust her even when he could not understand her. "But if we begin to fall in love, Snake Man, I will have to go back to New Mexico for a while to unburden myself from a heaviness I knew there, a heaviness that was a burden. I don't mean an old boyfriend. I don't have any leftover relationships in Taos."

Bridget studied Cale's eyes. They were intent, confused, attending—but they were not clouded. "I hate the person I was there and how I left. My demon won a victory there, and if loving you becomes something I must do, then I will have to go back to Taos and expel my demon. I need to be the person I truly am, for at least one day, in that place that hurt me so bad and then I will walk away from it and never go back."

Cale's eyes filled with guarded resignation. Bridget knew he was searching for a way to prevail against her dragons. She knew he had the blood of a slayer. "I don't care for any dessert, Baby, but I'll have a bite of yours—especially if you get the pecan pie with vanilla ice cream."

They spoke of Bridget's work and Cale's suspension of design efforts for the writing desk. They left the restaurant and drove to the Orange Peel music club. The former skating rink was thronged by enthusiastic patrons who lined the stainless steel bar and jammed the enormous dance floor. Cale and Bridget threw the passion, uncertainty, and frenzy of their burgeoning romance into dance; when the band blasted out its final crazed set, Cale and Bridget carried on a gentle, rhythmic slow dance until the drums had been packed in their cases. Returning to the motel room, they showered quickly then made love with the contentment of a couple who had settled something between themselves.

After a hearty breakfast the next morning, they explored the shadowy, overstuffed compartments of a musty antique store. Emerging back into the crisp, sunny day, they fed the pigeons strutting around Pack Square then had lunch at a fantastic hotdog joint. Walking northward to examine that part of town, they came to a large furniture store with huge windows.

Cale lingered to inspect the graceful lines of the eighteenth and nineteenth century reproductions that faced the street. "You might as well go in, silly," Bridget insisted as she brushed past Cale and went into the store. Cale was scrutinizing the detail of a roll top desk when Bridget called to him from the back of the store.

"Jack's cousin that you met in Halcyon. Odell. What was his last name?"

"Connor," Cale replied absently, wishing he had brought a notebook with him.

"They've got his stuff back here, Baby. You're going to be blown away when you see it."

Cale sprinted to the rear of the store and beheld an exquisite solid cherry highboy chest. A placard atop the chest read, "Odell Connor. Handcrafted furniture. Halcyon."

"Holy shit!" Cale exclaimed. "Jack said he was a master cabinetmaker but I would never have expected something like this. This is just beautiful. It's beautiful."

"I've never seen any furniture this well designed and well made," Bridget declared as she ran her hand across the chest. "The lines are so sweeping and graceful and the finish is so clear, but deep and rich. As an artist, I'm astounded. This is art in anybody's book."

"The guy has this much talent and yet he wants to get out of the business," Cale said sadly.

"Why?" asked Bridget.

"We only talked a little bit about it. He said he is getting too old to do the physical part anymore. But he doesn't want to up and quit on customers he's had for so many years. He said the problem is that new designs have

176

stopped coming to him. He wants to turn his customers over to a younger guy," Cale explained.

"It's a shame he feels like he has to quit," Bridget opined.

"It's a shame that these beautiful images have stopped coming to Odell," Cale reasoned. "It must be like having your life stop before you are done with it."

CHAPTER 12--TAOS

The delicate sweet fragrance of honeysuckle drifted into his shop on a warm evening in early May as Cale was studying his sketches for a new writing desk. That lovely smell conjured happy memories of childhood springs on Matthew's farm when the whole Earth was coming forth with promise. Spellbound by reverie, Cale barely heard the screen door slam; he looked up to see Hank running down the back steps.

"Cale!" Hank shouted wildly. "It's your sister Julia on the phone! She's crying something awful, man!"

Cale dashed into the house and snatched up the receiver. "Julia! What is it?" he cried frantically.

Julia's baleful sobs halted for a moment as she gasped then cried in an agonized voice, "It's Grandma, Cale. She's had another stroke. Marsh found her in Bride's Woods. I think we're going to lose her. Come home, Cale! Come home!"

"I'm coming, Julia! I'm coming now!" Cale shouted feverishly. The receiver fell from his hand and crashed on the floor as Cale bolted to his truck. The first blinding wave of tears came as he swerved south onto highway 611 and sped towards Adluh. Cale frantically wiped the tears from his eyes with one hand as a deep sorrow welled again and again, and he desperately tried to steer the speeding truck with one hand.

As the racing truck flew over the worn pavement towards the hospital and Julia's mournful voice echoed in his mind, Cale was suddenly cleaved coldly from the familiar land he was barreling through, as if excised from all known experience and pasted as an observer on a picture

178

of a truck cab rushing through the countryside. The things outside of himself did not feel outside of himself because it was the inside of himself he could no longer sense. For miles he zoomed down the highway, like a robot encased in a missile, scanning the road, nothing more. His mind, blocked by a curtain of panic, raised in consciousness just above the edge of bare perception.

He saw the steering wheel. He saw the road. He saw the deer jump before him.

Cale watched as the nose of the truck swung violently behind the deer. He felt his body jostle, then bounce, and the smell of burnt rubber stung his nose as the truck left the highway. He felt his shoulder slam against the door, then saw green stalks of corn fall before him in wavy crashes. His body lunged forward and he felt the steering wheel slam into his chest and the knuckles of his left hand strike the dashboard and the cool rim of the metal wheel pressing the flesh under his chin as motion ceased.

Cale heard a distant chirping and he stared at the red and blue lights that glowed before him. The chirping rang beyond the glowing lights and it was not of him--as the lights were not of him--and the sound was lonely, was terrible. The glow began to fade and he feared that he was passing into the desperate, rhythmic, eternal chirping, away from all light. The cadence of the chirping shifted as the light slowly fell--wavered, warbled, wailed, spilled into voice, calling him back to a house. In words that sounded like red-blue light, that gathered before him in an eerie glow, he saw a face: Olivia.

Cale jerked himself upright. In the dimming headlights, he saw cornstalks all around him. He glanced quickly at the rear view mirror and saw behind him a swath of trampled plants leading back to the highway. Suddenly he remembered the deer before him and the desperate situation beyond him. He extinguished the headlights and jabbed at the ignition switch.

179

"Come on, crank!" he pleaded as the engine rolled slowly, fired weakly then sputtered and died. The pungent, sweet smell of gasoline drifted into the cab on the night air and Cale knew that the engine had flooded when he crashed into the field.

As he switched off the key to wait for the excess fuel to evaporate, Cale felt a cold wash of sorrow engulf him. He longed to be near his grandmother, to take her hand, to ease her pain, to plead with her to cling to life, to tell her how much he loved her. Tears would not come to him now as he imagined Olivia on her deathbed at the hospital, losing her grip on her precious strand of being as he sat in the darkness in a strange field of early corn.

The moon suddenly rose, golden yellow and full, above the tree line and its rare yellow light spilled into the cornfield and flooded the cab of the truck. The loveliness of the opalescent illumination ennobled the young corn stalks and drenched the forest edge, urgently golden now. Wrought by this grand luminescence, Cale beheld land and sky and himself as one beauty: sublime in this moment, he saw the weft of leaf and root, earth and water, air and stone, ice and fire, love and honor, truth unyielding, heart and mind satisfied.

The golden light of moonrise silvered, then paled, and the forest edge and the corn stalks returned to the dusky night. Suddenly, Cale shuddered violently. Fear shot through him like exploding ice. For an instant, the last of the silvery moonlight hung on the young cornstalks as it had on the leaves and fronds in the jungle the night he had found them.

Sleeping without a guard, they did not hear him approach. Silvery faces of innocence, they were not much more than boys. They should have been home with their mothers. Their mothers would have bound their bare, bruised feet and stitched their ragged clothes. Their mothers would have shown them kindness and mercy.

180

Silver on silver, the moonlight had glinted off his knife as he had silently cut their throats.

"No! No! No!" Cale shouted to the innocent cornfield. "Please no," he sobbed, gasping wildly as the faces of the doomed youths flew at him from memory. "I had to!" he shrieked, forcing open the door and climbing out of the cab. He stumbled into the growing corn. "I was a soldier," he moaned as he crawled along the ground. "People die in war!" he screamed, writhing in the dirt. "People die in war!"

Cale raised up and, illuminated by the truck headlights, he saw the Earth covered with the skeletons of murdered corn. Bending over in agony, he pounded the soil with clenched fists. A deep burning sorrow welled up inside him, rippled through his abdomen, and erupted in his throat as he looked up at the faded moon and howled, "I could not save them!"

Confession stilled him. Cale cried softly now and rocked himself back and forth. His dark memories withdrew and he gradually grew quiet. He saw the dimmed light from his truck. He wiped his eyes, stood up and got in the cab.

Cale turned the key and the engine caught, spit, then idled smoothly. He backed the truck onto the highway, turned it towards the hospital and raced away from the damaged cornfield. The diminished moon hung above the checkerboard of lights in the windows of the small hospital as Cale swung into a parking place and hurried for the lobby door.

His mother gasped as Cale came into the quiet room where troubled family members gathered to receive or to convey fateful news about their loved ones. Ruth's eyes, tired and red from weeping, widened in alarm at his presence. His father's eyes, heavy with sadness, narrowed slightly in concern. Marsh's kind, sorrowful eyes told Cale he was too late.

"Cale! Your face is bleeding!" Ruth cried as she ran towards him.

Cale bayed her with his hand. "A deer ran me off the road, Momma, I'm fine."

Cale looked at Marsh.

"She's gone," Marsh said softly. "Julia won't leave her just yet."

Choked with sadness, Cale's voice faltered as he asked, "When?"

"Half hour ago," Marsh said gently as he took Cale by the shoulder. "But she didn't know anything, Cale. By the time I found her in Bride's Woods, she was already past knowing anything. The doctor said it was a massive stroke and at eighty-seven, she didn't have the strength to hold on." Marsh gripped Cale's shoulder firmly. "She had a good, long life."

Cale nodded and then smiled at his anxious mother. Ruth flew at Cale, hugged him tightly, then took a tissue from her purse and wiped the blood from his cheek.

Cale looked at his father. "I'm sorry, Pop," he said tenderly.

Sam briefly embraced Cale. "I'm going to miss Momma," he said sadly.

They stood silently for a moment before Cale said, "I had best see about Julia."

Cale heard Julia's gentle sobs before he opened the door. Julia raised her head slowly as Cale approached the bed where Olivia lay. Julia held her grandmother's arm and was softly stroking her grandmother's hair.

"I don't know if she heard me at the end," Julia said sorrowfully, "but I hope she did. I hope she heard me tell her how happy I was whenever she held Skye. And how grateful I was for all the love and understanding she had given me. I hope she heard me say how much I adored Grandpa and how sorry I was that he had been taken from her in that flood."

182

Cale touched his sister's face. "She knew, Julia, Grandma knew," he said reassuringly.

Cale looked upon his dead grandmother. Stilled by death, her face revealed much more of her Indian heritage than he had ever seen. Uncontested by happy, bright eyes, her brow seemed broader; draped flatly, with no mirth or scorn or joy or surprise to rumple them, her cheeks seemed higher and more sharply defined; unmoved and unanimated, her chin seemed wider and harsher somehow.

"And it should be this way," Cale thought, "this is only her body. Everything that she ever was is gone into memory now." That realization urged Cale to leave the body of his beloved grandmother because he suddenly knew that as long as he could see her body, could look upon the semblance of Olivia, the sense of Olivia would not come to him.

He leaned over the bed and gently kissed Olivia's forehead. "Goodbye, Grandma," he whispered.

He took Julia by the hand; seeing the intense purpose in her brother's eyes, she allowed him to lead her away from Olivia and down to the lobby where, along with their parents, they sat and waited for Marsh to make the necessary arrangements.

Ruth and Julia sat together quietly in the lobby; Cale and his father stood awkwardly looking out the windows to the forlorn parking lot until Marsh came and nodded grimly, indicating that the family had no further business at the hospital.

Julia climbed into the passenger's seat of Cale's truck and took his hand gently as Cale reached to crank the engine.

"Grandma had one clear moment after she got here, Cale," Julia said seriously, "and she whispered something to me."

Cale paused.

"She said 'Tell Cale not to look down'," Julia announced solemnly. "That's all she said."

"What does that mean?" asked Cale.

"I don't know," Julia admitted, "I never got a chance to ask her. She was only conscious for that one moment. That's all she said. And she said it clearly, and I know that's what she said. And it sounded like she didn't have more to say, like she was finished."

"Have you ever heard her say anything like that before?" asked Cale.

"No," Julia replied, "and it might not mean anything, Cale. She could speak clearly in that moment but that doesn't mean that her mind was clear."

"Don't look down from what, or at what?" Cale questioned as he cranked the truck.

"I don't know, Cale," Julia said earnestly, "but it must have been very important to her. It was the only clear moment she had. She must have been struggling to get to the point where she could speak those last words."

"Did you tell Marsh?" asked Cale.

"Yes," Julia responded, "but those words don't mean anything to him either."

As other family members and friends paid their respects to Sam and Ruth at the farm, Cale wondered uneasily about his grandmother's final message. For the next two nights, when only the immediate family remained in the farmhouse and stumbled over the awkwardness of death in disjointed conversations that recalled trivial memories in nervous words spoken more loudly than needed in an instinctive urge to dampen the shrill silence of Olivia's absence, Cale pondered his grandmother's mysterious advice.

As the eldest of the grandchildren, Marsh had the duty to dig the grave on Toenail Hill beside the granite headstone marking Matthew's remains. Three days after Olivia's body had been laid out, Marsh enlisted Cale;

within half a day, the ground was ready to receive the old woman who had loved it so deeply.

The following morning at ten o'clock, Sam led a small group of family and friends up the path to the top of Toenail Hill. As the plain pine coffin was lowered into the grave, each of her two sons spoke briefly in honor of Olivia, kissed Matthew's gravestone, then stood stoically watching as the remaining members of the processional tossed flowers onto the casket at the bottom of the pit. When the last bloom had descended, Sam soberly led the procession down the hill to the farmhouse.

Marsh and Cale tossed the thin poor soil into the grave then solemnly placed a wreath of roses atop the fresh mound of earth. Cale looked out over the land below. Instead of orderly fields, he saw the chaos of construction strewn atop fresh red clay. Rough roadways haphazardly cut across the land and here and there were new foundations and partially framed structures.

"There's no need to look at it. The farmhouse and the barns are all that's left, and with Grandma gone now, those will come down soon," Marsh advised his brother.

"I know but I'm not really looking at that. I'm thinking about what Grandma told Julia at the end."

"Don't look down?"

"Yes." Cale lit two cigarettes and handed one to Marsh. "What does that mean? Why was it important for her to tell me that?"

"I don't know Cale. Maybe she meant not to think less of Pop and Uncle Buck for bulldozing the farm to build Glory Bend," Marsh suggested.

"Maybe. But she could have said that," Cale replied.

"Does it matter if you know what she meant?"

"Yes. When she told me about her will, she told me that the farm would not be my home. That I only wanted it because my life had been so happy when I was at the farm

185

with her and Grandpa. I think she might have been trying to tell me where to look for a new home, but I don't know."

"Me either. But wherever it is, selling Swede's Pasture will give you the money to go there. Just let me know. I can get a buyer for it any time. We better get back to the house and do the family thing."

***

When Cale returned to the Potlatch, Boss met him on the front porch of the Kremlin. "Bridget's gone," Boss said solemnly as he pulled an envelope from his back pocket. "She split for Taos and she wanted me to give you this. Sorry, man."

Cale walked down to Spirit Lake, sat on a grassy bank and read the letter.

"Cale,

"Please don't be angry with me. I have not abandoned you. I care deeply about you. I told you I would have to return to New Mexico to face my demons. When you said we were starting to get heavy, I knew the time had come for me to work out my issues. Getting heavy is just a new way to say falling in love. I can feel that you are beginning to find a love for me in your troubled heart. I want to be able to fall in love with you. But first, I must settle my fear of abandonment. Please know this truth: I have not abandoned you.

Please keep me in your heart, Baby.

Bridget."

Cale was stunned. He felt numb and bruised. He had lost his grandmother and now Bridget had gone to New Mexico.

"Dear John?" he heard a soft feminine voice ask.

Cale glanced up and saw Mama Lucy with a look of nervous kindness on her face. He knew Boss had told her about the letter and she wanted to help.

186

"Not yet. Bridget went to New Mexico to work on some issues. She says she cares for me and has not abandoned me," Cale sadly explained.

Mama Lucy sat beside Cale. "Does she tell you the truth?"

"Yes," Cale admitted, "even if I don't want to hear it."

"Then I would believe her," Mama Lucy counseled. "If she had left you, if that were the truth, then she would have told you."

"I guess," Cale said grudgingly.

Mama Lucy's eyes brightened. "And she would not have asked Boss to save her room and her studio."

***

The second week in May, amid fanfare that included bright banners stretched across Station Avenue, colorful balloons attached to telephone poles, and gaudy mimes distributing fliers, the Colorado Café opened its doors beneath brilliant blue skies. The stream of students and professors that had flowed directly into the coffee shop all morning, now rippled before the lemon yellow awnings of the Colorado Café, swirled beneath the multi-colored wooden pony that hung above the gallery windows and spun into a lazy eddy of leisurely consideration. From this whirlpool of peering and gawking, some of the strollers were expelled across the street to the coffee shop and others were pulled through the door of the strange new emporium.

A few hours earlier, Hank had been the first official customer of the café. He had eaten breakfast at the table closest to the door into the gallery. The genteel class had not been astir at seven in the morning, so Hank's only company had been eager residents of the Potlatch who packed the café to get a free meal. Hank carefully observed the females among them then wandered into the gallery and sat behind the counter, hopeful that the day would bring him some cash and a new feminine acquaintance.

187

Slowly, the commune dwellers had given way to paying customers who occupied the purple chairs and placed their Turkish coffee, goat cheese omelets, whole-grain muffins and carob brownies on the yellow tables. The new patrons, cropped and coiffed students and curious, bespectacled professors, ate slowly as they gazed at the profusion of potted plants, macramé wall hangings, posters of bizarre fantasy, and smoldering incense vials while listening to wavering, dissonant strains of eastern music.

Around ten in the morning, Jack and Cale ambled down Rancileer Street towards Station Avenue. "Thar she blows!" Jack exclaimed as the café came into view and he saw people milling around the door and gazing into the gallery windows. "I do believe Hank will have lots of customers today."

"Good morning," Dargan called to them as the two roommates entered the café. "Breakfast for you dudes is on the house. Hank already had his before he opened the gallery. What'll you have?"

"Got any regular coffee?" Jack asked brusquely as he disdainfully read the menu from the chalkboard behind Dargan.

"I'm afraid not. We are a New Age establishment. We've only got Turkish coffee," Dargan replied.

"Tea?" Jack countered.

"Herbal," Dargan responded with a slight grin.

Jack grimaced. "I'll have an omelet and some orange juice," he said with a frown.

"I'll take coffee," Cale said. "How's business?"

Dargan shook his head and frowned. "We're getting more critiques than cash, but we're getting noticed."

"Any interest in the gallery?" Jack inquired officiously.

"Some," Dargan said as he turned towards the grill to prepare an omelet.

The roommates settled at a table which gave them a view into the gallery as well as the activity on Station Avenue. Jack scrutinized the approaching customers for any trace of interest in the gallery. Cale surveyed the interior rooms of the restaurant and appraised the work he had done.

Jack hurriedly ate breakfast then wandered into the gallery to help Hank with the customers he eagerly anticipated. Hank chatted with a man about a large piece of pottery the Gypsies had recently added to the Painted Pony's high-margin merchandise. Jack ignored the students who were idly milling about and marveling at the symbolism of the madly painted gallery floor; he gently assailed the one prospect who might have some cash.

"Cale!" Jack beckoned from the gallery as he smiled awkwardly at a young woman who was examining a nightstand. The buxom woman with short brown hair looked over her glasses, smiled warmly and eyed Cale with great interest.

"How much is this?" the young woman asked as Cale approached.

"Hi," Cale said. "The price should be on the back unless the tag fell off."

"The tag said twenty five," the young woman explained, "but Jack said that since I'm buying a photograph, there might be a discount on the nightstand."

Cale stared at Jack, who winced and turned slightly away. "Oh yes, there is a discount," Cale replied, "but we apply the discount over the total purchase. If you buy them both, we can take ten percent off the total price."

Jack grunted and took a few steps backward.

"That'll be great," the young woman said with a warm smile. "I'll take them both. How should I make out the check?"

189

"Just make it out to the Painted Pony," Cale answered, "and give Jack your address and the time when we can deliver it."

With a coquettish smile the young woman said, "My address is on the check. I live alone in an apartment and any time this evening after six is ok. I'll be home." Her warm fingers slid gently along his hand as she gave Cale the check, "I'm anxious to get it," she added in a husky whisper.

"Hot damn!" Jack roared as the young woman went out into the street and looked back at them with a suggestive turn of her hip. "We made a good sale, and she looks anxious for company."

"I didn't sell anything," Hank grumbled.

"Then make the delivery," Jack snarled. "She looks like more your type anyway."

Hank bristled. "And what type is that?" he demanded.

Jack appreciated the challenge from his normally timid roommate. He smiled and pulled on the ends of his moustache.

"The bored sensitive type," Jack conjectured, "who suddenly has a yen for a sonnet in her britches."

"Speaking of what women need in their britches," Cale said with a smirk, "Sharon at the diner--she did tell me her name when I went back--says you're overdue for a visit, Jack."

"Well, I just might head out there this evening," Jack said musingly. "That'll keep me occupied. Hank will be going after Miss Sonnet Britches. What are you going to do for sport tonight, Cale?"

"I've got a girl, remember, and she has given me plenty of sport. I'll be working in the shop" Cale said. He grinned at Hank. "Good luck with Miss Sonnet Britches. I think she's looking forward to a big delivery. Jack doesn't need any luck. Sharon's britches may be itching more strongly for internal rhyme than sonnets, but I'm sure Jack'll be happy to give her a scratch."

"By jing, I'll give her a rub!" Jack cried as Cale waved farewell to Dargan and went out onto Station Avenue.

***

Bridget waited for the last of the tourists to leave the Taos pueblo then she quietly entered the shop of a friend, a Tiwa artist whose family had lived at the pueblo for a thousand years.

"Hello, Richard," Bridget said softly.

The artist looked up from the receipts he was sorting at a cash register. He smiled warmly when he saw her. "Hello, Rabbit. It was a good day today. I sold many masks. This guy from North Carolina wants me to make a mask of Crazy Horse. He said Crazy Horse sent him a sign in the sky and the sign was confirmed by an Oglala medicine woman. He knew there are no pictures of Crazy Horse. He wants me to make him a spirit mask of Crazy Horse. That will be a challenge. I have to capture the spirit of Crazy Horse. How are you, Rabbit, you want some tea?"

Bridget nodded and Richard turned to a hot plate at the back of the room. "I'm good, Richard. Good but I need to get to a better place."

"Don't we all? You know there's nothing left of the commune, right?"

Bridget stared at the floor. "I know," she said softly. "That is all in the past."

Richard place two cups on the counter. "All?" His eyes penetrated her. He had known Bridget better than any of them. He had wanted her more than any of them. But she was outside the tribe. She was not Tiwa. It was forbidden to have her. He could only befriend her and mourn her. And he had done both, woefully.

"All," Bridget confirmed.

191

Richard poured the tea for them. "And yet here you stand, in a dusty old pueblo full of crickets and ghosts of the past."

Bridget sipped the fragrant beverage. "I want to make a mask."

Richard added sugar to his cup. "There are books."

"Is there nothing more to know than what is in books?" asked Bridget.

Richard stirred his tea pensively. "Depends. Are you trying to capture something or let something go?"

Bridget looked out at the sun sinking in the red sky. "Let something go," she answered softly.

Richard stared at her. She was more beautiful than ever. "How long have you known that he cannot help you let it go?"

Bridget spun and confronted him. "You have scary powers of observation."

Richard smiled sadly and shook his head. "No, Rabbit. I am just a man who has been in love so I know what it looks like. This man you think of has real power. He is not like the one at the commune. He has moved you all the way back to New Mexico."

Bridget dropped her head and gazed at the earthen floor. "I know," she muttered.

Richard looked upon her as her eyes were downcast. She could not have been his in the old days just as she could not be his now. If he told her what she needed to know, he would never see her again. Either way, he could not have her. Ever. Helping her now would be the only way he could make love to her and his heart had ached to make love to her so many times before.

He let her see his raw desire for a brief moment then turned away. He closed his eyes and imagined touching and kissing and licking her naked body. He pictured her writhing in expansion and wriggling to enfold him in her electric wave of liquid release.

192

"Listen to me, Rabbit," Richard began in a slow, measured, tender voice. "There are three kinds of masks. The life mask is how a person appears when he has life. A death mask is how a person appears when his life is gone. A spirit mask is how a person appears when his medicine spirit possesses him."

Richard turned and touched Bridget's shoulder gently. "You must make your spirit mask when the spirit you fear is upon you. You can dry it in my kiln. When it is done, take it to a spot in the desert that you love. Smash it to pieces and you will release the spirit that haunts you. Then you will stop running forever. Then, Rabbit, you can go back to him."

CHAPTER 13--HAND APPARENT

In late June, the day before the summer solstice, Cale drove out to the Potlatch to examine the corn fields. Mama Lucy limped out to greet him.

"Your corn is looking good," Cale told her, gesturing towards the healthy green plants. "Not only will the Potlatch folk eat well, but fresh corn will be in high demand in the food co-op. Assuming Boss solved the irrigation problem?"

Mama Lucy nodded. "He has. If you need him, he's in the Shuttlepot talking to Jugs about more shelving for Xanadu."

"Got a second, Boss?" Cale asked when he arrived at the camp of the yellow yurts.

"Sure," Boss replied as he stepped aside to chat with Cale.

"I need a few days off, man. I want to go trout fishing in the mountains and try to stop thinking about Bridget for a while."

"Sure," Boss agreed. "Take whatever time you need, man. We don't have any major projects now. Besides, you got the monkey off my back when you planted the field crops for Mama Lucy. Where are you going to fish?"

"Jack told me about a great place for wild trout in the Halcyon Valley of the Blue Mountains."

"Don't catch 'em all," Boss quipped.

"I'll be lucky to be able to concentrate on fishing at all," Cale responded with a frown.

Boss put his hands on Cale's shoulders and looked directly into his friend's sad eyes. "Bridget is a decent woman. Don't give up on her."

Early the next morning, Cale struck out for the mountains on a highway that followed the Glory River northward. Beyond Saluda, the land began to rise and the current in the river grew more turbulent as it coursed more steeply. Cale thought about Bridget as he watched the grey clouds growing heavy in the western sky. He gripped the steering wheel tightly as he remembered something Bridget had said about Noordwjik.

"'Some people only live when the wind fills their sails, and other folks only drift in leeward waters. And you don't know if the drifters have no sail or if they just can't find the wind. You can't see if you helped any of the drifters because, when you have found your wind, you must turn into it and sail. Those without sail don't know what wind is, but the hopeful sailors will see your tack and know there is a gale in this life.'"

As he passed through Jack's hometown of Halcyon, a break in the clouds of the dark sky ahead gave Cale his first glimpse of the cascading summits of the front range of the Blue Mountains. Rain suddenly enveloped him as he raced headlong into the towering peaks. Cale became apprehensive as the narrow road became twisted and its sharp turns, shallowly gouged from precipitous slopes, took him beneath the gloomy canopy of leaden clouds.

Cale had never ventured into the upcountry, and as his truck lurched around ever sharper bends, he longed for the calm surety of the broad-shouldered, gently rolling highways of the Red Bank country. Suddenly, torrential rain slashed at the windshield, falling in great sheets driven by howling winds that hammered the truck. Blinded by the dashing rain, slipping now ever slightly in the sharp crooks of the road, Cale felt the grisly edge of peril bite into his gut. Still he knew, in the midst of this ferocious mountain tempest, up was the only way he could go on that road so thinly wrought along its gnarled course that it would not permit re-direction.

As the truck crested the eastern Continental Divide, the storm dissipated into a brief, sputtering squall. The rain ceased, the clouds broke, and the sun streamed down upon the glistening Blue Mountains. Loosened from the grip of the steep climb up the mountain and the violence of the storm that had been trapped in the piedmont by the abrupt lift of the land, Cale's truck flew into the brilliantly clear air of a magnificent highland valley.

The sight of the long valley, flowing into the waves of stunning blue peaks surrounding it, amazed Cale. As he gawked at the imposing splendor of the Halcyon Valley, he pulled his foot from the accelerator, shifted into neutral and let his truck glide into that wondrous beauty. As his truck coasted to a stop, Cale steered it onto the shoulder of the road. When it came to rest, Cale shifted into gear, shut off the engine and stepped out into this wild new land. The air was crisp and laden with the smell of grass. In the faint breeze, he heard the gentle rustle of water.

Cale hiked across a narrow meadow to reach the banks of the Glory River, where, astonished, he stopped and gazed at the tumbling current of limpid water. The river he had known and loved since he was a boy, because it had been dark and unknowable, was, in this mountain valley, filled with clear water. Revealed, it was more beautiful than anything he had ever seen and he felt as if his heart would spill into it and be swept away. Lured by this magnificence, Cale carefully climbed down to the river's edge.

The current was strewn with boulders and was broken by great rock ledges which had been sharply scalloped by the relentless flow. Deep runs appeared as rippling filaments of grayish-green which, in descent, melded into strands of dark gray. He breathed deeply and the chilled vapor rising from the water smelled of mineral and moss, of secret origins and paths yet to travel, of things known and discovery pending, of sheer being brimming with passion.

Suddenly, a flash of silver in the current broke his studied fascination. Instinctively, his eyes fell to the hunt and a moment later he saw another silvery flash, trailing a pinkish-purple iridescent streamer. Peering into the water, he saw trout swimming and a crayfish scuttle beneath a rock.

Cale reached into the river, drank the sweet liquid, and stared into the water. The rocky riverbed glowed with streaks of yellow and white from the small round stones that lay mixed with glinting bits of mica and jagged grey slabs of broken shale. Sunlight shimmered on sparkling stones and illuminated the golden sands and silvered pebbles of the river bed with a rare dancing light. That precious glow reflected in Cale's eyes as he saw the heart of the river: sublime, mysterious, life-giving beauty in dispatch.

He could see the awesome beauty of the river, and he could feel the great power of his love for it. Inside, he was vibrantly alive. Cale splashed into the river and knelt. He kissed the crystal water again and again. "I could not save them," he whispered, "but I did not condemn them."

Cale rose slowly and walked out of the river. He returned to his truck and continued his journey until he came to the fork in the river Jack had mentioned. Following the left fork, he soon arrived at an old millstone that marked the head of a trail. He parked his truck on the shoulder, put on his fishing vest, grabbed his bamboo fly rod, and hiked the overgrown footpath.

The road disappeared quickly behind him as he entered a deep cove. At the towering hemlock Jack had described, Cale waded into the clear water and began to fish. His technique was too clumsy for fish who could see everything in the sparkling water, so he focused on improving his casting as he ranged farther into a deep cleft in the soaring peaks. Suddenly, a red trout raced past him and held in the current ahead, just where the river turned sharply to the right.

Cale approached the rare trout and made several casts. The fish ignored the brightly colored fly that fell into the current. On the fourth cast, the fish moved upstream sharply. Cale followed. The trout moved again and again and Cale kept pace, managing a cast or two before the fish swam forward. Then Cale noticed that the river was no longer before him.

He had entered a thick, dark forest and faced a large plunge pool into which the river fell in two separate streams over the face of a towering granite wall. The trout lay at the tail of the pool where the water flowed out. Cale's first cast spooked the fish, and it swam to the far side of the pool where the waterfall created a thunderous current. Cale studied the swirling current and the large rock where he knew the fish was seeking prey, confused or injured by the by the furious whirlpool beneath the falling water.

Suddenly, Cale felt an eerie presence. The hair on the back of his neck stood up; he drew his knife and studied the terrain. Raucous jays, crows, and squirrels fell silent. The wind stilled. Not a creature moved. Cale could no longer hear the thundering crash of the two waterfalls and the waters of the pool ceased their turbulence and lay as flat as glass.

The crisp, chilled landscape of the steep mountainside contracted, and the smoky depths of the forest loomed menacingly intimate. As it had in the jungle, time and being froze in his blood, and terror raged in his mind as he waited for the coming to appear. Then he saw the eyes. The eyes saw him. He braced. A strange man-like creature slowly emerged from the gap between the double waterfalls and stood in the misty pool.

Cale beheld the noble face of a man and the serious countenance it bore, enveloped by streaming gray hair and a long gray beard, was knowing and tranquil. A great deerskin robe with sleeves of holly draped the tall figure. Two shining antlers towered magnificently above the creature's head. The figure did not move, but he regarded Cale affectionately, as if he welcomed Cale to some appointed moment in his domain.

Cale watched the regal being with awe, for the creature seemed to possess the power of the mountains. Cale stared at the figure's glistening eyes and in them he saw the precious light he had discovered in the river. Cale sheathed his knife and gazed at the majestic creature. The creature extended his arms toward Cale and Cale saw that his upturned hands were made of beautifully sculpted and polished wood. The marvelous being crossed his arms above his head, touched his massive antlers, and melted away into the two waterfalls.

A hidden covey of quail flushed and filled the forest with a furious roar as they fled. A startled whitetail deer broke from cover and bounded downstream behind Cale. Disturbed crows cawed and squirrels barked nervously from their perches. The wind freshened and the red trout disappeared.

Cale wiped his eyes then stared at the incredible twin waterfalls. Two clear seams of shimmering smooth water, separated by a couple of yards, swept over the sheer face of the rock, mingled with currents of air in descent, and crashed into the pool below. Then Cale realized that what he was seeing now—just as with the mysterious creature moments before—was not water, but pure imagination flowing over the edge of consciousness into the pool of creation.

When the picture flashed in his mind, his hands shook so badly Cale could barely retrieve the small notebook and pen from his vest to make the sketch. When the lines went down on the paper, he knew he had captured it, he knew it would be beautiful and he was filled with such joy that he screamed with delight as he splashed out of the cove and hurried down the trail to his truck.

***

Jack and Hank were not at home when Cale returned to Grace House. He was disappointed that he could not share his exciting news, but Cale was more eager to work than to talk. He threw his gear in a corner, grabbed his drawing materials and settled at the kitchen table to render a formal design for the writing desk he had conceived in the mountains. Glancing at the hasty sketch he had made while standing in the stream, Cale easily recalled the vivid image of the desk he had imagined while trying to understand the apparition that had emerged at the waterfalls.

He drew a small cabinet whose sloped front door opened and rested flat on a cylindrical joint to become a stable writing surface. Inside the cabinet, he fixed a panel that housed three small drawers and enclosed three slots on a raised shelf. Atop the cabinet, a small delicate railing ran along the back and the two sides but stopped midway in the front and curved inward and downward like the spout of a pitcher.

Veneer techniques were crucial to the cascading image the desk must project. Beneath the gap in the railing, Cale drew a book-matched, tight grained pattern in the middle of the sloped front door to represent the turbulent center of the waterfall. On each side of the central current, he inked slip-matched sections of a more open grain that suggested a calmer flow. The sides of the desk were depicted with random-matched panels of varying grain and color that resembled the rocky cliff over which the water tumbled.

Next he drew the narrow frame that formed the base of the cabinet and the tall thin legs, tapering slightly inward, on which the frame rested. The face of each leg was incised with tiny vertical gashes and an occasional horizontal slash. Beneath the legs, Cale drew the sheen of the polished wood floor on which the desk stood.

When the carefully detailed drawing was complete, Cale lit a cigarette and walked out to his shop. "I did it!" he remarked triumphantly. "Jack won't turn this baby down. But I'll never be able to build it here. I'll have to find someone with a real shop who will let me use it to build my desk." After he ground out the cigarette on the floor of the garage, Cale returned to the kitchen.

Crossing the threshold, he closed his eyes and slowly felt his way to the table. He touched the drawing pad to be certain he was standing directly in front of the desk design. Cale wanted, when he did look at it, to see, captured in wood, a ribbon of water spilling over the edge of a rocky cliff and plunging into a sparkling pool. Cale opened his eyes and on the paper saw this: the sheen of the polished cabinet top spilled through the lipped railing and fell down the sloped front door, twisting in the light grain of the veneer, and plummeted past the cracked markings on the tapered legs to crash on the shiny floor below.

Cale was ecstatic and ached to share his excitement, but his roommates would not return home until after they had eaten supper in the cafeteria. Bubbling with excitement, he went to his room to get a pack of cigarettes before treating himself at the 611 diner. Atop his dresser, he found a letter from Bridget. Cale ripped open the envelope and read the words slowly.

"Dear Cale,

"I hope you are well. I am pleased with the work I am doing. An artist friend of mine at the Taos pueblo has been encouraging me to look at the story in faces, and that made me wonder what the story was in my own face. I've been working on self-portraits, but I don't like any of them yet.

"I hope you are finally doing work that you like. Recently, I had an experience like your rainbow stallion

201

dream. New Mexico is famous for visions, and I had one while I was looking at the mountains. Suddenly, I saw a huge hand floating in the sky. It looked like it was made of burnished copper. A single hand, just hanging in the air, then quickly it was gone.

"When I know my own story and can deal with it, I will be ready to come back to the Potlatch. I think of you often and I really care for you.

"Please try to understand,

"Bridget."

Cale tossed the letter aside and gazed at the painting of the scrimshander. Bridget was right. He wanted to capture some of the beauty of the world with his hands. Olivia was right also. He had to find the things he loved before he could make a home. He had always known that he loved the river and he loved farming. Now he knew he loved the creation of beautiful furniture. And he knew one more thing: he loved Bridget. His insides were on fire.

Cale went out for supper. He thought about Bridget and rejoiced that he had her affection at all--but his heart ached to have her near. The joy of his celebratory meal was punctured by memories of the woman in New Mexico who beckoned to him painfully with her absence. When he returned to Grace House, Jack and Hank were sitting in the parlor.

"Well, mate," Jack began merrily, "tell us the tale of your adventures in my neck of the woods."

Cale smiled broadly. "I caught a really big one. I'll show you," Cale replied as he hurried to his room. Jack looked puzzled when Cale came back with a drawing pad. Standing before Jack, Cale flipped back the cover and revealed his design for a new writing desk.

Jack leapt to his feet. "By thunder, that's a fine piece of work!" he exclaimed. "It's beautiful, Cale. This is art."

Looking over Jack's shoulder, Hank added, "Cale, this is the real deal. Have you been holding out on us?"

"No. It just came to me and I can't wait to get started! But I can't make it here. I need a real shop to do this kind of work," Cale exclaimed excitedly.

"This is a far cry from what you have been doing. What the hell happened to you up the mountain?" Jack insisted.

"Do tell," Hank added eagerly.

"Best I know is," Cale began happily, "I came unstuck. First, I was in the most beautiful place I have ever seen--thanks to Jack. The river up there is absolutely clear. You can see what a river actually is.

"Anyway, I was chasing a red trout. I had never actually seen one before. I followed it upstream into this hidden cove. It led me to this incredible double waterfall."

"That's Mirror Falls," Jack interjected, "the Glory River is on one side and the Yellow River is a few feet away. The bottom of those falls is where they join."

"Now, I had not been smoking anything," Cale continued, "but I saw a strange creature emerge from those waterfalls."

Jack regarded Cale intently. "What kind of creature?" he asked cautiously.

Cale was surprised by the question. "It looked like a tall man with long gray hair and a beard. It was wearing a deerskin coat with sleeves made from holly--but it had two huge antlers coming out of the top of its head."

Jack looked stunned. "Go on."

"When the creature came out from between the two waterfalls," Cale continued, "everything got quiet. The critters quit stirring and there was not a sound. I couldn't even hear the waterfall crashing into the pool. And that rippling pool suddenly lay down flat like glass. The creature showed me his hands and they were made of some beautifully carved wood. Then he crossed his hands above his head and disappeared into those waterfalls.

"That's when I saw it. Gawking at the two waterfalls, I had this idea of imagination spilling over the edge of consciousness. Bam! A picture of the writing desk popped into my head. I have no idea how it happened."

Pensively, Jack stroked his moustache. He regarded Cale with studied earnestness. "I do," he said with conviction.

CHAPTER 14--ODELL

As the summer deepened in July, the Potlatch was in full flower. The Physic garden burgeoned with ripening red tomatoes, lustrous purple eggplant, lemon yellow crookneck squash, deep green cucumbers and swollen chocolate bell peppers; fragrant herbs grew on delicate stalks, spread broad leaves and sprouted feathery wisps; bounteous florid blossoms filled the garden border and perfumed the air along with sweet wafts of honeysuckle and the crisp, clean smell of magnolia petals. In the fields, the corn plants stood tall, the cabbages flared broad, crisp green leaves around bulbous heads, the foliage of the beans and potatoes was bushy and dark green, and the watermelon and cantaloupe vines had set tiny lime-colored melons.

On the northern edge of the farm, myriad bright green little orbs hung on the trees in the apple orchard. The white frames of the beehives hosted thousands of frantic bees whose golden produce had been recently uncapped to fill the glistening jars of oozing honeycombs that enticed a growing clientele to purchase more foodstuffs from the Co-Op in the Red Barn.

Fallow fields were thick with tall sedges, tasseling grasses and brightly colored wildflowers. The blackberry hedgerows separating the pastures where small herds of cows, sheep and goats grazed were laden with dark clumps of fat fruit. The springs that fed Spirit Lake, cleared of weeds and stones by Boss and Dakota, bubbled vigorously--irrepressible, clear and sweet.

Cale inquired of the few people he knew in Saluda about the use of a woodshop to build his new writing desk but no one was able to help him. He took his new desk design to the Potlatch.

"Damn!" cried Jugs, "it's no wonder you and Bridget got together. You are an artist too. It's beautiful, Cale. Have you started building it yet?"

"No, man, I need to find a real shop," Cale replied. "My crummy shop in the garage is ok for making the stuff for the Painted Pony. To make this desk, I need access to a real woodshop. I was hoping you boys might know someone around here who would let me use their shop. I can pay."

"I don't know anybody," Jugs confessed. "We've got plenty of shop space here at the Potlatch, but it's just empty space. We don't have the other stuff you need."

"I don't know anyone either," said Dakota.

"Sorry, man," Boss answered.

That evening, as Cale entered his shop to work on a nightstand for the gallery, he glimpsed a patch of white in his nail apron and he knew that the crisply folded sheaf had come from Claire. He opened the clean linen paper and read the words that had been carefully written in the center of the sheet.

"Sometimes you can teach an old bitch new tricks. Available for lessons Friday night 8pm."

As he turned to flip the note onto his workbench, Cale glimpsed a tuft of purple fabric in his nail apron. Claire had also left him another pair of her panties. He removed the crumpled lingerie and held the crotch to his nose. He inhaled the musky scent of Claire's womanliness and remembered how she had been when he had gone to her.

But Claire was not Bridget. Both women urgently compelled him as a man but only Bridget drew his heart to her. He would visit Claire but he would deny himself consoling pleasure with her. He knew that not having sex with Claire would be more difficult in the moment than in the imagination but he believed that Bridget had not forsaken him. He would not abandon her.

Cale chuckled. Claire would be angry when he refused her but she knew many men in town and she might be willing to help him find a shop. He reasoned that if Claire was willing to fuck him she should be willing to help him with something truly important.

Claire was much less sympathetic than Cale had anticipated. Her eyes hardened and her face flushed with vengefulness when Cale declared his devotion to Bridget. Her vanity was not bruised: Claire knew she was gorgeous, intelligent and interesting. Cale's simple act of fealty jabbed sharply at Claire's secret pain: she lived without honor and would die in that condition. The fury of her revulsion, though aimed at herself, was focused squarely at Cale.

"Let your little girlfriend find you a suitable shop," Claire decreed icily as she showed him the door.

Early the next morning, Cale bought a lock and a hasp; before going to work, he secured the garage. Claire would not help him find an adequate workplace to build the new writing desk and his own shop, as poor as it was, might need protection for a while.

***

The dog days of August brought sweltering heat to Saluda, yet the roommates still took their morning coffee at the turquoise dinette table in the sunny kitchen of Grace House. "Did you hear about that big hurricane coming up from the Caribbean?" Hank asked while Jack fiddled with the window trying to devise a way to force a breeze to enter the room.

"No. What about it?" Cale replied.

"The forecasters say it may come our way," Hank replied, "and it's a really big one that they say will get even bigger."

"Do tell," Jack said as he abandoned his project.

"Could it really hit us?" Cale inquired with concern.

"I've heard that conditions are favorable for it to come ashore and make a beeline for the piedmont."

"Damn," Cale remarked sharply.

"What's the matter?" Jack demanded irritably, "you don't live at the coast."

"No, but I hope that hurricane doesn't go near Adluh. The development my daddy is building on my grandpa's farm will raise the price of the land my grandma left me. I can sell that land one day and buy my own place, if that hurricane doesn't wreck Glory Bend," Cale explained.

"You still want to be a farmer?" Jack asked pointedly.

"I'd like to have a small place where I could farm a little and have a shop where I could make furniture. But it's got to be on the river. After seeing the Halcyon Valley, I think living there would be my first choice--if I ever have a choice."

"Hum," Jack muttered. "I may have an idee on the matter, mate, but I'll have to ask you a serious question and I need a true answer, on your honor," Jack said gravely.

"What question?" Cale demanded.

"Did that new design for the writing desk come from your heart like you said, or did you copy it from one of the books I gave you?" Jack asked sternly. He glanced at Cale's fierce eyes and added, "Ain't no shame in copying till you get the hang of things."

Cale approached Jack and looked him straight in the eye. "When I saw the desk in my mind, standing in that stream after I had just seen the creature, my whole body shook! I had created something beautiful in my head and I knew I had to build it. When I imagined myself actually making it, I felt pure joy. Now that I have drawn it, I will build it. Out of my head, with my hands."

Jack appraised the look on Cale's face then turned to Hank. "Longfellow, can you take care of the gallery by yourself this weekend?"

Hank nodded confidently. "No problem." Now that he was dating Miss Sonnet Britches and she was attending summer school at the college, Hank had no desire to leave Saluda.

"Ol' Jack's a'scheming," Cale declared with a crooked smile.

Jack grunted. "You remember that talk you had with Cousin Odell about his shop?" Jack bluntly inquired.

Cale only nodded. He intended to draw Jack out into the open now.

Jack's eyes assumed a delicate look as he considered his gambit. "There ain't nothing Cousin Odell don't know about making fine furniture by hand."

Cale finished his coffee then slowly lit a cigarette. "Granted," he said as he blew a strand of blue smoke into the brilliant sunshine.

Jack poured another cup of coffee for Hank and himself. "Working side by side with Cousin Odell could shave years off a journeyman's learning time."

Cale fiddled with his lighter. "Affirmative," he said.

Jack was irritated that Cale would not give him an indirect approach to the subject. He tugged on his moustache. "Cousin Odell lives in paradise and paradise lives in him."

Cale leaned out the back door and thumped his ashes. He chuckled because now he was intrigued. Jack had pulled it off. Cale returned to his seat and gazed directly at Jack. "Say sooth," he demanded.

Jack put his elbows on the table. "The way to Cousin Odell's house is nothing but a goat trail for the last five miles. He doesn't have a phone, a mailbox or electricity--doesn't want them neither. Plows with mules,

209

keeps his milk and butter in a springhouse, and can see the Milky Way in his backyard every night.

"Since you met him at Aunt Rose's, I've written Cousin Odell. If you was to ask him, he would let you build the new writing desk in his shop. He could probably rustle up a few orders for that desk from his customers. If you was to ask him, that is."

"And this weekend is as good a time as any," Cale concluded.

"Granted and affirmative," Jack said. "Are you up for it?"

Cale nodded. He flicked open his lighter, lit it, and placed it in the center of the table. "What man could deny paradise?"

"Good. You know where Aunt Rose's house is. Mosey on up on Friday, as soon as you knock off. I'll drive us to Cousin Odell's in the Bismarck on Saturday."

***

Friday afternoon, while Dakota and Boss were busy at the Potlatch, Cale was working alone in one of the houses in College Hill that Dargan had purchased. While replacing the wainscoting in the dining room he heard a key in the lock. He tightened his grip on his hammer as he turned to see who had opened the door. A beautiful young woman came through the door clutching a large pizza box and a carton of beer.

"Hi, Cale," she said dreamily. "I'm Meredith. I'm Dargan's chick."

Cale was stunned by the young woman's beauty. Her face had shimmering blue eyes, long strands of silky blonde hair, smooth creamy skin, slender cheeks, and a delicate mouth easing into a soft chin that gave her a look of exquisite loveliness. In the instant that she regarded him intently, Cale saw that Meredith had both expected to allure him and had also confirmed her affect by the look in his eyes.

210

"Thank you," he said awkwardly, "but you didn't have to."

Meredith smiled seductively. "Dargan told me you were trying to finish this job today because you were taking a few days off. I thought if I brought you a bite to eat, you wouldn't have to go out for lunch. Dargan would have done it himself, but he's gone fishing at the coast. He said the approaching hurricane will make the fishing great but the sunbathing lousy. That was his lame excuse for leaving me all by my lonesome self--even though he knows how I get when I'm without him."

Meredith drew close to Cale and handed him the pizza and beer. Then she stood before Cale in a diaphanous white sundress. As she brushed her hair back with both hands, her large breasts pushed against the cloth and appeared fleshy against the thin fabric and her brown nipples were distinct. The light behind her shown through the frock and clearly revealed her shapely legs; the florescent flood from the work light in front of her defined a tuft of hair at her crotch. She caressed her hair slowly, allowing Cale a long, uninterrupted gaze at her voluptuous body. Her nipples hardened as she watched him look at her.

"Besides, I wanted to meet you," Meredith said firmly.

Cale glanced up into her eyes without apology and saw that she was presenting herself to him, then he resumed his deliberate examination her body. She and Claire were in the same league.

"That pizza won't be hot for long," Meredith said softly. "You should eat it now, while it's warm and gooey."

Cale looked away from her. "There's no place to sit," he explained.

Meredith gently touched his elbow. "I can sit on the floor," she said.

Cale nodded, sat on the lustrous bare wood and put the pizza and beer in front of him. Meredith stood across from him, her back against a wall, and slowly sank into a squat. Her dress rose as she settled; when her buttocks rested on her heels, the hem was above her knees and her naked crotch was exposed to Cale's view. A long moment later, she sat cross-legged and tucked her dress around her folded legs. She took a slice of pizza from the box and a bottle of beer from the carton. Cale did likewise.

Meredith licked the slice of pizza and pushed the melted cheese into a mound at the tip. Then she held the slice tilted above her chin until the soft white blob slid off the sauce, hung by its extruding tail, then plopped into her open mouth, draping its creamy streamers across her full red lips.

"Umm," she murmured then hungrily curled her mouth around the tip of her beer bottle, sucked softly and slowly swallowed.

"So what do you think of the Potlatch?" Meredith asked when she had eased the bottle from her mouth.

Cale glanced at her still erect nipples. "It's a little different than I am used to."

Meredith tilted her head back against the wall. "It's a really far out place," she said with a sigh. "So peaceful and so beautiful outside," she continued, "a home for people who are peaceful and beautiful on the inside. Can you dig that?"

"I don't know," Cale said with a hint of reproach. This woman was younger than Claire, but she walked the same path. Meredith was accustomed to being indulged by men. She dropped her head and stared at Cale with narrowed eyes.

"Don't know or don't want to know?" she inquired accusingly.

"Don't need to know. I'm just doing a little carpentry," Cale retorted sharply.

"Carpenters build things, man." Meredith took another beer, opened it and stared at the brown glass bottle.

"We live inside our own bottles, you know. We each build our own bottle of reality and we float in it for the rest of our lives."

Meredith could see that she had aroused Cale. He couldn't or wouldn't take his eyes off her tits. She was pleased. He was good looking. Dargan had gone to the beach without her. Meredith raised her bottle of beer and continued her rap.

"If we build a dark one like this, then we can't see the other bottles, or the great sea all the bottles are floating in or the creatures inside the other bottles. Don't you ever think about the kind of bottle you are building for yourself?

"Or will you just keep the bottle that your parents put your mind into? Don't you want to make it for yourself so that it will be big enough and clear enough to hold what you want to know, what you want to do, what you want to experience and explore? So that it will have enough holes in it that your heart and mind can pick from the garden of life enough of the fruits of passion that your bottle will float in the memory of others when your spirit has been emptied by death?"

Cale regarded Meredith's bulging nipples and sly eyes. "Do you have some warm, gooey passion I could put my bottle into?" he asked frankly.

Meredith's eyes glistened and she slowly moistened her pursed lips with her fleshy pink tongue. "Right here and now--on the floor?"

"That's reality, isn't it?" Cale insisted.

Meredith brushed her nipples lightly with her fingertips. "Yes," she said longingly, "that's my reality."

"What dark bottle will you put Dargan in while I'm putting my bottle into you?" Cale demanded angrily.

"Hey, man, you're really bumming me out," Meredith protested.

Cale stood and dismissed her with a sharp wave of his hand. "You're leaving. I've got work to do--so this place will be beautiful on the inside."

Meredith staggered out of the house and a few hours later, Cale finished the work, climbed into his truck and headed for the mountains. He came to Halcyon, crossed over the crystal Glory River, and turned onto a narrow road that ran across the shoulder of a large mountain. He soon arrived at a large white house that sat on a knoll above a broad field of Christmas trees at the foot of the mountain. As Cale pulled up behind the Bismarck, Jack burst through the back door and ran out to greet him.

"Welcome back to the mountain!" Jack called warmly. "Come on in, Aunt Rose has hot coffee and warm cobbler."

Cale followed Jack through the door, which opened into a small dining room whose outside walls were lined with numerous windows that captured the panoramic view of the mountains. A short, stout woman with tousled gray hair, wearing large glasses, a simple frock, and an apron stood in the kitchen that adjoined the small dining room.

"Good to see you, Cale. Thanks again for fixing my old tractor," Rose chirped happily.

"You're welcome," Cale said.

Rose indicated that he should be seated at the table. "I've got some hot coffee, with cream still warm from the cow that gave it, and some blackberry cobbler. The berries are huge this year. You must be hungry after that long drive from Saluda."

Cale and Jack settled at the oblong oak table. Rose served them, then settled herself facing them. "Have you ever been deep in these mountains before?" she asked. When her guest shook his head, Rose continued, "Well, you're gonna see the best part of them tomorrow. Jack tells me he's taking you to visit Cousin Odell. I 'spect you've not

214

seen anything like that before," Rose advised as she chuckled heartily and cut the golden-crusted cobbler.

***

"Odell lives right far back in the mountains," Jack announced the next morning as he and Cale finished their breakfast at Rose's table.

"Odell knows you're coming," Rose noted as the young men climbed into Jack's car. "I wrote him to expect visitors." Rose handed Jack a small box filled with glass jars. "Jack, you mind that you give my best to Acrilee. And these squash pickles. Odell always did love my squash pickles."

Cale and Jack headed north out of Halcyon and traveled the narrow, winding gravel back roads that led them across the Yellow River and into the highest and most remote region of the Blue Mountains. They passed no farms in the densely timbered mountains and saw but few isolated cabins.

Just after noon, they turned into a rocky lane that soon became a mere trail that took them into a deep fold in the mountains and ended in a small meadow where a rude cabin faced a small shop and a modest barn.

An old man with long gray hair and a long gray beard emerged from the barn and waved a greeting.

"How you faring, Cousin Odell?" asked Jack as he approached the old man.

"Fair to middlin', Jack, fair to middlin'. How's Rose gittin' on?"

"Same as always, Cousin Odell. She keeps me fattened up with her vittles. If I didn't have business to tend to every once in a while, I'd get too big to get out the door."

Odell laughed softly. "My old woman keeps a good kitchen too. That's why I have to work in the shop."

"Cousin Odell, you remember my roommate Cale," Jack began, "he fixed Aunt Rose's tractor."

215

Odell removed his tattered felt hat. "Good to see you again, Cale. Come on in the house. The old woman's just putting dinner on the table."

When they went inside, Odell introduced the visitors to his wife, Acrilee. The elderly woman stood nearly six inches taller than her husband and her long white hair reached to the top of the apron she wore around her waist. She beckoned them to a small table in the kitchen, then turned to her husband.

"Put your teeth in, Odell, we've got company," Acrilee insisted.

When Odell returned to the table, Acrilee served them country ham, butterbeans, boiled cabbage, escalloped potatoes, and yellow corn bread.

"If you'd like some sweet milk, Odell can get some from the springhouse. It'll be cold and it ain't no trouble," Acrilee offered.

When no one asked for milk, Jack began to explain to Acrilee the reason for their visit. "Cale here makes furniture with hand tools, too, and he is mighty interested in seeing how it is done in the old way."

Odell smiled. "Well, everything we do around here is done in the old way. We live and farm in the old way and I make things in my shop the old way. Don't have to, of course, they got electricity and cars in these mountains--I just never wanted any part of it. I got candles and lanterns and mules and a wagon. And I reckon I got peace of mind."

"Yes, old man, you're quite comfortable, I reckon," Acrilee said curtly.

"You complaining after all these years, woman?" Odell demanded quickly.

"Not so as you'd know it, old man. I figure I'm comfortable too. I've seen that electric life and I don't cotton to it. It feels cold to me. It seems to me it ain't about loving things as much as it is about having things that don't need you to put any heart into them. I believe they call it

216

convenience. I call it cold-hearted and I don't see no contentment in it.

"We got creature comforts here but we got heart comforts too--the quiet beauty of the land, the pleasure of working with a good team of mules, the satisfaction of knowing when the day's work is done so you can delight in your rest. I got no complaints."

"Jack told me you cut your own timber," Cale said to Odell.

"I got oak and fir and walnut and some maple. I cut what I need," Odell replied, "and then I cure it out for a couple of years."

"You might as well show 'im the shop, Odell. They didn't come all this way to listen to me jabber," declared Acrilee as her guests were finishing their noon meal.

Acrilee remained in the kitchen as Cale and Jack went out to the shop with Odell. Cale marveled at the interior of the wooden building. On the far wall hung planes, gouges, chisels, saws, and a variety of small templates. A long workbench ran along the front wall beneath a row of windows. Cale stared at a strange contraption in one corner of the room.

"That's my treadle lathe," Odell explained as he placed his foot on a metal rocker at the base of the device. "I got the treadle from an old sewing machine. This hickory sapling is screwed to this post. It's just bent over right smart and hooked to this leather strap. You just put a piece of wood through a loop in the strap. Pushing down on the treadle while the hickory is pulling up makes the hickory give and that spins the flywheel at the back of the treadle and that spins the wood caught in the strap. With that wood spinning, you just shape it like you want, same as you would on an electric lathe."

"That's incredible," Cale remarked as he studied the lathe.

"No flat land toys and trinkets, but just look at this fine furniture, made with hand tools, in the old way," Jack exclaimed proudly.

Along the back wall of the shop, Cale saw a drop leaf dining table made of cherry, a triangular corner table made of oak, a sideboard made of yellow pine with designs of inlaid maple, and a magnificent double chest of drawers made of walnut.

Cale hurried to the back of the shop to examine the stately walnut cabinet. The piece stood about seven feet high and was faced with book-matched burled walnut veneer. The top chest featured chamfered pilasters at the corners and the pediment consisted of carved molding, a filigreed fretwork that rose in two symmetrical crests terminated with carved rosettes and a carved oval finial. Cale was astounded by the beauty of the cabinet.

"You made this, here," Cale stammered, "with hand tools from trees you cut in the mountains?"

Odell looked away shyly. "Yes, sir, I did that."

"It is absolutely beautiful," Cale said in amazement.

"I feel like it's some of my best work. I'd be glad to show you around the place, if you'd like," Odell offered.

Cale and Jack followed the old man out to the barn and Cale listened intently as Odell explained how he carefully dried and turned the lumber that was stored in long racks along the walls.

"My nephew cuts the logs into boards for me with that pit saw out back. I'm gittin' too old for that now. I do all the squaring and planing here in the barn before I take the lumber into the shop. That little fire pit yonder is where I heat the hide glue to do the joining. Another thing I do in the barn here is I make my own wood stains. And, of course," Odell added with a laugh, "I keep a few cows in the barn too, in the winter."

They walked out behind the barn and Odell pointed to a ridge. "I get walnut from a stand of black walnut trees in there. The pine, oak, and maple I get from just about anywhere."

"It's hard to believe it all happens here, on your place," Cale observed.

Odell tapped himself on the chest, above his heart. "The first part happens in here, when you get a craving to put some of the light inside you out in the world where it can shine on other folks."

Odell then rubbed his head. "The second part happens in here, when you can see something beautiful that you can make. The easy parts are drawing it out, getting the lumber, and joining everything. Somehow, it all flows together. It comes out of me, is made by my own hands, goes away when somebody buys a piece but it still stays with me, for having done it at all. Let's go in now and have some dessert. I'll get some cold milk on the way," Odell said with a smile.

Acrilee brought out a warm apple stack cake as they gathered at the table again. "Speaking of being fed," Jack said seriously, "I hear that Hand paid a visit to Rafe McNeil."

Odell tapped on the table with the handle of his fork. "Rafe has been ailing right smart since he got hurt putting up hay. He ain't been able to work and times were gittin' hard for him.

"Well, the other morning, his oldest boy found a deer hanging from a tree in the yard. It had been gutted and dressed out. And there were six ducks hanging on the back porch and they found a leather sack by the back door. When they opened that sack, they found a bunch of rocks and there were small emeralds and rubies sticking to some of those rocks.

"Rafe can sure use that meat and he can sell those gem stones and get a little cash. Nobody saw him, but it must have been Hand, sure as the world."

"I 'spect so," affirmed Acrilee, "ain't no one else gonna leave fresh game and rough gem stones to help a body."

"Who is Hand?" asked Cale.

"According to the experts in the flat land," Acrilee said quickly, "he ain't nobody and he couldn't be at all."

"Nobody knows how long Hand has been in these mountains," Odell explained, "but stories of his visits go back to the first settlers. He could have left things for the Indians before that, but nobody knows. Precious few people have ever seen him, but those who have all tell the same tale.

"He is a tall creature who looks like a man. He has long gray hair and a long gray beard. Like me, except that he has a lot more hair and it's a lot longer than mine. He looks exactly like a man, except that he has two large antlers growing out of his head and his hands are made of wood.

"He only visits good folk who are suffering from bad luck. He leaves them things that come from nature-- meat from deer and rabbits and ducks and geese, gem stones clinging to rocks, ginseng, wild grapes, trout."

"Some folks say he's some kind of missing link," counseled Acrilee, "because he's half way between the animals and mankind. Nobody's ever accused him of any meanness, so he must be a lot closer to the animals than he is to humans. A few unwed mothers have tried to blame Hand for getting them in a family way, but nobody pays that kind of talk any mind."

"Whenever folks have a powerful need, in a moment that can change their lives forever, Hand appears. It's just always been that way and I 'spect it always will," Odell surmised.

Cale's eyes widened in astonishment. He took a quick drink of milk and glanced at Jack.

Jack laughed a very satisfied laugh. "Tell them, Cale. Do tell."

Odell and Acrilee stared at their guest with expectant eyes. Jack only brought visitors who were interesting to him and Jack's unique outlook on things guaranteed that these infrequent gatherings were worthwhile.

Cale felt his face burning and knew his embarrassment was visible. "I saw him," he said hesitantly, "at Mirror Falls."

Odell sat up straight in his chair. Acrilee put her hands in her lap and her lips moved silently. Jack grinned from ear to ear.

"He emerged from the small space between the two falls," Cale began nervously. "Everything got quiet. I couldn't even hear the falls. The water lay down flat. He wore a coat of deerskin but the sleeves were made of holly. His antlers were huge and magnificent. Around his neck he wore a silver necklace. In his left hand, he carried a longbow. Both of his hands looked as if they had been carved from a beautiful wood. He seemed to be welcoming me. Then he crossed his hands above his head and vanished into the falls."

Odell's eyes flashed at Jack. "You been telling tales in the flatland?" Odell asked suspiciously.

"Not a peep, cousin, not a peep," Jack confessed.

Odell scratched his head. "If you don't mind me asking, did you have some great need at that time, Cale?"

"Yes, sir, I did. I had been trying to come up with a design for a fine piece of furniture, a writing desk. My first attempt, as Jack can tell you, was an awful mess."

"I don't mean to pry," Odell said delicately, "but did Hand leave you anything that helped you?"

Cale relaxed. He nodded and took another bite of cake. "Yes, sir, he did."

Odell was intrigued. He leaned on the table and gazed directly at Cale. "Never mind the sir, Odell and Acrilee is how we go. Would you be able to tell me what Hand left you?"

"It was incredible, Odell. After he disappeared, I stared at those falls. Then I saw it. It came to me all at once. I made a quick sketch standing there in the water. I rushed home and drew the design."

"The drawing is in the car, he could show it to you if you want to see it Cousin Odell!" Jack cried happily. "And there's a package from Aunt Rose."

Odell nodded and Cale excused himself and went out to the car.

Jack waited for Cale to reach the Bismarck. "Cousin Odell, the design that Hand helped Cale to see is crackerjack. And Cale's dying to build it. But he doesn't have a real shop where we live, just a jackleg workbench nailed to the side wall of our sorry garage. Hand ain't never visited none of our kin, Cousin Odell, but it could be Hand is trying to pay you a visit now."

Odell cocked his head. "How so?"

Jack stroked his moustaches. "Even though he showed himself to Cale, and not you, Cale said that Hand seemed to be welcoming him to the mountains. Cale had a powerful need for a beautiful design and Hand gave him that. You have a powerful need to turn your shop over to a younger man who will carry on the old way. Hand is calling a budding young cabinetmaker, who works in the old way, to these mountains just when you need to find such a feller. That can't be a coincidence."

Jack studied Odell's face. The old man was interested but not convinced. "Could be, Cousin Odell," Jack urgently continued, "that Hand had in mind helping Cale with his problem and helping you with yours at the same time. Folks always say you should make the most of Hand's gifts. He don't trifle with fools."

Acrilee nodded her assent. It had pained her that Odell had been struggling to find an honorable way to lay his tools aside. She knew that her husband's powerful spirit could not abandon the creation of beauty without seeing that passion arise in another. "You could let him build the first one here, old man. We got room."

Odell's eyes sank, as if he were looking upon his own death. Fear flickered in the depths of his gaze. Acrilee rose and stood behind her husband. She could see that he trembled. Acrilee bent forward and kissed Odell softly on the shoulder.

"You told me yourself that you admired his good sense in fixing that tractor," Acrilee began softly. "You could teach that boy a few things about sending beauty into wood. I'll swan if you don't love to show a body how things should be done! If it works out, and you like the boy, you could help him get settled in his own shop. Then your customers could turn to him and you could devote your every minute to getting in my way around here. Could be Hand is paying us a visit now by getting Jack to bring this boy to see you, old man. Study on that. Shush! Here he comes!"

When Cale returned, Acrilee was giving Jack a second helping of cake. "Would you care for some more?" she asked her guest.

"Thank you, Acrilee, I would. It's delicious," Cale said as he handed a small box to Jack.

Jack took the parcel from Cale and offered it to Acrilee. "Aunt Rose sent these squash pickles along for you. And she sends her best."

Acrilee chuckled. "Odell will be tickled with these. I can cook near everything we got in these mountains but I can't make a pickle worth spit. You thank Rose for me, honey."

"Yes, ma'am, I will," Jack said respectfully.

223

Cale handed the drawing to Odell. The master craftsman studied it carefully. He lifted his empty glass and Acrilee filled it with milk. "This is a fine piece of work, son. A fine piece."

"Thank you," Cale said awkwardly.

"I was wondering how many of that desk you were figuring on making," Odell began seriously, "because I believe some of the customers that have been with me a long time would want a piece like that."

"And I'll need a couple for the gallery," Jack added.

Cale was surprised and pleased with the interest in his work. "Once I make the measured drawings," he said shyly, "I could make as many as I need."

"Do you have the wood and the veneer and the stain and the finish—and the set up to apply them?" Odell asked.

"No, Odell, I don't. My shop is too rough for this piece," Cale confessed. "I don't have a place to build it yet."

Odell took Acrilee's hand. "Folks in these parts think highly of a visit by Hand. To us old timers, it means the man visited is a fine man who needs a little help changing his circumstance."

Cale nodded.

"You remember I told you I am now too old to saw my timber from logs?" asked Odell with a smile.

"Yes," Cale replied.

Odell chuckled. "Well, I'll soon be too old to do much in the shop at all. So my proposition is this. You can use my shop to make the first desk. I've got every kind of wood, glue, stain and finish you could need. I can show you some of the tricks I learned along the way. We've got an extra room so you can stay here, room and board for free. You already know how Acrilee can cook.

"The only thing I ask in return is that you make one desk for me. I'll use it as a sample to show some customers. If we get along and you have a strong mind to continue handcrafting furniture, I might be able to help you get a start. Ain't got no electricity. Just work, shelter, friendship, and peace of mind.

"Of course, now and again, Acrilee might ask you to fetch water from the well and milk and butter from the springhouse. I might need you to spell me hoeing the garden. And we might put in a little time fishing and hunting in these mountains.

"If things go to suit you and you decide you want to light in these mountains, I might be able to locate a small place and dicker my way to a good price for you.

"No need to decide anything now. I just wanted you to know my thinking on the matter. A friend of Jack's is always welcome here. You sleep on it a spell. Ain't got no phone, but you can write to me and tell what you think. We'd be proud to have you in these mountains. We already know Hand wants you to be here."

CHAPTER 15--HALCYON

As Cale and Jack drove back to Grace House they heard on the radio that the hurricane Cale was concerned about had weakened when it hit Redd Isle and had lost most of its punch crossing Cape Indigo. The dissolving storm had limped inland only as far as White Lake but the Red Bank country had been soaked by torrential rains for almost a week before the skies cleared. The Glory River was nearly at flood stage but was expected to crest before it came out of its banks.

"Well, mate," said Jack, "I guess your little nest egg in Adluh is safe now. So what do you think of Cousin Odell's proposition?"

"I think you're a damn scalawag, Jack!" Cale retorted sharply. He waited until Jack curled his lips in perplexity then added, "and I'm damn glad of it."

Jack's face eased into a smile and flowed into a grin. "Cousin Odell is a proud man. He knows he needs to let go of his business but he feels a duty to his customers. His kind of craftsmanship is fading. Nobody wants to work with hand tools anymore. The fact that he made you that offer means he wants to test your mettle, not your skills. He knows he can teach you a thing or two. But nobody can teach devotion.

"I know what he has in mind, 'cause maybe I put a little idea in his head. You use his shop, work as an apprentice, pick up some new skills while you work on your own new designs. If he likes your work and sees that you have a love for it, he could transfer his customers to you. Not only that, Cousin Odell is well known in the mountains and is a shrewd horse trader. He could help you find a little place on the river in the Halcyon Valley--and make sure you don't pay too much for it.

"I'd study on his proposition real hard if I was you. You could have the life of a real cabinetmaker--if that's the kind of life you want."

***

When he returned to work at the Potlatch, Cale requested a meeting with Boss, Dakota and Jugs. "Jugs can't leave his pots just now. What's up?" Boss asked.

"I'd just like to get your perspective on something I'm thinking about," explained Cale.

"Are you sure it's wise to deliberately ask us what we think?" Dakota teased.

"Yep," said Cale as he pulled a quarter from his pocket. "Heads, we meet in the Kremlin after supper, tails we meet in Paha Mata. If it rolls across the floor before falling flat, we meet in the Shuttlepot."

***

After enlarging the co-op space in the Red Barn to accommodate Boss's thriving barter enterprise, and enjoying a meal of pork stew and cornbread, the three young men went to the Blue Grass Lodge. When Jugs arrived, Cale declared, "I'm thinking about moving to the mountains."

Boss and Dakota looked at each other in surprise. Dakota replaced the joint he had taken out of his shirt pocket. "Why, man?" asked Boss sadly.

"I've got a chance to go for something I really want," answered Cale. "Jack took me up to the mountains to visit his cousin Odell. Odell is a master cabinetmaker. He makes everything by hand in his shop. He lives way back in the mountains. He doesn't have electricity because he doesn't want it.

"He's getting old and wants to pass his business on to somebody who will continue his traditional craftsmanship. He's offered to let me apprentice at his shop

227

and wants me to build several copies of my new desk. If everything works out, he could help me find a little place on the river in the Halcyon Valley. He might even help me get my own shop started by sending his customers to me."

Cale glanced at Dakota's medicine bow, hanging from a lodge pole. Dakota was devoted to a way of life that had not faded but had been crushed out of existence. "I've got a shot at getting my own place where I could do a little farming and do a lot of cabinetmaking. I think I've got to take it but I wondered what you boys thought."

Boss removed his Fedora and drummed it on his knee. "You know we'd hate to lose you, man."

"We'll still be friends. And I would always help out here if you got into a jam."

"I know, I know," protested Boss. "It's like you've got a chance to have your own Potlatch--a place where you live by doing the things you love."

"That's exactly what it is, man," agreed Dakota. "When I was fourteen, I had to go into a sweat lodge to seek my vision for the purpose of my life. The vision I asked for came."

Dakota removed the medicine bag he wore around his neck, carefully opened it, and took something into one hand. He raised that fist, kissed his palm, and closed his eyes. He continued in a slow, solemn voice.

"I was in this beautiful land of rich green hills, sparkling lakes and deep forests. On the top of the highest hill, a big fire was burning. But the flames were not like normal flames. Their light was clear and bright and it was colored like a crystal with the power of the sun caught inside of it.

"I walked up to the fire. It had no warmth. I touched it and my hand was not burned. When I looked up from the fire, I saw thousands of lodges on the hills. Most of the lodges were painted black, but some were painted red.

Dakota rose, eyes still closed, and stood facing north. "Then," he said brightly, "a wondrous song, a fantastically beautiful song, began to ring in the hills. Suddenly, the people came out of their lodges. They folded their lodges and dragged them up to the big fire.

"When they were all gathered by the fire, the people began sticking their hands into the fire. The black lodge people took charred wood from the fire and put it into their mouths.

"The red lodge people took flames from the fire and put them into their mouths. When the red lodge people were done, the big fire was not big any more, it was a regular fire."

Dakota faced eastward and spoke as if beseeching, "Then the people departed. The black lodge people went into the earth and disappeared. The red lodge people scattered through the hills.

"Now, when I looked out over the land, I saw, on every hilltop, a big fire and many red lodges. Then I saw nothing but the inside of the sweat lodge and my vision was gone."

"What did it mean?" Jugs asked earnestly.

Dakota returned the object in his hand to his medicine bag and hung it around his neck. He did not open his eyes. He pivoted until he came south. His voice was calm and soft now. "I saw the fire first, which means that the fire is the most important thing in the vision. The fire was not the fire that burns wood. It had no heat and did not burn my hand.

"At first, I thought the fire was life. But everyone is born with that. So, there couldn't be two kinds of people if the fire was life itself. Then, I understood that the fire stood for a society of fire, people who live with fire in their hearts.

"The beautiful song was the understanding each man gets that he must choose the way in which he will live

229

his life. The black lodge people chose to live their lives according to the shadows that they had already put over their own spirits. That is why they went into the earth. They were not willing to live with fire, so they could not live in the land of men."

Dakota pointed his shoulders to the west and finally opened his eyes. "The red lodge people had chosen to live according to the bright spirit within them. That is why, when they reached into the big fire, they took flame. The black lodge people only took charred wood. All the people had the big fire in common, but only the red lodge people shared the big fire with each other.

"The black lodge people went away but the red lodge people went to other places in the land. They established new camps around new council fires.

"My vision told me that the society of fire lives on as long as there are people willing to share the flame. And that the people who will not share it go away. That will happen here at the Potlatch. The ones who are not living with fire will go away."

"But Cale is thinking about leaving," Boss challenged.

"Yeah," Dakota answered somberly as he sat on the dirt floor of his lodge.

"The grass is always greener," taunted Jugs.

Cale noticed Dakota's happy eyes.

Dakota smiled. "But, my vision says our society of fire will go on."

"Our society of fire?" Cale questioned.

"Why did you want to speak with us?" Dakota asked pointedly.

"Because you would tell me if my thinking is screwed up," Cale replied frankly. "Boss would urge caution until a real plan emerged and Jugs would just say it is stupid--if it is."

"You came," Dakota said graciously, "to share your dream. That's the difference. A community is a group of people who have something in common. They don't actually have to do anything. People who live around a lake have the lake in common, even if they never fish in the lake or go in the water.

"But a society only happens when people choose to share something. In my dream, all of the people were a community who had fire. They had the fire in common. But only the red lodge people were a society who lived fire.

"The world calls the Potlatch a commune. The people who live here describe it as communal living. And they are right. We all have the Potlatch, the farm itself, in common.

"But a society of fire, man, that's something different. In living here as we have, the four of us, we are a society of fire. We live with passion, with purpose, and welcome that spirit in others. Wherever we go, I know each of us, man, will keep his council fire burning."

Jugs offered his hand to Cale. "I'll make sure of it, man. I'll make four firepots that will hold a fire even in the rain so we can take the council fire with us any time we need to. You've got to go for it, Cale."

Boss tipped his Fedora. "It is the ultimate plan."

Dakota gestured up towards the sky. "It is time," he said solemnly, "for the Snake Man to leave the nest."

***

Early in the morning of the following Saturday, Cale left Grace House headed for Adluh. As he approached the farm, he could see the roadways that wound through the gently rolling hills and the framed ribs of the houses that were rising along the freshly paved streets of Glory Bend. He turned into the gravel road that led to the empty farm house where his grandparents had lived, drove past it and stopped at the base of Toenail Hill.

He walked up the path, sat down between the graves of Matthew and Olivia and looked out over the land that his heart had called home from childhood until he had returned from the war. All of the magic he found in life he had learned here: the power of beauty to transfix and to expand the very dimension of reality; the force of truth to identify something certain and to reveal the moral depth of experience; the command of honor to know the truth in every act and to act in accordance with that knowledge; the majesty of love in coupling kindness and belonging, in uniting passion and pursuit, in satisfying the desires of the body and the restlessness of the mind, in billowing the sails of the living as they course through the wildest seas and inescapably tack to the end of days.

Cale recalled Olivia's deathbed message. Don't look down. He stared at the raging current of muddy water swelling the Glory River almost out of its banks. Such a torrent had pulled Matthew downstream, had violently taken him far below his home, down from the love of his wife, down from his sons, down from the farm, down from his sacred cornfields, down and drowned.

"That's what you meant!" Cale exclaimed as he touched Olivia's grave. "Don't look downstream! Don't point your heart to what is lost. Let your heart point you to what should be."

Cale looked at the farm that had been destroyed by the building of Glory Bend. Except for the house Matthew had built with his own hands, the only trace of the original farm was his own land, Swede's Pasture. He had come back to this place to let it go. He was not ashamed. He was not sorrowful. He was not angry. Cale was proud. He was going home.

Marsh arrived as Cale surveyed the burgeoning development.

"Saying a final goodbye?" Marsh asked gently.

"I think I figured it out," Cale replied, "what Grandma meant when she said don't look down. I think she meant don't look downstream because that's where she lost Matthew in the flood. She was telling me again not to follow Matthew. To make my own way to the life my heart truly wants to live."

"I think you're right," Marsh agreed.

Cale stared at his brother. "I'm going to write Odell and accept his offer to use his shop. I am going to ask him to help me find a small place on the river in the Halcyon Valley. So I am ready to sell Swede's Pasture. You said you could get me a buyer any time."

"I can and I will. But it's a big step. Are you sure you want to take it?" Marsh asked.

"Yep," Cale declared, "designing the new writing desk was a big step too, a breakthrough. And it was the most exciting thing I have ever done. Building it will give me the same satisfaction as farming—doing something I love. Seeing it will make me feel like I do when I look at the river or tall standing corn--admiring beauty. But designing it was a pleasure all its own: creation of beauty.

"I've got a chance to learn from a master, like I learned farming from Matthew. But Odell's kindness gives me something else: the chance to start walking my own path. I have to take it. I can't wait to take it."

Marsh hugged Cale. "You've come a long way since you got home from the war, little brother."

"I guess you're right," Cale responded. But my way will be easier now. It's leading me home."

"Then let's go to the grill and tell everybody the news. Pop can help us figure out how much your land should be worth. Then we have to sell it fast before another hurricane comes through here and makes us all dirt poor."

After telling his family the news, Cale returned to Grace House. Jack was sitting on the front porch fiddling with one of his cameras. Hank stood on the steps. He was wearing an ironed shirt and his hair was neatly combed.

"Hot date with Miss Sonnet Britches?" Cale inquired.

"It will get hot later," Hank said, "but we're going to the movies first. I know Jack's date will be hot right off the bat."

Jack chuckled. "It took quite a few visits but I finally talked that waitress filly at the 611 diner into going out with me."

"Where are you taking her, besides to bed?" asked Cale.

Jack searched his pockets for a pipe. "Turns out, she's an amateur astronomer. We're going to the planetarium."

"I'm going somewhere myself," Cale announced.

Jack set his camera aside. "Do tell."

"I'm about to write Odell and accept his offer. I just got back from Adluh. I asked my brother to get a buyer for my land. You boys will be losing a roommate."

Jack leapt to his feet crying, "By jing, you're setting the right course now, mate!"

"Congratulations!" exclaimed Hank.

"Just don't forget the Painted Pony once Cousin Odell makes you famous. I'm going to need your stuff so I can raise my prices," Jack admonished.

"I won't," Cale promised as he opened the front door. "One get some, two get some, Cale gets none," he said before going in the house.

Cale quickly wrote a letter to Odell thanking him for the opportunity to work with him. He also mentioned that he was selling his land in Adluh. His hands shook slightly as he sealed the envelope and put a stamp on the letter. Then he lit a cigarette, took a fresh sheet of paper, and wrote to Bridget.

"Dear Bridget,

"I am glad your work has a new dimension. I have had a vision also and a hand is involved. I think it is important that you saw only one hand. I believe that it was your own hand and that your vision means there is something you must give yourself that you cannot get from anyone else.

"My life has suddenly erupted in an exciting way. My insides are free from the cold. My creation problem has been solved. I am moving to the mountains, to a glorious place on the river. All of this came about in an incredible way, which I will tell you when I see you again.

"My grandmother was right. Once it thawed out, my heart did show me what my mind loves. I always knew I loved the river, farming, and working with wood. But there is one more thing I know I love. You. I love you, Bridget.

"I hope one day soon your heart will be open and free and you will count me as one of the things you know you love. If that day comes, we will find a way to put our homes in the same place.

"Cale."

***

The first week in September, Cale returned from work and found a letter on his bed. He eagerly snatched it up, hoping the small white packet was from Bridget. He had not heard from her in many weeks, and he regretted that he had no way to phone her. A post office box in Taos was his sole connection to Bridget and he ached to be touched by her, only if by script.

Bridget knew the number of the phone at Grace House, but she had not called him since she left the Potlatch. Some lonely days, the isolation from him that Bridget had deliberately imposed felt like a test but he did not believe it was. Bridget felt very far away because she was: across a great stretch of land and an even greater personal divide. She did not want the intimacy of voice to distort that breach. If she came back to him one day, it

235

would be because she had closed the gap. The waiting was hard but at least now his work gave him satisfaction.

When he glanced at the rough scrawl on the envelope, Cale knew it had not come from Bridget's hand. The message it contained was brief.

"Cale,

"Me and the old woman are proud that you will be visiting with us a spell. Your room is ready.

"Odell."

***

Jack was happy and concerned when he and Hank came into the parlor after having supper in the cafeteria and Cale told them about Odell's note.

"I'm pleased as punch," Jack declared loudly, "but the thing is, mate," he added softly, "school is back in session and I'm a mite low on your inventory. The Gypsies are giving me enough of their stuff but I would like to stock up on dorm furniture before you head to the hills."

Cale puffed up his chest and pulled on his thin moustache. "I've got a proposition on this matter, lubber."

Jack chuckled at Cale's imitation of him. "Do tell," Jack said quietly.

"I'll make up some stock before I ship out," Cale offered, "but the paint job will be yours. Deal?"

"Ahoy, captain," Hank called gleefully, "methinks you've run aground."

Jack considered alternate courses. There were none. He hated painting but Cale's items were big sellers. Cale would soon deliver his artistic work from Odell's shop and Jack would be able to raise the prices on everything.

"I always meant to take up art without a camera," Jack grumbled. "Voluntarily, that is. Deal."

***

In the middle of September, Cale packed his belongings and made the journey to Odell's farm. He was welcomed cheerfully and quickly settled into a small

236

bedroom in the cabin. After supper, he and Odell went out to the porch to smoke.

"I 'spect the quiet will rattle your nerves for a few days," Odell counseled. "And everything being strange will make you feel like a cat that just woke up in a world without mice and dogs."

"It will take some getting used to," Cale admitted. "Mostly, I just don't want to get in the way."

Odell tamped his pipe. "No need to fret about that. We are glad to have you here. Besides, we are set in our ways. We go to bed early but that don't make no never mind. You do as you please. The lamps burning in the cabin won't bother us. You've got your work to do.

"If you was to hear a bear rumbling around in the cabin when you're in your bed, it's just me and the old woman snoring. We do have bears in here--and panthers-- but they go after my livestock. Must be tastier than me and the old woman."

"You ever shot one?" Cale asked.

Odell stopped rocking. He dropped his head as he tried to recall a distant memory. "Years ago. A bear got into the barn and got one of my calves. The poor critter screamed, and I went to running with my rifle and lantern. I followed the drag marks as far as I could. When the bear got into heavy timber, I stopped and waited for the sun to come up. I followed the blood trail and bear sign until I found where he had covered up the carcass.

"I knew he would come back to finish the meal. He did and I finished him. We had a heavy mast crop that year. No need for that bear to kill my calf. Bear meat ain't my favorite but it's a mite sweeter with a side of justice."

"Do you still hunt?"

"I do when the smokehouse gets lean. You a fair shot?"

Cale thought about the critical shots he had made at great distances, through heavy cover and dark shadows. "I can get the job done."

Odell emptied his pipe. "I guess I'll turn in now before the old woman figures I've wandered off somewheres."

Cale sat on the porch as the darkness around him deepened. The moonless night slowly disclosed a vault of myriad stars twinkling more brilliantly than he had ever seen. Even on Toenail Hill, the cosmos had not presented its dazzling maw so intimately. His body felt ever earthbound, but his spirit flew up into the stream of crystal lights and marveled at the vastness of their infinity and the cold certainty of their eternity.

"Dying fire is the heart of the universe," he thought, "but living fire is the heart of man. If we fail to keep it burning, we will all go into the earth like the black lodge people. Council fires will turn to ashes and we will have no need of warriors."

Over a breakfast of country ham, grits, and eggs, Cale and Odell discussed the design for the cascade writing desk and selected the woods to be used for the frame, the case, and the cabinet. Odell agreed to show Cale how to plane and true the wood by hand. "I'll be telling you some stuff you already know but I can't separate it out, so you'll just have to skip over it in your head while I'm telling it. If you're going to work with hand tools," Odell insisted, "then I've got to show you how to draw a very sharp edge--and keep it while you're working. Later we'll get into working with veneers, putting on a stain, polishing and handling shellac. I 'spect you'll be wanting to try turning on my treadle lathe. I'll turn the pieces for the first desk and you can watch. Turning is the crown and glory of the whole thing."

Cale was an eager student and by the time the weather turned cold enough in October for more than a cooking fire in the hearth, he and Odell had finished the first desk. That night, as Odell and Acrilee slept, Cale sat before the flames and wrote to Bridget.

"Dear Bridget,

"I have moved in with Odell and Acrilee. The mountains are beautiful and their life is so simple that they seem to be a part of the hills.

"I am learning a lot very quickly. When the second desk is done, I will try to send you a picture of it. I hope your work is going well.

"Your silence frightens me. I worry that my confession of love has driven you farther away from me. The truth will either bring us together or keep us apart but it will not change.

"Cale."

Cale placed the letter in an envelope and addressed it with the post office box number Bridget had given him. He wanted desperately to be with her. But even if he drove to Taos, he would not be able to find her. Asking about a beautiful female artist in Taos would be like seeking an Irishman in Boston.

He stared into the hearth as if the dancing flames could explain why Bridget had not wanted him to be able to breach her exile. Cale believed she was a truthful woman and she said she cared for him. Why was her struggle taking so long? Had she returned to see an old boyfriend? How could she deal with her fear of abandonment only by going back to Taos?

Cale had no answers. He longed to have Bridget with him now, to see his work, to share his joy, to make a home in the Halcyon Valley. He decided to turn in. Tomorrow would be another day of learning. Each day Odell poured out knowledge of wood, grains, joints, shapes, stains, finishing, glue, and polishing. Cale could feel the urgency in the old man's voice, the desire to pass on his passion before he was felled by death.

As he reached to turn out the lamp, Cale saw it hovering in the hearth: a beautiful sideboard with arched doors and bright inlays suggesting fire. Cale got out of bed and quickly drew the hearth-styled piece. Trembling with excitement, he extinguished the lamp.

Cale sat in the darkness. He was away from Matthew's land. He was out of the Red Bank country. He had moved beyond the Potlatch and Grace House. He had left the jungle behind.

He had let go of those he had killed--all of them. His heart and mind were united, and he was pursuing a life devoted to the things he loved. His work was genuinely himself: he would not abandon it and it would not abandon him. But Bridget could leave him and he had no way to pursue her. Cale desperately wanted to hear from her, to have a sign of her heart.

At breakfast the next morning, Cale told Odell about his idea for a sideboard and showed him the sketch. "I'll do the design drawing tonight."

"You're on your way now, son. We'd better get to hunting up a place you can call your own," Odell said proudly.

The next morning, Cale and Odell began working on the second cascade desk. Starting just after supper and working until the moon had risen and set, Cale drew the design for the hearth-style sideboard. He was thrilled and fatigued and stumbled into bed. He dreamed of Bridget: in a distant valley, he saw her fighting some dark monster while his own feet were entangled in a slithering web of dead letters.

***

The desert was particularly cold as Bridget drove out of Taos toward Tres Orejas. The sun had been up for a while but had not yet cleared the mountains. The gravel road maintained by the county was uneven and washed out in many low spots but it led to a lonely rise that offered an unbroken view of the broad, scrubby desert basin. Unbroken was the attribute she needed this frosty morning.

Bridget stopped her van atop an isolated mound and looked out over the crumbled rocks, sand and sagebrush that stretched away from her to the ring of mountains that encompassed the high desert plain. This was the spot where she had read and re-read Cale's letter about the meaning of the hand she had seen in the sky at Ranchitos.

He had suggested the hand was her hand. Bridget had felt that Cale was right. The image in the sky did feel like it was a part of her. She had thought and thought about what seeing one of her hands in the sky could possibly tell her about her fears. Then, while sitting in the Adobe bar in Taos marveling at the cowboy from Wyoming who was doing his best to pick her up, whose overpowering lust was charming in its awkward sincerity, Bridget had finally understood the hand floating in the sky.

Watching the cowboy display his best seduction preamble, Bridget had felt like a spectator. As a spectator, she had suddenly realized that with one hand she could not applaud. In that one thought, the icon of pain that hung in the center of her heart was suddenly clear: in her whole life she had never been able to applaud herself.

On a tattered bar stool among startled strangers, Bridget had howled with the pain of that insight. She had never felt worthy of love. All the sounds of her childhood had been heralds of departure: packing to leave, making ready to move, securing the next career grade, shuttling to the next duty station, emptying out the current quarters, wiping away the history, forsaking the unworthy. Her growth marks had been left on a dozen different door jambs; her drawings had been taped to numerous refrigerators; her puppies, goldfish and marigolds had all been left behind.

As a child, her life had constantly been erased by her parents' restlessness. Nowhere she had ever been and nothing she had ever done had been celebrated. She had never been left behind but her life had always been.

Girl Bridget had learned that she could not applaud anything she did because everything she did would be left behind. Eventually she learned that she herself was not worthy of applause. Before she had breasts, Bridget had grimly concluded that she did not deserve love. So she had never loved herself--ever.

Her heart, as all human hearts, exists only for love, so it had never realized itself, had not been allowed to be, had not unfolded its yearnings in raiments of affection, had not reflected joy back into the darkest canyons of her being. Childhood for Bridget had been the cold, unending, unspeakable, unshakable, unknowable sorrow of a passionate heart that cannot dwell.

The cowboy had apologized profusely when she had burst into long, sorrowful wails but she had no way to explain that he had been faultless. Moaning, blinded by tears, she had stumbled out into the street and made her way to the plaza and held onto a tree.

Weeping inconsolably, Bridget had lost her grip on the tree and crumbled to the ground, desperately sobbing without making a sound. She did not fear abandonment. She was terrified of being forever unlovable. Her trembling body had parted the tide of happy tourists that swirled around her and the cowboy had found her.

Terrifying loneliness, dimensioned in her mind as if it had existed for eons, erupted from Bridget's throat as the frightened cowboy had knelt beside her, gently grasping her violently quaking shoulders. Forlorn memories had freshly ripped her spirit from her body and Bridget's long screams had been anguished and grave. The cowboy had helped her stand and had tenderly led her to a coffee shop.

He had listened to her for hours, aching to figure out how to fix what he had not broken, desperately trying to halt her tears. When she had finally breached the fathomless sorrow of years of painful insignificance, the cowboy had accepted her smile. He had insisted on following her back to her apartment and had bid her farewell with a reluctant wave. That lusty, decent cowboy would never know what he had done for her.

Following the revelation in the plaza, Bridget had worked on her spirit mask for most of three days, resting only in brief naps. Richard had approved of the mask but would not listen to the story of its creation.

Now she had come to this spot to do what must be done. Bridget took the mask, carefully stepped out of the van and walked out into the desert until she came to a large boulder. She had timed her trip well. The sun was about to rise above the mountains.

Bridget stared at the ugly, misshapen countenance of the mask. The forsaken eyes and the drooping mouth that could not say the word for cherishing made her shiver. This monstrous creature had been her soul but it had not been of her devising. The sun crested the mountains and streams of golden light struck Bridget's eyes.

"I am Bridget Chattan!" she shrieked. "I matter and I always have!" Bridget hurled the mask against the massive boulder and the sculpture shattered, its shards falling among the rocks and pebbles of the ancient desert floor. Her ardent conviction freed her in that instant and she stood in the wild land as a fully human woman. She looked upon the mosaic of her despair and saw, not bits of freshly fired pottery, but a faint imprint of Cale. A powerful wave of love swept into her heart and Bridget's knees buckled.

Bridget steadied herself against the boulder. The pure, true, golden light of the desert filled her heart and her mind. Bridget was herself, resplendent in spirit, brimming with love. And she had two duties.

She would take care of one of them now. Bridget hurried back to her van. She had promised to buy breakfast for a certain cowboy. Speeding back to town, Bridget yelled thanks as she passed the brightening ancient pueblo; the man inside, who still searched the shadows of his heart for his own peace, did not hear her words of tribute.

***

The second cascade desk was finished in the middle of October and Cale loaded it onto his truck and drove to Saluda. "Seems like I ain't seen you in a coon's age," Jack declared when Cale walked in the Painted Pony just before closing time. "How you getting along with Cousin Odell?"

"Great. He is teaching me stuff as fast as I can put it into my head. And living way back in the mountains is fabulous--except for the outhouse part," Cale replied.

When they brought the desk into the gallery, Jack positioned it so that pedestrians could see it clearly. "It's a lovely piece, mate, a lovely piece," Jack mused. "Got anything new?"

"Why Jack," teased Cale, "I thought you'd never ask." Cale spread the design for the hearth-style sideboard across the desk. "Top drawer!" Jack thundered. Suddenly, he slapped his knee and bent forward in hearty laughter. "I was just remembering that pitiful first writer's desk you brought to me."

"A lot has changed since then," Cale said thoughtfully. "Where's Hank?"

Jack checked his watch. "By now, he's probably lifting his girlfriend's skirt. Speaking of which, are you getting any mud for your turtle?"

Cale shook his head. "Bridget is still in Taos. I haven't even heard from her in a long time."

"Do tell," Jack said sadly.

"I say to myself that she hasn't left me. She wouldn't do that without at least saying it was over. I say it, but that's not how it feels," Cale confessed. "When I sit in Odell's shop at night, worn out from a day of learning and accomplishment, and I'm aching to tell her about it, to share my exhilaration with her, to--she feels gone then, long gone."

"There's something you should study on," Jack said sympathetically. "Bridget is a powerful female. Physically, she is fetching. Artistically, she is amazing. Intellectually, she has vision.

"Emotionally, she is wounded. She keeps you at bay because she needs to see things clearly--with her heart. Keeping you close would roil up her insides so much she wouldn't have a chance to see the thing that's plaguing her. When she spots what is, she will whip it. She's got grit. That girl's got grit aplenty. You study on that."

***

When the chilly winds of late October began to blow, foundations had been set on dozens of footings at Glory Bend and routes the streets would take had been deeply cut into the red clay. As his men prepared to lay solid beds inside the gouged tracks of the roadways that had obliterated old cornfields, Marsh felt a sad relief that Cale was not a witness to the final disappearance of Matthew's farm.

***

In early November, Cale began work on the sideboard. Odell watched carefully as Cale planed and trued the wood and laid out the joints he would fashion. "I heard about a piece of land we ought to take a look at," the old man said as he suggested a slight revision to the frame corner joints.

They stopped by the post office on the way to inspect the property. Cale received a letter from Marsh indicating he had found a buyer for Swede's Pasture. Cale was elated by Marsh's news but the farm he and Odell examined was not what he was seeking. The land and the buildings had been badly neglected and the property was too close to a main road. Still, Cale was happy the search for his own farm had begun.

A few days before Thanksgiving, Cale went to Adluh and negotiated the final terms of selling his land. He arranged the closing two days after the holiday. When the transaction had been completed, Cale and Marsh walked to the top of Toenail Hill.

"We'll start selling in the spring," Marsh said as they looked out over the development. The marina, boathouse, restaurant, club house and most of the homes were finished. As he looked upon it, Cale did not want to remember what this land had been but remembrance came.

An empty foundation stood on the ground where Matthew had built his farmhouse. Into that sturdy home, meant to last for many generations, Matthew had brought his bride, Olivia, to join him in a life of purpose he had first glimpsed in southern France. From bare red clay, Matthew had built the rich dark soil in which his beloved corn could grow tall and bountiful.

Glory Bend allowed no connection to the earth, the river, the sky. The people who inhabited the modern lodges his father had built would walk above the ground on concrete and asphalt, would ride above the water in boats, and gaze beneath the sky as the glow of their electric lights illuminated the shiny objects from which they wove their lives--never knowing that they had obliterated the heavens.

"I don't see momma's dream house," Cale said sourly.

"Pop won't build it until the money starts rolling in. He's mortgaged to the hilt," Marsh explained.

"Is this going to get momma out of the grill?" Cale asked.

Marsh nodded. "After these houses start selling, she won't need to work. I don't know what either one of them will do with themselves. They've never known anything but work. Have you found a place yet?"

246

Cale lit two cigarettes and handed one to Marsh. "No, I looked at one but it wasn't right. We will start looking again as soon as I get back."

"You figuring on space for two?" Marsh inquired delicately.

"I don't know. I haven't heard from her in months. When she went away, she only left me a post office box number. She doesn't want me to be able to call her and she doesn't call me."

"Has she left your ass?" demanded Marsh.

"I don't think so. She's not the type to cut me loose without a word," Cale insisted.

"But that word could be a Dear John, right?"

"That's what keeps me up some nights. How long could it take to confront your fear of abandonment?"

"Depends, little brother."

"On what?" challenged Cale.

"On whether or not she knows what was abandoned."

Cale stared at Marsh. "I told you, her father was always moving from one duty station to another, abandoning any friends or relationships or roots that Bridget had put down."

"But her parents never abandoned her," countered Marsh. "They uprooted her but they took her along with them. So how did Bridget become afraid she would be abandoned?"

"Beats me. I'll ask her--if I ever hear from her again."

***

Early in December, Odell received the first order for a cascade desk. Cale worked on the desk during the day and the sideboard during the night. The first snow came to the mountains in the second week of December.

247

"It's going to be a tough winter," Acrilee predicted as she pulled a pan of biscuits from the oven. "When we get snow this early, look out!"

Odell split a hot biscuit and slathered butter on both halves. "Don't 'spect winter will interfere with your travel plans none, old woman."

"That just shows how much you know, old timer," Acrilee retorted, "I'm studying on how I could run off with this handsome young man at Christmas."

Odell smiled at Cale and sipped his coffee. "You aim on fattening him up like you did me?"

Acrilee swirled in a half circle and flipped up the hem of her apron. "Could be I've got a mind for romance. You never know what a mountain woman might be scheming."

Odell scraped a lump of plum jam onto one half of his biscuit. He put the halves together, squeezed gently and stared at the biscuit as it oozed a delectable seepage of buttery jam. "Could be the very next body that knocks on our door would be his girlfriend, come all the way from New Mexico. I'd just have to hang my head and say that Cale was away, romancing my old woman because she had studied a way to outfox the change."

Acrilee swatted Odell with her apron. "Shush! You old fool!" she exclaimed as she left the kitchen.

"I heard tell of another place on the river," Odell told Cale. "It's got some bottom land for your corn. The house is supposed to be in good shape. And it has a shop. Not a wood shop. The old boy was a mechanic. But it won't take much to make it right. It's rough going to get to but no worse than coming here. We'll be at a stopping point on these two pieces pretty soon. We can ride out and look at it then."

"Sounds good." Cale replied.

Before following Odell out to the shop, Cale went to his room. He opened the Christmas card he had bought for Bridget. Inside he wrote the brief note that, mindful of the words of Marsh and Jack, he had been composing for several days.

"In this season of joy and light, I wish you happiness, vision, and resolve. Celebrate yourself.

"Merry Christmas.

"Love,

"Cale."

***

The snow that had troubled Acrilee lasted only two days, but the weather got steadily colder. On the morning of the winter solstice, Odell made an announcement at breakfast.

"We'll be going for a little ride today. We have to fire up the stove in the shop though so that first coat of finish can dry. Acrilee, darling, I need you to chuck a piece of wood in the shop stove every so often 'til we get back from looking at a piece of land."

Acrilee poured red eye gravy over Odell's grits. "Calls me darling when he needs something," she complained. "Most times it's just old woman. Gravy?"

Cale nodded.

"Word is," Odell began, "this old boy was a good farmer. Kept his fences tight and his pastures clean. Had a stroke real bad and had to go into a home. His kids live in the flatland and they don't give a damn about farming."

After breakfast, Cale helped Odell tend to his stock. Before the two men climbed into Cale's truck, Acrilee came out of the cabin and handed Odell a small basket. Cale slowly drove down the rocky path to the state road. When they reached the Glory River, they took the highway that led northwest, following the sparkling current. The mountains grew taller, more rugged, and bluer. Farms disappeared and cabins grew sparse. Cale became more excited.

249

Finally they turned onto a gravel road that wound its way through a gap in the mountains. "That's it!" Odell cried when they rounded a bend and came upon fenced pastures. "Drive real slow."

They scrutinized the fences and the vegetation that grew in the pastures. Turning into a lane that led to the farmhouse, they crossed a small creek, passed a large barn and came to a small unpainted clapboard house. Behind the house stood a large wooden building with small glass windows.

As soon as he stepped from the truck, Cale smelled the river. He hurried past the shop and came to the swiftly flowing water. On the far side of the river, the land rose sharply into a towering ridge. The river hugged the base of the ridge and the broad crop fields and pastures stretched away from the water and rolled gently into the gap.

"I love it!" Cale cried as he ran back to the shop.

"Slow down, young feller," Odell admonished. "First impressions count a lot more with females than with farmland. There's only sixty acres in here, but we got to walk it. Can't buy a pig in a poke. Looks like you might have black walnut up on that ridge yonder."

Before they ate lunch in the cab of the truck, they climbed the ridge and walked the pastures. After eating, they peered through the windows into the empty house. Cale jabbed his knife into the siding, porch posts and window sills. Odell examined the foundation and verified that the chimney was plumb.

Cale located the position of the septic tank and the leach field and confirmed that the ground was not soggy. The two men met in the shop.

"I would have to put in larger windows," Cale commented as he studied the outbuilding.

"You got electric here," Odell countered.

"I know," Cale responded as he tested the mounting of the workbench, "but Bridget will need natural light."

Odell rubbed his chin. "I 'spect you'll wait 'til she gets here. A woman has to have things just so."

Cale sat on the bench. He would have to make a decision about this place without thinking about Bridget. She might triumph over her fear and then not want to live in the place he had chosen. She didn't even know he had a decision to make. She had not communicated with him in a long time. Silence does not make the heart grow fonder.

"What do you think about this place?" Cale asked as he lit a cigarette.

Odell pulled a pipe from his coat pocket and tamped it. "Seems to me," he said before putting the stem between his teeth, "it has all the signs." He struck a match, puffed, and continued, "Of a good farmer being suddenly stopped in his work. Don't see neglect anywhere. It's a good property. The house and the fields have a southern exposure. Question is: does it call to you?"

Cale walked out of the shop and stared at the house. "Would my heart be glad," he wondered, "if I looked up from my work in the shop and saw the fields and the river and the mountains and there was no Bridget? I have always loved the river and I love it more upstream, where I can see what it is made of. I have always loved farming and I can make a good corn crop in these fields.

"If Bridget never comes or if she comes and then leaves, this would be it," Cale muttered.

Cale walked past the house to the river. He knelt and put his hand in the cold water. He looked downstream and saw past the sunny fields and the enclosing mountains to where his life had been; to his father's scheming house and his grandfather's spirited farm; to the large holly tree that grew atop Toenail Hill; to the council fire that burned in Paha Mata; to a bedroom in the Kremlin where a woman had stolen his heart.

He turned and looked upstream. He imagined blue smoke rising from the chimney of the house and the

251

stovepipe of the shop. In the pastures he envisioned a few cows, and in the fields he pictured corn, green and tall, in silk.

It was enough. Alone, this farm could not give him joy, but it would make him glad. Here, alone, he could make the life he wanted and hope that more happiness would come. He walked back to where Odell awaited him. "Yep," he said and got into the truck.

Driving homeward, Cale and Odell discussed the purchase of the farm and agreed on a price Cale should offer. Odell suggested that he meet with the seller and strike up an informal deal. "No need to pay for lawyers until you've got something to buy," he concluded.

Odell described the farm to Acrilee at supper and she was happy that Cale was satisfied with the place. "We would be neighbors, in the mountain way, if you was to own it," she said merrily. Acrilee smiled at her husband. "The old man knows trading. If it can be got at that price, he'll see that you get it."

Odell blushed. Acrilee's eyes sparkled as they had when she became his bride. He was embarrassed because he knew he had given her a hard life and she had stuck by him. And she had loved him, every minute of every day. He feared death, feared it mightily, because it would deprive him of Acrilee. Odell did not know if God existed or what God was, but he knew what Acrilee was: devoted love and pure joy in being alive.

CHAPTER 16--TURNING

At sunup the next morning, Cale quietly put two presents under the Christmas tree near the hearth, slipped out of the cabin, let his truck roll away from the house before cranking it, and began the drive to Adluh. His Christmas card to Julia had explained that, after celebrating Skye's first birthday and Christmas with the family, he would leave for Saluda to spend the remainder of Christmas Day with his friends at the Potlatch.

Cale arrived at his father's house, placed his gifts under the tree, and joined his family for breakfast. Julia sat with her fidgeting son in her lap. "What's it like living way back in the hills?" Julia asked Cale.

"I must like it," Cale replied, "I'm going to make it permanent. I put an offer on a little farm. I'll tell you all about it after we open our gifts."

The absence of Matthew and Olivia made the celebration of Christmas less festive than usual, but Skye's playfulness lifted the somber attitude of the adults. During Christmas dinner, Cale told them of his life with Odell and Acrilee, the learning of old skills and the excitement of new designs. He did not mention, and no one asked about, his relationship with Bridget. After dessert, he suddenly rose to leave.

"Can't you stay just a little longer?" Julia beseeched him as Cale hoisted his nephew and kissed him on the cheek.

"I gotta go," Cale insisted.

Julia hugged her brother. "My Christmas wish for you is that she comes back to you," Julia whispered.

***

Cale delighted when he crested the hill that overlooked the Potlatch. When he parked in front of the Kremlin, Mama Lucy hurried as best she could to greet him.

"Cale! Merry Christmas! Everyone's so glad you came!"

She hugged him tightly then stood back to look at him. "You don't look any worse for going us one better," she surmised.

Cale laughed. "How am I going you one better?" he asked.

Mama Lucy frowned. "We have electricity. You don't. That puts you closer to the land."

"Closeness is in the heart, Mama Lucy," Cale rejoined, "not in the power supply."

"What's wrong with our power?" Boss demanded as he came out on the porch.

"Judging by your Christmas lights, I would say nothing," Cale replied.

"I've got something for you, dude," said Boss as he nudged Cale towards the far corner of the porch. He gave Cale a large envelope.

Cale trembled when he saw the post mark--Taos. He opened the envelope slowly and removed the Christmas card. He looked inside and read Bridget's words.

"Merry Christmas Baby,

"You have taken a big turn in your life and so have I. But it is not away from you. I know I am making it harder on you because you can't talk to me or come find me. But I have more to leave behind than I knew. When I leave it, I have to leave it for good and I have to leave it all. If you still love me, you will want me to give all of my love to you. I now know the source of my fear but I must get this long, deep pain out of me.

"Please keep me in your heart, Baby.

"Bridget."

254

Cale put the card in his pocket. "Why did she send it here?" he asked Boss.

"Don't know--unless she just put it in the batch with all the other cards she was sending to the Potlatch," Boss replied.

"Could be more," Mama Lucy suggested. "Maybe it means she wanted Cale to get this news in the place they were once together."

"Hmm," Cale said. "So, Boss, what's the Christmas plan?"

"Boss always has a plan," Mama Lucy sang as they went into the kitchen and sat at the table.

"It's pretty simple, really," Boss explained. "The Gypsies have been making presents for the kids for months. They also took responsibility for the decorations. The Diggers, of course, are in charge of the food. And the Lodgekeepers have organized the events."

"Events?" questioned Cale.

"Yeah," Mama Lucy said happily. "They built a bonfire and sang carols by the lake on Christmas Eve. Right now, they are taking the children on a Christmas Walk through the woods so the kids can leave little presents of food for the animals. And tonight, they are going to make a huge council fire and dance."

"It's going to be far out!" Boss exclaimed.

"I believe it, dude," Cale replied. "Where do you want me to help?"

"Since you are staying in Paha Mata, you can give the Lodgekeepers a hand getting ready for tonight. But the main thing is that everybody wants to see you, man. Visit all the camps and make merry. It's Christmas, dude!"

Cale made his way down to Paha Mata. Dakota greeted him eagerly, "Merry Christmas, Snake Man!"

Cale shook hands with his friend. "Merry Christmas, Dakota."

"I was just going to exercise our horses. Want to ride?" Dakota asked.

"Sure," Cale agreed as they went to the corral. Dakota caught Gretchen's horse and handed the reins to Cale. Then he mounted his own horse and they went out by Spirit Lake.

"Did Boss fill you in on our Christmas plans?" Dakota asked as the horses walked slowly on the trail.

"Yeah. He said since I'm bunking in Paha Mata, I should give the Lodgekeepers a hand tonight. Sounds like a good time will be had by all."

"Maybe for the last time," Dakota said solemnly. He stopped to let his horse eat some grass.

Cale lit a cigarette. "What do you mean?"

"You know as well as I do that most of the people living at the Potlatch are hiding from something. The war, their parents, bad credit, a criminal record--something.

"You also know the folks who are really living with purpose here. Me and my camp, Jugs and his camp, Mama Lucy and half of her camp, Boss and maybe a tenth of the folks who hang out in the Kremlin. And Bridget--but she's not here right now.

"The thing is, even though they are playing games at the peace talks in Paris, there are peace talks. We've been reducing our combat troops for some time now. The war won't be over tomorrow but it is not the threat to people's lives it used to be.

Dakota looked away toward his camp. When he turned to glance at Cale, his eyes were sad.

"The bottom line is that the pretenders are talking about pulling out. They call it checking their other options. They have found something that makes them want to run. They have learned that a new place does not make you a new person.

"On top of that, Dargan is not getting the bread out of the café and the shops that he had hoped for. He's the

256

biggest pretender of all. He and Meredith have not been here for weeks. They've been relaxing in the Cayman Islands. Dargan will turn thirty-five next March and he will have unrestricted access to his trust fund. He will be loaded and he will not piss around with this little commune. He has just been biding his time until he could lay his hands on all that cash. The Potlatch has been his entertainment. Let's run 'em!"

Dakota kicked and his horse broke into a run. Cale immediately prompted his roan to chase Dakota's Paint. They circled Spirit Lake at a full gallop, slowed to a canter and passed through Mudville and the Shuttlepot before easing into a trot and finally walking back into Paha Mata. Gretchen took the winded horses to the Rock Barn.

"You hungry, man?" asked Dakota as he fed the council fire.

"I could eat. You got some gourmet Sioux Christmas cuisine?"

"Hell no!" Dakota cried. "The Diggers cooked real Christmas food. Boss has called a secret meeting of the serious folks in the Shuttlepot. There was no reason for it to be a secret. All the pretenders went home to have Christmas with their mommies."

"Cale! Welcome, dude," Jugs cried as Dakota and Cale entered the largest yellow yurt. "We've got turkey, sweet potatoes, green beans, a couple of pies, and hot apple cider--help yourself."

Cale shook hands with Jugs then sat with Dakota. They ate in silence for a while then Boss addressed the group. "Thanks for coming. I know there has been a lot of talk about the Potlatch closing."

"What's the plan, Boss?" the group chanted. "What's the plan?"

Boss chuckled. "The plan is--"

The yurt became quiet. Everyone stared at Boss with hopeful eyes, hopeful that a plan existed that would keep their homes safe, their way of life going.

"There is no plan," Boss reported sadly. "I have asked Dargan if he is committed to keeping the Potlatch open, and he just won't say."

"Why the fuck not?" demanded Jugs. "We committed to live here. To make it possible for others to live here."

"I know, I know," Boss admitted. "We all knew he was a trust fund baby when we started. Face it, we didn't do this for Dargan, we did it for ourselves."

"Fucking A we did," Jugs shouted, "and it is working. The Painted Pony is a real, functioning gallery. Xanadu is making it as a head shop. Boss' food co-op is a great success. And goddamn, man, Mama Lucy's raised enough food to feed an army."

"Everybody loves Mama Lucy," the group said in joyful unison.

"She feeds all of us," Jugs continued. "The Colorado Café is serving stuff the Diggers have raised. Boss uses their stuff to trade for other great stuff. The Potlatch is making itself go now, man. So why wouldn't it keep going? Why would anybody fuck it up?"

"It's not just Dargan, man," Dakota observed. "People are not as scared of the war as they used to be. The little pussies think maybe now they can safely resume their lives of suburban pleasance. They didn't come here to live differently. Those fuckers came here to hide.

"I'm not waiting on Dargan to make up his mind. I'm saying right here and now that I will be moving Paha Mata. My people are raising the money to buy some land that we will own as a tribe. Because that is what we are. You know Dargan will close the Potlatch down and move his playground to the Caymans or Tuscany. But Paha Mata will survive. Paha Mata is real!"

258

"The Diggers don't have a pot to piss in," Mama Lucy confessed. "If Dargan closes the Potlatch, we'll have to disband."

"If the Potlatch closes," Jugs declared, "I will try to buy it. I have committed to making this land my home. The clay here is perfect for my pots. And I love this place. My family is not rich but they would be willing to help me. If Dargan decides to close the Potlatch, I will do my damnedest to buy it from him. The Shuttlepot is real too."

Mysteriously, the group turned to Cale. He had been a respected leader at the Potlatch and he had left and was making his way. "The only thing I can add is something my grandmother told me when she took away the family farm that I had always wanted to one day call home.

"She said that home is not a place. Home is the way you live your life, according to the truest things you know in your heart and mind. She said that the things your heart and mind love will lead you to a place where you will put your home. Maybe they will lead you to more than one place. She was right. That's why I'm in the mountains."

***

As night fell, Cale helped the Lodgekeepers build a huge bonfire. Dancers emerged from the lodges and moved around the fire joyfully, celebrating Christmas in the place they knew as Paha Mata and rejoicing in Dakota's promise that Paha Mata would continue to live in a place none of them yet knew. In their happy songs there was a definite sense that in the new year they would be turning, turning towards home.

***

The new year of 1973 came in very cold and very dark. Work on the sideboard progressed quickly then paused as Cale and Odell discussed the final finish they were considering for the piece. They were debating the qualities of Odell's favorites as Cale drove them into town to collect the mail.

"Damn it's cold!" Odell exclaimed as he returned to the warm cab of Cale's truck with an envelope. "You better get a lawyer, son," Odell remarked as they left the tiny post office.

"Why?" Cale asked casually. "Did your customer find fault with the desk we sent them?"

"Not so far as I know," Odell replied flatly, "but the old boy I talked to will sell you his farm, the way we talked about it. He gave his word on it. If I was you, I would get a lawyer and I would get a new survey, lickety-split. We're about to be neighbors."

"Fantastic!" cried Cale. "Thanks, Odell! Thank you very much."

"No need to mention it. No need at all," Odell said quietly.

When they got back to the cabin, Cale immediately told Acrilee the good news. "This calls for a celebration," Acrilee declared. "I'm going to rustle up a big buttermilk apple pie. That's the old man's favorite. I'm tickled you will be close to home, Cale. Me and the old man are very fond of you." She kissed Cale on the cheek.

"Got your mind on romance again, old woman?" Odell asked.

"Pie ain't the only dessert you're liable to get tonight, old man. Now fetch me some apples from the root cellar and some buttermilk from the springhouse."

Cale winked at Odell. "Like we were talking about in the truck, I'll be working late in the shop tonight. Real late."

That evening at supper, after they had happily discussed the prospects of Cale becoming a neighbor, Acrilee saw a dark look come into Cale's eyes. When that look remained for more than a moment, Acrilee asked, "What's troubling you, son?"

"I'm excited about getting my own place, Acrilee, I truly am," Cale said hesitantly.

"But?" Acrilee questioned.

"But I would be happier if I wasn't going to be alone," Cale lamented. "In her letters, Bridget says she cares for me and she asks me to keep her in my heart. But I haven't heard from her in a long time. She went away to work out some problems. She says she did that so she can come back to me and love me like I love her. But she won't let me call her or visit her. Maybe she doesn't love me anymore and that's why I haven't heard from her."

Acrilee tapped Cale's hand gently. "Love is the only thing we have to live for. I guess it stands to reason that it would roil us up more than anything else. And we mess it up more than we mess up anything else. But when we get it right—" she paused and gazed tenderly at her husband "—well."

Acrilee adjusted her dress. "You see, a woman is very messy about her moods. She just can't seem to hoe the row with them. But a woman is very tidy about her heart. Love is second nature to a woman and she keeps it to close account. Close account. She knows if she loves you or not, she always knows that real clear. If Bridget loves you, Cale, she will come to you. In her own sweet time she will come. Love is too glorious to pass by."

Odell gazed at his beautiful wife. Loving Acrilee was the marrow of his life, as it was for all men. "The old woman is right, son," he said lightly. "Love flows into purpose because that is the only way it can live. If she does love you, you will know her purpose soon enough."

***

The next morning, Odell admired the finish Cale had applied during the night and the two men polished the sideboard. Cale was proud of the elegant furniture he had designed and they had produced. Odell was confident he had a ready buyer for the sideboard. "It'll bring top dollar, that's for sure."

***

261

Marsh's lawyer was able to help Cale expedite the purchase of the farm, and on the day of the closing Marsh arrived in Halcyon with Cale's tractor chained to the deck of a flatbed truck. As soon as the deed was recorded, Marsh followed Cale to his new home on the river in the Gunpowder Range of the Blue Mountains.

Marsh was amazed at the clarity of the river. He was impressed by the quality of the pastures, the tilth of the fields, the sturdiness of the fences, the soundness of the house and shop, and the beauty of the towering mountains that enclosed the farm. "Matthew would have loved this place!" he exclaimed. "I know one thing for sure. Come summer, your corn will be standing tall in that rich bottomland. Congratulations, brother! I'm really happy for you."

"A lot of this is your doing, Marsh," Cale declared, "and I am very grateful. If you hadn't forced Pop to lay out the golf course next to Swede's Pasture, I wouldn't have had the cash to buy this place." Cale hugged Marsh. "You got me back on my feet and I'll never forget it. Thank you."

"Hell," Marsh replied, "that's what big brothers are for. Besides, I may come up this way one day myself. I love the Red Bank country but this is a few notches above home. And I heard that Halcyon doesn't have a baseball team."

Cale backed his tractor down off the flatbed and parked it beneath a lean-to attached to the barn. Marsh then moved the flatbed up the driveway so Cale could back his pickup against the front porch of the house. They strapped Olivia's massive cast iron cook stove to a large dolly, rolled it into the kitchen and connected it to the flue.

"It makes me happy to see Grandma's stove sitting in a farmhouse kitchen again. It just seems right," Marsh proclaimed. Cale kindled a small fire in the cold stove while March retrieved a box from the cab of his brother's truck.

262

"Winters will be very cold this high up," Marsh observed. "And the growing season will be a lot shorter than down home."

"I know," said Cale as he set a pot of coffee to brew on the warming stove.

"What kind of stock are you figuring on running in here?" questioned Marsh.

"A couple of cows with some sheep behind them," Cale answered.

"Why sheep?"

"You just said how cold it going to be. Besides the cows always leave plenty of grass for the sheep. The sheep crop it close."

"No pigs?"

Cale shook his head. "I'll be spending most of my time in the shop. Cows and sheep don't need much tending to. I can trade for pork."

Cale poured coffee for them. Marsh lifted his cup in a toast. "From this day on, this stove will no longer be called Grandma's stove, it will be called Cale's stove because it sits in Cale's house."

Marsh lit two cigarettes and gave one to Cale. The brothers sat on boxes in the living room and looked out at the frosty mountains.

"You could use some chairs," Marsh teased as he drank his coffee.

"I've got to wait on Boss," Cale replied.

"Why?"

"Because, Construction Boy," Cale explained, "Boss has planned a house warming for me this Saturday. My friends might bring an old chair or two. Something to get me by until I make my own."

"Good," Marsh judged.

When they finished their coffee, they went out to begin unloading the trucks. When the last box was inside, Cale turned on the oil furnace and it started with a boom.

They arranged the few pieces of furniture, hung the clothes in a narrow closet and stowed the groceries in the kitchen.

They left the house and took the tools to the shop. Noticing the woodstoves at each end of the building, Marsh commented, "It's a good thing that old boy laid in a good supply of seasoned wood."

"Yeah," said Cale. "The house should have warmed up a little by now."

The brothers went in to the kitchen, had some more coffee and smoked. Cale carefully stoked the fire in the cook stove so the great iron appliance would warm slowly. "What should we fix for supper?" Cale asked when Marsh returned from his truck with a sleeping bag.

"Well, you've got those pork chops," Marsh replied.

The house warmed up long before the cook stove was hot enough to fry the chops and cook the rice and peas the brothers ate for supper. The wind came up a bit just after dark as Marsh and Cale opened a bottle of bourbon.

"To my brother's house," Marsh proclaimed, "long may it stand."

"Here, here," Cale answered.

"I guess Grandma's advice was on the mark," Marsh surmised as they drank.

"Don't look down," Cale said, echoing Olivia's words.

"You didn't look down. You went about as far upstream as you could go. And became a damn fine cabinetmaker. I never saw that one coming. I'll bet Grandma didn't either. But she saw something coming for you that wasn't going to happen at home."

"What she saw," Cale explained, "was what home really is. It is not something you can be born into or inherit. It's something you have to find--inside yourself. Then you can take it any place."

"Speaking of taking it, I've got to take it to bed," Marsh said. "Or better yet, take it to bag. Goodnight, brother."

"Goodnight, Marsh. Thanks for everything," Cale called as Marsh trudged out of the kitchen and into the living room.

Cale banked the fire in the cook stove, put out the lights, went into the bedroom and crawled into his cold bed. This house did not yet feel like home but having his brother with him was a start.

During the night, Marsh was awakened by a strange noise. The sound was a forsaken moaning, as if someone were desperately crying. Then the night wind howled around the house. Marsh rolled over and slept soundly until morning, though he dreamed of a planet that had been hurled away from its sun and disappeared into unfathomable darkness.

Just after sunup, Cale fired up the cook stove and the brothers had a breakfast of bacon, eggs and coffee. A heavy frost covered the ground and the sky was filled with low gray clouds.

"Pay attention to the radio," Marsh advised as they ate. "If you get a January thaw, you might be able to turn your fields. We haven't had a really hard winter yet but everybody says it's coming."

After breakfast, they went out to the shop and started fires in the two stoves. "What else do you need me to help you with before I hit the road, little brother?" Marsh asked.

"I guess there's nothing left to do, except get used to the place. And you can't help me with that," Cale responded.

When Marsh left, Cale began to organize the shop and build racks to store the wood he would get from Odell to fill orders for Odell's customers. He kept busy in the shop because it already felt like it belonged to him. He knew the house would take much longer. The kitchen at least, with his big cook stove, was beginning to be his.

***

Just before noon on Saturday morning, a small caravan, led by the Bismarck, arrived at Cale's farm. A van, a station wagon, and a VW bus pulled into the driveway behind Jack's car.

"This is it!" Cale proclaimed as Jack and Hank, Boss and Mama Lucy, Dakota and Gretchen, and Jugs and Sable stood in the freezing cold and gazed at the land.

"This is heaven, man!" Boss proclaimed.

"This is God's country, pure and simple!" Jack thundered.

Hank embraced Cale. "It's fantastic, Cale. I know you'll be happy here. What a gorgeous view of the mountains. And you can see the river."

"Well done, mate," Jack said. "I'm right proud you've become a man of the mountains."

Cale shook hands with Jack. "If you hadn't told me about the Halcyon Valley, none of this would have happened."

"Do tell," Jack said with a wide, happy grin.

"You did it, Snake Man," Dakota said as he grasped Cale's shoulder. "You've got your own camp. What are you going to call it?"

Cale thought for a minute. "Home."

"Of course," Dakota said, "that's the universal name for all warrior camps."

"I love your place," Mama Lucy said urgently, "but I think the women need to get in out of the cold. We brought lunch. I believe the men could quit talking for a minute and take the gifts in the house."

"Lunch will have to be buffet style," Cale added. "I don't have any chairs."

"You do now," Boss conceded, "and a table too. Everybody chipped in and we paid a visit to the thrift store.

It's genuine crap but we've got the general provisions for setting up a household."

"Boss always has a plan," the Potlatch folks sang.

Under Mama Lucy's direction, the table and chairs were moved in the house, utensils were placed in drawers, dishes and pans were stored in cabinets, and linens were stacked on shelves in the hall closet. The food was warmed while Boss tapped the beer keg.

"I don't know what to say," Cale confessed as his friends were about to eat. "I appreciate your generosity, your help, and your friendship."

"I want to make a toast and an announcement," Dakota said as he stood. "A while back, I told Cale that he and his friends at the Potlatch were a society of fire, were a group of people who lived sincerely by the fire of their passions and shared that life with others who also lived by fire. Cale now makes his camp here by the river in the Gunpowder Range. In the spring, the Potlatch will close.

"I will move Paha Mata to some beautiful land on the Yellow River in the next range over, the Blacktop Range. Boss and Mama Lucy will be joining us. Jugs, you have the floor."

Dakota sat and Jugs addressed his friends. "In the spring, the Potlatch will close but it will become the Shuttlepot. I have made a deal with Dargan to buy the place. The clay there is perfect for my pots. I am going to build kilns and throw pots in the Rock Barn. In the Red Barn, I will have my retail shop. The Kremlin will lose its name and just be home for Sable and her potter.

"I promised Cale I would make four firepots that would hold a fire, even in the rain. Boss has his, Dakota has his, I have mine, and Cale, yours is now sitting in the yard, beside the path you take to your shop. Like all the others, the fire that is burning in yours this very minute was kindled with coals taken from the council fire in Paha Mata."

267

"I have a little something for you too, Cale," said Jack. He presented Cale with a new axe.

"Thanks, Jack."

"I had a hard time thinking of a gift for this man," Hank began, "then I remembered his portrait. He is a scrimshander. They wouldn't be caught dead without a good knife." Hank handed Cale a new pocketknife.

"I appreciate it, Hank. Thanks to all of you," Cale began. "Now this place will really feel like my home because I have shared it with my friends. Let's eat."

***

Later that night, when his house was quiet again, Cale sat in his kitchen with a cigarette and a cup of coffee and wrote to Bridget.

"Bridget,

"I hope you had a very good Christmas. I have moved into my own place now. I have orders to fill for Odell's customers, and I will build the furniture here in my own shop. My farm is beautiful and the river runs close to the house. I have designed and built a cascade writing desk and a hearth-styled sideboard. I know now that my scrimshander's hands will be busy for the rest of my life.

"I hope your work is going well. You will always be in my heart.

"Cale."

A few days after he mailed the letter to Bridget, the weather warmed up enough that Cale could crumble the soil in his hand. He worked quickly to turn his fields so that the weeds and the clods would be exposed to the frigid days that were coming.

He had barely finished the work when a terrible snowstorm blew through the mountains. The river froze along its banks and Cale used a lot of wood to keep the shop warm enough to work. Making his way from the shop to the house through the bitterly cold wind, Cale was glad he had not yet bought any stock. Come the spring, he could not let the shop occupy all of his time because the land would need a lot of work to put in his corn and a garden. When the sun strengthened in the spring, his life on his farm would be turning towards his other love.

CHAPTER 17--CRIPPLE GOAT

Throughout the tempestuous, icy winter, Cale established two daily rituals. In the morning, he took his coffee down to its banks and stared at the heart of the Glory River. Watching the clear current, he remembered how his insides had been so darkly clouded by the war that his heart could not shine in his mind.

Day and night, he tended the council fire in his firepot. Watching those glowing coals, he thought of Broadus. Still missing in the jungle, Broadus could not risk fire. Abandoned, in peril, denied the comfort of a crackling blaze, Broadus could exist as not much more than a scared, isolated animal desperately searching for the way home.

Working in the shop gave Cale great satisfaction and he often thought of Bridget when he paused for a smoke. His last letter remained unanswered. He still believed she thought of him but wondered "Does she think of me when she is painting, talking with friends, or lying alone in bed? Does she reach out to grab memories of him or did he just flow into her mind?"

***

In March, Dakota called to tell Cale that Paha Mata had been resettled in the Yellow Mountains. Dakota invited him to come for a visit and, at the end of the week, Cale made the short journey through the mountains.

"We are actually now more like the camp of my ancestors," Dakota explained as Cale looked beyond the lodges to the fenced meadows where several horses roamed. "The tribe would always have members who were not born into it but were adopted into it. Boss, Mama Lucy, and the Diggers who came with them are more into dirt

270

than Indian culture but they want to plant here, with us, and they observe our traditions."

Boss and Mama Lucy showed Cale the broad fields beyond the meadows where they would plant corn. "We will make two plantings," Boss explained, "about two months apart. Sweet corn and field corn. We will harvest the sweet corn first, for us and the food co-op. The field corn will be cut to feed the stock."

"That sounds like a good plan," Cale said.

Mama Lucy tapped Boss with her cane. "Boss always has a plan."

On his return from Dakota's new camp, Cale swung the truck into the driveway and paused. He glimpsed the house nestled against the mountain, the river flowing behind it, and the shop that stood nearby. As he stared at the scene before him, the elements shifted and a picture emerged: home.

***

In early April, Cale disked his fields, laid off rows, side dressed the rows with rotted manure, planted corn and set out a garden. By mid-April, spring retreated as cold, wet weather descended on the mountains. A heavy frost lay on his land a few days before corn plants emerged from the cold soil. Cale was very troubled when the bad weather reached into May. "Grandpa," he said aloud as he walked his cornfields, "I might have planted my first crop too early."

Cale could see that the crop was stunted. The corn could recover size later but it could not heal itself from slowed internal development. Cale knew that late June would be an anxious time. If the corn tasseled and shed its pollen before the silks had emerged, the crop would be lost.

"How bad is it?" asked Marsh when Cale phoned him that evening.

"The stand rate is fine," Cale responded, "I didn't lose any plants to the cold. They were stunted but they are

271

starting to recover from that. But if the development is off, they may shed their pollen before the silks have emerged."

"How well do the fields drain?"

"I haven't seen any problems there."

"How many leaves do you have now?"

"Fifteen."

"Shit. It's going to be close. Call me when you get good brace roots."

Fear of the failure of his first corn crop mingled with his uncertainty about Bridget's continuing silence and Cale sensed he was on the verge of a catastrophic loss. The next morning, he took his coffee to the river and flung the dark liquid into the crystal water.

"What good is clarity if all I can see is what I'm about to lose?" he shouted into the chilly morning.

For several weeks, Cale could not focus his thoughts. He thought of Bridget constantly now. Why didn't she write? Had she broken both arms? Did she have nothing to say? Could she not see how mean her silence was? Even if she was working on her masterpiece, she could find ten minutes to drop him a line. Did she just not care anymore?

Cale began to drink again. He had long dreamed of the first corn crop he would raise on his own land. Now he feared that crop would be a bust. Maybe his love for Bridget would be a bust. He was on the river. He was far upstream from the Red Bank country. He was a cabinetmaker. He was home. He should be happy. Cale's production in the shop slowed but he made scheduled deliveries to Odell.

"It hasn't been as cold here as it has at your place," Odell said as he paid Cale for furniture he received. "You are a little higher than we are. If your corn silks on time, you could still make a crop. Are you running any stock?"

"No," Cale responded. "I'm on new ground. I don't want to run any stock until I know I can make a corn crop."

"Corn silks are like everything female," Odell advised. "If they give themselves to you at the right time, all is well. If they hold back too long, all is lost."

Cale thought about Odell's words as he drove home. "Has Bridget been holding back so long that her feelings for me are lost? Does she just not know how to tell me?"

***

On June thirteenth, Cale called Marsh. "My corn tasseled and now I've got good brace toots. No silks have emerged."

"Ok, now listen carefully," Marsh replied. "Your pollen drop started two days ago. It will last two more weeks. I hope you've got some wind."

"Negative," Cale reported. "It has been very hot, dry and still."

"Hold on, Cale. You should be getting afternoon thunderstorms now. They have wind. This dry spell will break."

The morning of the summer solstice, Cale was very despondent as he drank his coffee by the river. The air was hot and dry. He worked in the shop until lunch. As he sat on the porch eating a tomato sandwich and drinking iced tea, the air suddenly freshened. In the distance, he saw large clouds forming. He put his glass in the kitchen sink and walked out into his cornfields.

The corn had recovered rapidly from the cold, wet spring and was now head-high as it should be. He walked deeper into the field and the house disappeared behind him. The corn was silking, but the silks were much shorter than normal. The corn only had a few more days to shed its pollen and Cale needed wind to carry the pollen to the silks to fertilize the kernels.

The clouds were growing fat and black. The first day of summer would surely bring him wind. The corn began to stir as Cale smelled rain. The corn rustled in a crisp breeze.

"Yes!" Cale cried. "Yes!" "Yes!"

Suddenly he recalled the time Matthew's corn had taunted his memory and he thought he had been thrown back into the jungle. That would not happen to him now. He had freed himself from the war. This was his corn. Even if the crop failed, it was his corn and he was home.

The rain did not come even though the clouds were very heavy and very dark. The strengthening wind whipped the tall green plants but Cale did not rejoice. The crop was being pollinated but the wind was too strong and the rain had not yet come and the sky was as dark as night. Suddenly, Cale realized what was upon him: hail!

Cale sprang towards the house and ran hard through the broad field. He fought for breath and his calves burned. Lightning crackled in the deadly sky and a dazzling bolt struck the river. Hail broke from the sky in a furious white torrent, striking his flesh as Cale tore through the madly flailing plants.

He was hit in the face and his back was stinging. Cale could hear the hail striking his corn. He remembered running through the killing fields while those behind him fell. But Cale was not running for his life now. He was running for home.

The blizzard of icy pellets howled across the land. Cale sobbed as he saw his first crop being cut to the ground. "No! No!" he screamed powerlessly as the butchery around him intensified. He had lost Matthew's land to Glory Bend, he had lost Broadus to the war, he had lost Bridget to an unconquered demon in the New Mexico desert.

"No," he shrieked as he looked at the broken stalks of corn he could not save. Cale thought of the young soldiers who had died savagely in the moonlight. "I already paid for that! A million times I paid!" he shouted to the dark sky as he topped the final rise and the house came into view. Cale stopped and bent forward, gasping violently.

When the hail whipping his back slackened and rain began to fall, Cale raised up and gazed sadly through his ruined fields at the storm's receding fury. He turned away from the sorrow of his fields and faced the house. Bridget stood on the porch.

"Bridget!" Cale called desperately as he loped slowly toward the house. He crossed the driveway and bounded up the steps. He stopped to look at her. Beside her stood Infinitus. Bridget's green eyes were nervous.

"I want to come home," Bridget said tentatively, "if you meant what you said in your letters."

"Bridget," Cale exclaimed, "I love you so much. I missed you so badly. I have things to tell you, to show you--are you sure?"

Bridget put her hands on Cale's shoulders. "Because I was going through so much, I put you through a lot. But I faced my fear and it is gone now. I love you, Cale. I came back because my home is the things I love--painting and you. Like your grandmother said, your home will lead you to a place. My place is here with you."

Cale took Bridget in his arms. He kissed her deeply then held her close while she sobbed softly. "It was me," Bridget murmured. "That's who I was afraid of. I was afraid of being abandoned by me because I did not love myself.

"And I didn't. All those years of tearing up relationships and leaving friends behind. I learned not to love me because I was always leaving the scene and being replaced. I wasn't someone anybody should love."

Bridget wiped her eyes with the sleeve of her blouse. She held Cale's hands.

"I had to learn how wrong I had been. I had always blamed my parents for my fear but it was always me. Your letter about the hand I saw in the sky made me realize it was my hand that was missing. It was about me, not them. I needed to love myself, to feel I was worthy of love. Once I was able to do that, my fear went away.

"My relationship with my parents has changed. I realized that they did not love me as they should have, that they are limited by their own ambition. I confronted them. They see it now and I think they are sorry. But it is too late for them to change.

"You helped me so much. Just knowing that you were sticking by me while I struggled, that gave me the strength to see it through. I knew you were a good person and that you loved me. I needed to love myself so I could accept your love and return it. And I do. I love you, Cale."

They kissed once more, held each other tightly, then Cale took Bridget inside. "The cobbler's children have no shoes," said Cale as he gestured to the sparsely furnished living room. Bridget followed him through the small house. When they came to his bedroom, she saw the scrimshander painting hanging over his bed.

"You helped me see something about myself, too," Cale said. Suddenly, he heard the soft rain falling on the roof. "We'd better get Infinitus."

They brought the steamer trunk in from the porch and put it in a corner of the living room. "I can finish it now," Bridget said happily, "now that I am home."

"Boss told me," Cale explained, "where he got the big windows I put in the Red Barn to make studio space. I will get some and put them in the shop, on the south side, and you will have plenty of light to paint."

"Thank you, Baby. Speaking of Boss, I have something for you out in my van."

When they went out on the porch, the rain had stopped, the sun was shining brilliantly and it was getting hot quickly. The river sparkled. "Close your eyes," Bridget insisted.

Cale heard the creaking as the door on the van opened. Then the brief sound of something dragging reached his ears. He detected a slight rustle.

"Now open."

Resting on the ground and propped against Bridget's leg, Cale saw a large wooden sign. Painted on the broad plaque was a holly tree beside a field of corn, above which, in a blue sky, floated a red hand. The lettering above the illustration read CRIPPLE GOAT STUDIOS.

"Boss said you didn't have a sign for the shop," Bridget explained, "and studio applies as much to painting as it does to cabinetmaking.

"It's wonderful!" cried Cale. "Thank you. Let's hang it."

Bridget leaned the sign against the van. "Ok. After."

"After what?" asked Cale.

"After we get reacquainted," Bridget said in a low silky voice.

Bridget took his hand and led Cale into the bedroom. In their nakedness, they touched each other delicately, then eagerly, then passionately, then joyfully, and their memories of loneliness, desperation, anxiety, and failure were soothed and passed away. Quietly embracing, they rejoiced in togetherness, in binding the most urgent reaches of the heart with the promise to love, to aid, to understand, to celebrate and to comfort.

Finally, Cale spoke. "I guess I had better check the damage."

"What damage?" Bridget asked sleepily.

"When I ran back to the house, and I saw you on the porch, I was running from a vicious hailstorm. I need to see if I have any corn left."

They got dressed and walked out to the fields. The evening breeze had come up and Cale struggled to light a cigarette as they walked the rows. Half his crop lay in the

277

dirt. The other half swayed gently and he knew that pollen was being shed from the tassels and caught by the silks.

Cale and Bridget returned to the house and hung the sign above the door on the shop. Cale took Bridget down the short path to the river. She was astounded by the clear water.

"The river is so beautiful here. It is nothing like this at the Potlatch," Bridget remarked.

"The heart of the river is the same everywhere," Cale insisted, "it just has more things floating on it downstream."

They walked over to the large brown pot that sat between the house and the shop. "Jugs made this for me. The fire burning in it now was started with coals from the council fire at Paha Mata. As you can see, it will hold a fire in the rain. This is my council fire. I will never let it go out. You hungry?"

Bridget nodded and followed Cale into the kitchen. When she saw the massive cook stove, she asked, "Is this Olivia's stove?"

"I got it when she died," Cale answered. "It still sits in a farmhouse and helps feed a man who grows corn. I guess I need to stoke it if we are going to cook."

While the fire came up in the stove, they went outside and added wood to the council fire. Sunlight rimmed the horizon but in the darkness above, the first stars had come out.

Cale saw that Bridget was watching the smoke rise from the firepot. Her green eyes shone with the golden light he had seen in the heart of the river. Cale imagined that the light in Bridget's eyes mingled with the smoke from the firepot and the cook stove, and that the smoke, now golden, drifted down across Saluda and across the Red Bank country. Incorporating wisps of smoke from scattered council fires, Cale pictured the marvelous aerial ribbon as it sailed above Toenail Hill, down to Cape Indigo and beyond to Redd Isle.

Then, over some lone island in the wild ocean, Cale saw the blue wisps from a lost warrior's desperate fire rise above the jungle and join with the golden smoke. The unified plume rushed upwards and crashed into the sky, spilling a golden light that made the world home for all who could see fire with their hearts.

THE END

Other Books by the Author

The Estrangement of the Rain God
State Rebellion
Squeach and the Magical Starfish

Enjoy Other Fine Books from Righter Publishing Company

Thrillers, detective stories, short story collections, children's books, inspirational works, poetry collections, family histories, science fiction, romance, literary fiction, local histories, personal memoirs and self-help.

Go to www.righterbooks.com

www.ingramcontent.com/pod-product-compliance
Lightning Source LLC
Chambersburg PA
CBHW050926030726
47503CB00007BB/2492